ARK

A Native American artifact points the way to one of the greatest legends in history!

Archaeologist Dima Zafrani receives a mysterious package containing fragments of an unknown text that proves the existence of the lost Book of Noah. Pursued by a shadow organization known only as The Trident, Dima crosses paths with former Navy SEALs turned treasure hunters Dane Maddock and Bones Bonebrake. Can the three find the legendary Noah Stones before the Trident can harness their power?

Join Maddock and Bones on another action-packed adventure as they set off on a quest for the Ark!

PRAISE FOR DAVID WOOD
AND THE DANE MADDOCK ADVENTURES

"A page-turning yarn blending high action, Biblical speculation, ancient secrets, and nasty creatures. Indiana Jones better watch his back!" Jeremy Robinson, author of SecondWorld

"Dane and Bones.... Together they're unstoppable. Rip roaring action from start to finish. Wit and humor throughout. Just one question - how soon until the next one? Because I can't wait." Graham Brown, author of Shadows of the Midnight Sun

"What an adventure! A great read that provides lots of action, and thoughtful insight as well, into strange realms that are sometimes best left unexplored." Paul Kemprecos, author of Cool Blue Tomb and the NUMA Files

ARK

A DANE MADDOCK ADVENTURE

DAVID WOOD

Ark, A Dane Maddock Adventure

Published by Adrenaline Press
www.adrenaline.press
Adrenaline Press is an imprint of Gryphonwood Press
www.gryphonwoodpress.com

Cover art by Drazenka Kimpel, cover design by Kent
Holloway Book Cover Design

ISBN-10: 1-940095-65-4
ISBN-13: 978-1-940095-65-3

BOOKS BY DAVID WOOD

The Dane Maddock Adventures
Dourado
Cibola
Quest
Icefall
Buccaneer
Atlantis
Ark
Xibalba
Solomon Key (forthcoming)

Dane and Bones Origins
Freedom
Hell Ship
Splashdown
Dead Ice
Liberty
Electra
Amber
Justice
Treasure of the Dead

Jade Ihara Adventures (with Sean Ellis)
Oracle
Changeling

Bones Bonebrake Adventures
Primitive
The Book of Bones

Jake Crowley Adventures (with Alan Baxter)
Blood Codex
Anubis Key (forthcoming)

"On that day all the springs of the great deep burst forth, and the floodgates of the heavens were opened. And rain fell on the earth forty days and forty nights." Genesis 7.11-12

PROLOGUE

1362
Somewhere on the Atlantic Ocean

The sea was angry. Waves battered the wooden sailing ship, pitching it to and fro and threatening to upend it with each wall of water that broke across its bow. Rising high on every swell and crashing down into every trough, the ship creaked and groaned as it struggled on its Sisyphean journey toward the land that, according to the charts, lay somewhere close by.

"I swear we haven't moved in an hour." Godfrey shouted above the howl of the wind and the rush of the waves. He stood, arm twisted into the rigging to hold him in place, and watched the horizon for any sight of land. It had to be there.

"Oh, we've moved plenty. Up and down, side to side." Despite his lighthearted words, Hugo's face was a mask of grim determination. "The gods of the sea are toying with us."

"Don't blaspheme," Godfrey said. "Not even in jest." He looked up at the sky as if he expected God Almighty to smite them. Given the current state of things, it would make for a fitting end.

"Do you think He's angry?" Hugo's eyes flitted skyward before returning to the sea. "Because of what we did?"

"What did we do?" Godfrey knew exactly what Hugo meant, and his comrade's words echoed his own deep-seated fears, but he was not ready to concede. "We recovered holy relics from the clutches of the Saracens, and we are taking them somewhere far beyond their reach. We are doing His work." That was the best rationalization he could summon at the moment. He wasn't sure he believed it, though.

Icy droplets of rain smacked him in the face, each

like a chastisement from above. Salt spray burned his eyes and parched his lips. The taste reminded him of the story of Lot's wife.

Don't look back. Don't think of home.

"I don't know," Godfrey said. "Sometimes I think we should have pitched the whole cargo into the sea. Then no one could ever lay hands on it."

"The Lord has a plan," Hugo said with more confidence than he felt. "Someday these things might be needed to serve His purpose. Until then, we will stand guard."

"Maybe it's the stones." Godfrey looked down as if he could see into the hold. "You know what they are."

"I know what the old man claimed them to be, but scripture tells a different story. I know which story I choose to believe."

The ship suddenly pitched, sweeping both men off of their feet. They held fast to the rigging as the craft once again came perilously close to capsizing. When it righted itself, neither man bothered to stand.

"We won't survive many more of those." He glanced up at the main mast. "The wind has picked up and it's beginning to play hell with the rigging. We should tell the captain to furl the sails before the mast breaks."

Hugo couldn't hide his surprise. "How does a knight know so much about sailing?"

Godfrey managed a smile. "When I was a youth, I ran away from home. I worked on a fishing boat for a year. I drank in the filthy seaside taverns, enjoyed the company of some of the filthiest whores you'd ever want to know. That was the best time I ever had."

"Are you winding me up? You're a man of God."

"I am now, but I wasn't back then. As a matter of fact, if we make it through this, I just might…" Whatever Godfrey might or mightn't have done was lost, along with Godfrey, in the wave that broke over the gunwales and swept him out to sea.

"Godfrey!" Hugo struggled to stand on the slippery, shifting deck. In a flash of lightning he caught a glimpse of Godfrey's white tabard amongst the waves. In the next flash, he was gone.

Another wave swamped the deck, bringing Hugo down hard on his knees. The impact sent dull pain lancing through his legs and up his spine.

"Lord Almighty, send us a miracle," he prayed.

The only answer was a sharp cracking sound from behind him. He turned but already knew what he would see. The mast was breaking. The ship was done for.

"The relics must be saved," he said to no one in particular.

He clambered down into the hold and retrieved the one box about which he cared the most. Inside lay the mysterious stones. He had his doubts about the story surrounding them, but they clearly held tremendous power—power that could only come from God. They must be saved.

Tucking the box under his arm, he made his way back out onto the deck, which now swarmed with activity. Sailors were fighting to cut the rigging free before the mast gave way completely. Hugo suspected it was far too late.

As if the sea could hear his thoughts, the largest wave yet crashed into the side of the ship. Hugo fell face-first, his precious box spilling its contents down the sloping deck and into the water. He managed to snatch one of the stones, but everything else was lost.

In a flash of lightning, he caught one last glimpse of the horizon before the ship finally capsized. What he saw there remained etched in his vision.

Land!

A shock ran through him as he slid off the deck and plunged into the icy depths. Cold blackness enveloped him as he felt the strong current sweep him away.

He was a poor swimmer, but he managed to kick off his boots to free himself of their weight. Paddling for all he was worth, being careful not to drop the stone, he finally broke the surface. He had time only to suck in a single gasp of air before he went under again.

Only the thought of saving the precious stone kept him going. It became, in his mind, a holy commission from the Lord Himself. Save this last remaining relic— the only bit of their cargo that remained. He continued to swim, keeping his head above water just enough to stay alive.

As he felt his strength wane, something struck him a glancing blow on the crown of his head. A plank! Probably a bit of the broken remains of his ship. He grabbed it with both arms and held on for dear life.

The current swept him along, and he let it carry him. No point in sapping what remained of his energy fighting against it, particularly when he didn't know in which direction the land lay.

He watched, searching the horizon for another glimpse of the shoreline he'd spotted just before the ship went down. Finally, he saw it. It was a small island, so agonizingly close he felt he could reach out and touch it, but it wasn't truly as near as all that. He kept his eyes locked on the spot, savoring the glimpses each lightning flash revealed.

Too soon, the current bore him past the island and into dark, open water. As he watched its receding outline, he wondered if he would ever see land again.

Hours later, or perhaps it was days, he awoke to a burning sensation on the back of his neck.

Am I in hell?

He opened his eyes and rejoiced to see white sand all around him. He had made it to land. And then another thought struck him—the stone! Did he still have it?

His left hand was balled in a fist, clamped down so tightly that he was forced to use his other hand to pry his fingers open. There it was. He had saved it. Perhaps the Lord smiled on him after all.

"Thanks be to God." He rolled over onto his back and breathed deeply of the morning air. He didn't know where he was, but he was alive. That was what mattered the most. He closed his eyes. He could easily fall asleep, but knew he ought to move off the beach and find water, food, and shelter. A shadow passed across his face and he snapped his eyes open.

Three reddish-brown faces stared down at him.

Perhaps he was in Hell after all.

CHAPTER 1

Robert couldn't possibly drink another cup of Turkish coffee. It was delicious, without a doubt, but he'd been jittery even before wandering into the tiny cafe in this dirty corner of Dogubeyazit. Besides, he'd sat in one place for too long. He should get moving again.

He handed a few bills to the man behind the counter and watched them disappear. The man gave him a quick smile, mischief dancing in his eyes, and turned away. Oh well, getting back change was the least of his concerns right now.

"Excuse me, but can you tell me how to get to…"

The man shook his head. "No English," he said, his back still to Robert.

"That's all right, then. Thank you."

He stepped out of the dimly lit shop and onto the dark street. No one seemed to be about at what would have been considered an early hour back home. That was fine with him. He tucked his hands into his pockets and resumed his search for the way back.

Every shadow made him jump. The tiny shadows that flitted across the windows lining the darkened street, dancing across the corners of his vision. The flat, distorted shadows cast by the moonlight. All were dark and foreboding. But it was the moving shadows that were the worst. The long thin shadows that swept across him with every vehicle that passed along the main street. He imagined each one was a hand reaching out to grab him.

"Pull yourself together, Robert. You're letting your imagination run wild."

But that wasn't entirely true. Someone was after him, though who it was, he could not fathom.

He'd suspected it for a while. Several times today he'd seen the same car parked in various places he visited. He'd told himself it was a mere fancy, but when he'd returned to his hotel this evening to find his room ransacked, he'd run. That had been a mistake. Now he was lost.

"Just keep on the move," he told himself. "Stay out of sight until you get to your car. You'll drive to the airport, get on the plane, and you'll be out of this place."

Something rustled in the alleyway to his right and he let out an embarrassingly high-pitched cry. He whirled around, ready to flee again.

It was a cat, probably after a mouse. Nothing more. It gazed up at him, judging him with its wide-eyed stare. Even it knew he was a craven.

Why did I come here, and alone to boot? I'm not cut out for this cloak and dagger business.

Of course, it hadn't seemed like anything other than a scholarly endeavor at the time he decided to make the trip. He was merely following up on an old legend he'd uncovered. To his great pleasure, it had proved to be true, and what he'd discovered was remarkable. Better than that, it was a tantalizing clue that might lead to the greatest prize imaginable.

At least he no longer had it in his possession. By now, it would be miles from here, on its way across the ocean. He considered calling Dima and warning her to be on the lookout for a mysterious package, but something told him not to. He didn't know who was after him, or how they'd found out about his search, but if they were to catch up with him, he supposed they could check his outgoing calls and target her next. He couldn't allow that to happen.

He took a left turn at random, cutting through an alleyway. He checked his watch. It was ten o'clock. A long time until his flight out but he'd feel better if he found his way back to his hotel and his vehicle soon.

Several times he'd considered walking up to any of the doors he'd passed and asking directions, but paranoia kept him on the move. If he'd seen a taxi or a police officer, he could have flagged them down, but no luck. He'd really made a mess of things.

He just needed to make it to the airport. They had security. There he could safely hide in plain sight until his flight departed.

Why hadn't he simply hopped in his rental car and driven away? He knew why. He was a coward and completely out of his depth. A day of rising tension and fear had led him to snap.

He quickened his pace and came out on a familiar street. His hotel was not far from here! Perhaps another mile. His spirits buoyed, he set out down the street at a slow jog. When his hotel came into sight, he quickened to a trot.

Almost there.

He was so focused on his destination that he didn't see the figure lurking in the shadows off to his right. A powerful hand closed around his wrist and another clamped down over his mouth. He tried to cry out, to struggle, but the unseen figure held him fast.

"Mister Crane." The speaker's breath was hot on Robert's neck. "We have some questions to ask you."

CHAPTER 2

"The winner by knockout and still champion, Angel Bonebrake!" The crowd packing the arena roared as, in the center of the cage, the referee raised Angel's hand high in the air. From his seat in the front row, Dane Maddock clapped and whistled. For a brief instant their eyes met and she winked.

Bones Bonebrake, Angel's brother and Maddock's business partner and best friend, elbowed him in the ribs.

"How does it feel to know your fiancé can beat the crap out of you?"

Maddock smiled. The truth was, he was still in a daze over his engagement. For years he thought he'd never marry again, but the beautiful Cherokee girl with the vocabulary of a sailor had other plans.

"I can still kick your ass, Bones. That's what matters."

"Keep dreaming, Maddock." He looked around at the attendees who were already filing out of the arena. "I suppose we should get out of here. She's going to be busy with post-fight interviews and all that crap." Bones caught his sister's eye, waved, and then pointed to the exit. She smiled, gave him the thumbs up, and then blew Maddock a kiss.

"Do you think she's the first mixed martial arts champion to blow kisses in the ring? That's not very badass." Bones asked as they pushed their way into the lines of people making their way to the exits.

Maddock rolled his eyes. "Can we talk about something else?"

"Sure. Let's talk about the wedding. Which one of you is going to wear the dress?"

Maddock silenced his friend with a frown, but it didn't last. Upon leaving, Bones spent the drive from his uncle Crazy Charlie's casino, where the fight had taken place, to his mother's house, speculating about what Maddock's and Angel's children would look like.

"Don't get me wrong, but it's going to be weird if I have a bunch of short, blue-eyed blond nephews. I mean, I can teach them how to pull chicks and all that other important stuff you don't know anything about, but there's nothing I can do about the DNA. We'll just have to hope they get that from my sister."

At a hair under six feet tall, Maddock was hardly short, but most people look small alongside the burly, six foot five Bones. The big native had lorded his height over Maddock, literally and figuratively, since their days in the Navy SEALs.

"We haven't even talked about a wedding date and already you've got us having kids? Slow your roll," Maddock said. The engagement was so new, he wasn't at all ready to contemplate anything beyond that.

"Maybe you missed a couple of health classes, but you don't have to get married before you…" Bones broke off in midsentence and tapped the brakes as his mother's house came into view.

"What is it?" Maddock asked. Neither silence nor slow driving could be classified as typical Bones behavior.

"Something's not right. Mom's still back at the casino with Angel, so Grandfather's the only person home. He goes to bed at, like, eight o'clock and he never leaves a light on." Bones pointed to the front of the house, where a faint light was barely visible through the front curtains.

"Maybe he left it on for us?" Maddock offered.

"And waste ten cents worth of electricity? Not a chance."

Bones pulled his Dodge Ram pickup over to the side of the road and parked. They hopped out and moved quickly toward the house. As they drew closer, Maddock spotted a shiny white SUV parked behind a clump of trees a short distance away.

"Do you recognize that car?" He pointed at the SUV.

Bones shook his head. He quickened his pace and Maddock had to double-time it to keep up.

"I'll take the front door, you take the back." Maddock keenly felt the absence of his Walther, but he had seen no need to take it along to the fight. He wouldn't have gotten it past the metal detectors at the casino in any case.

A covered front porch ran across the front of the modest, ranch-style home. Neatly trimmed shrubs and flower beds bursting with life lined the porch on either side of the front steps. Bones' mom had a green thumb.

Maddock crept up the front steps, careful not to tread on the second, which he knew to be squeaky. By the time he reached the front door he could just make out unfamiliar voices. He moved to the front window and peered through the tiny slit between the drawn curtains.

Two well-dressed men, one a hooked-nose fellow of Middle-Eastern descent; the other a tall black man with a shaved head, stood over Samuel Bonebrake, Bones' grandfather. The old man sat in a kitchen chair placed in the middle of the living room, his face a mask of serenity.

"Come on, you obstinate old codger, you are wasting our time," hook-nose barked. He leaned in close and whispered something in Samuel's ear.

"Questioning him will get us nowhere, Ahmed. He won't talk unless we persuade him," his partner said. He spoke in a light Jamaican accent that would've been pleasant to the ear in other circumstances. He looked down at Samuel, smiled, and drew back his fist.

Maddock sprang to the front door and turned the knob.

It was locked.

Twice he heard fist meet flesh. The second time, the old man cried out. Maddock threw his shoulder into the door and it burst open. He heard another crash as Bones forced his way in through the back. The intruders looked up in surprise, but each reacted in an instant.

Before Maddock could close the gap between them, both drew automatic pistols and opened fire. Maddock dove behind the sofa, bullets shredding the upholstery just above his head and tearing into the sheetrock wall.

"Come on, Tyson! Let's get out of here!" Ahmed shouted. Still firing, the two men ran out the front door.

Maddock sprang to his feet and, for a moment, considered chasing them, but he knew he would be a sitting duck.

"Bones, are you all right?" He turned to see his friend standing beside his grandfather, checking him for injuries.

"I'm fine. Here." Bones dug into his pocket, took out the keys to his truck, and tossed them to Maddock. "Pistol's in the writing desk."

While Bones attended to his grandfather, Maddock yanked open the drawer of the nearby desk and snatched up an old Ruger Single Six Convertible .22 revolver and a few spare bullets. He dashed out the front door just in time to see the SUV roar past the front of the house. From the passenger seat, Ahmed blazed away with his automatic.

Maddock dropped to one knee, bullets whizzing past his head and smacking into the door and wall behind him. He had time for one aimed shot which shattered the SUVs rear window before the vehicle was down the street and out of sight.

He sprinted to Bones' pickup truck, intending to give chase, but stopped when he drew close. The front right tire was flat, and a quick inspection showed a bullet hole in the sidewall was the culprit. Ahmed was either very lucky or an excellent shot. Either way, any hope of catching the two intruders was now lost.

He tucked the revolver into his belt and stalked back to the house, cursing all the way.

Inside, Bones had moved his grandfather to the sofa. The old man lay stretched out with his head resting on a cushion, holding a bag of ice against his forehead. Blood trickled down the side of his face. Bones looked up when

Maddock entered.

"What happened?" Anger burned in his eyes and his body trembled with scarcely contained rage. Maddock was almost glad he hadn't caught up with the two intruders. He shuddered to think what Bones would've done had Maddock somehow managed to detain them.

"They shot out the tire. For what it's worth, I got the license plate number."

Bones spat a curse and his grandfather raised a crooked finger.

"No language like that in my house, Uriah," he rasped.

"Yes, Grandfather." The irascible Bones was perhaps the most irreverent person Maddock had ever known, but his respect for his elders was absolute.

"I don't suppose you know who they are or what they wanted?" Maddock asked.

The old man shook his head. "I have never seen them before, but I do know what they wanted."

Bones frowned. "And what was that?"

"They are looking for our family treasure."

CHAPTER 3

"**Another late night,** Miss Zafrini? Maybe you need to schedule some other sort of nocturnal activities." Hank flashed a crooked grin over the top of his Maxim magazine and winked.

Dima forced a smile. She knew the middle-aged security guard to be harmless and that his attempts at flirtation were intended to be flattering, yet it galled her that she had to put up with it. She had complained about him before and gotten nowhere. Even now, in the twenty-first century, working at a major university, she was still expected to take his clumsy overtures as complimentary rather than creepy.

"You know me, Hank. Too busy for any of that foolishness." She hurried out the door before he could make one of his usual comments about her long legs, glossy black hair, big brown eyes, or olive complexion. He had actually reached his peak the previous evening when he assured her that he knew Jordanians were not terrorists. "Freaking redneck," she muttered as the door slid closed behind her.

Outside, the humidity wrapped around her like a blanket. Even at nine o'clock at night Atlanta was a veritable steam room. Oh well, she'd known what she was getting into when she moved here, but the position in the university's archaeology department had been too good to pass up. Or so she had thought.

Inside her battered Honda CRV, she blasted the air-conditioning and the new Volbeat album in equal measure and spent the drive home cursing her lazy department head who kept dumping his projects on her so he could spend time "training" his new grad assistant. Rumor had it, tonight's instruction was taking place at the Marriott Marquis. She had considered tipping off his wife but she had no idea under what name he booked his room. Besides, his marriage wasn't her problem. She had enough concerns of her own to be getting on with.

By the time she reached her apartment she had tired herself out and a dull feeling of discouragement had settled upon her. Perhaps she should move back home. At least there she'd be around friends and it would get her mother and father off her back.

Passing through the empty lobby, she checked her mailbox and was surprised to see among the circulars and credit card offers a small box with no sender's name or return address. She wondered what it might be. She never received mail from home, much less packages. Her parents had finally mastered the Internet and now did their pestering through cyberspace.

The box was light; so light, in fact, she wondered if it might be empty. She gave it a shake but heard nothing. Weird.

Her apartment was decorated in a style she liked to call "too busy to care." The sofa, her lone piece of living room furniture, faced the television set which she hadn't gotten around to removing from its box. As long as she set it up in time for football season, she would be fine. A single, framed photograph hung on the wall—a family portrait from her teen years. Four faces smiled back at the camera. She didn't like to look at it, hated to in fact, but she displayed it out of a sense of obligation.

In the kitchen, luxuriously furnished with a card table and two folding chairs, she tossed the junk mail in the garbage, poured a glass of red wine, and contemplated dinner. Cold pizza or salad from a bag? It had been a long day and even tearing open a plastic bag felt like far too much effort. Pizza won out.

Sitting down at the table, she pushed aside the half-finished puzzle she'd started on Valentine's Day when her date stood her up, and carefully opened the box. Inside, encased in layers of bubble wrap and pressed between two sturdy squares of cardboard, she found a Glassite envelope containing scraps of old vellum covered in faint writing, and a note. She took a bite of pizza, grimacing at the cardboard texture of the stale crust, and began to read.

Dima,

I know this isn't the proper way to care for or transport an ancient document but I needed to get it to someone I trust, someone who can work on it with me. You're an expert at this. I have one more stop to make, but I'll get to you as soon as I can. Feel free to begin working on it. I think you'll find it's right up your alley. Have fun!

Robert

Robert Crane was an old friend and colleague. She hadn't seen him for years and was surprised he even knew her current address, much less setting her a task without first touching base. And what was up with this note? Robert had never been the secretive type, but this message was maddeningly vague. Maybe it was a prank. When translated, the fragments inside the envelope would probably spell out an insult. That would be more Robert's style. She could still hear his infectious laughter. The man loved his jokes. Oh well, she could use a laugh.

She held up the envelope and examined the sheet inside. Her heart began to race. If the document was a fake, Robert had outdone himself. A quick inspection with a magnifying glass convinced her that this was the genuine article. Warming to the challenge, she grabbed her laptop, a pad, and a pen and set to work. A few minutes later she had already translated a few phrases.

called the name of that son Noah ... began to multiply on the face of the earth ... in the earth in those days, but they were not of man...

So it was something from the Bible. More accurately, something extra-Biblical. She knew the book of Genesis contained no story of Noah's birth. It came to her in a flash and the breath caught in her chest. Her slice of pizza slipped from numb fingers to fall forgotten onto a paper towel.

"It couldn't possibly be. There's just no way."

She hastily typed the phrases into her web browser, took a deep breath, and tapped the enter key. The search results left no doubt.

"Robert," she whispered, "if this is a joke, you are a dead man."

CHAPTER 4

"Mister Bonebrake, we need you to tell us everything you can remember about this treasure." Maddock sat at the kitchen table with Bones, his grandfather, Angel, and Bones' mother, Miriam. Behind Miriam, Bones' uncle, "Crazy Charlie" Bonebrake, paced back and forth, one hand resting on the grip of the 357 Magnum he wore on his hip, and a dark look in his eyes.

They sat in the small kitchen of Miriam's home where the attack had occurred the night before. It was a quaint, cozy place with dark wood cabinets and yellowing linoleum. The room smelled of coffee, bacon grease, and Lysol. It reminded Maddock of visits to his own grandparents' house when he was younger.

"It's all right," Miriam said to her father-in-law. "You can tell us." Miriam Bonebrake was a handsome woman, tall with delicate features and big brown eyes. It was plain to see where Angel had gotten her good looks.

Samuel shook his head. "There is no need to discuss it any further. Those men are gone and I don't want to cause trouble for the boys." He twitched a crooked, liver-spotted finger at Maddock and Bones.

Angel smirked. "Grandfather, these two are perfectly capable of finding trouble on their own. Believe me." She reached over and took Maddock's hand. Her diamond engagement ring twinkled in the morning sunlight that shone through the window. Maddock still couldn't believe his good fortune. Thank God for beautiful women with bad taste in men.

"We have a lot of experience in treasure hunting," Maddock said, turning his thoughts from the lovely lady at his side. "It's our profession."

"And we know how to take care of ourselves." Bones bared his teeth in something just short of a grin. "Besides, these men want the so-called family treasure, whatever it is, and they clearly think you're the key to finding it. They'll keep coming back until they get what they want."

"Unless we find it first," Maddock finished.

"You don't know that."

"With respect, Grandfather," Bones said, "yes we do. We've dealt with situations and men like this before."

Samuel let out a sigh of resignation. "All right, but I want a cup of coffee first."

"I got it." Angel rose, gave Maddock's shoulder a squeeze, and went to refill her grandfather's mug. Maddock couldn't help but stare at her. He loved her big eyes, her fine cheekbones, her long brown hair, her trim, athletic figure…

"Dude." Bones elbowed him in the ribs. "Can we focus here? We've got a situation."

"Sorry about that." Grinning, Maddock took out his phone, turned on the voice recording feature, and slid it across the table. Meanwhile, Bones borrowed a pad and paper from his mother and prepared to take notes.

When Samuel finally had his steaming mug of coffee, he took a sip, savored it for a few seconds, and finally began the story.

"Esau Bonebrake was the brother of my great-grandfather," the old man said.

"So I'm not the only one who got stuck with the weird Bible name?" Bones asked.

Samuel carefully placed his mug on the table, folded his hands, and fixed Bones with a stern look. "Uriah, if you insist on interrupting me with your juvenile comments, the story is going to take a long time to tell, and at my age, time is not on my side."

"Ass," Angel whispered to her brother.

Samuel turned his eyes on her and she quickly adopted a look of contrition. "Sorry."

"Esau was an unusual man," Samuel said, resuming the narrative. "He kept mostly to himself, never married, and spent most of his time in the mountains." Samuel seemed to anticipate Maddock's thoughts. "That in itself was not out of the ordinary for the mid-1800's, but there is no doubt he was an eccentric. He was a treasure hunter."

Bones grunted and mimed stabbing himself in the heart, but everyone ignored him.

"He also collected stories and legends the way Angel collects dolls."

"Dolls?" Maddock arched an eyebrow at Angel.

"They're vintage," she said, as if that explained everything. "Now stop interrupting Grandfather's story."

Samuel smiled. "One of the stories that was passed down through our family spoke of an ancestor who had discovered an item of power. The details have been lost, but Esau took it for the truth and spent years searching for it until he finally found it. At least, he claimed to have found it. If anyone else saw it or knew what it was, I cannot say. He called it the 'family' treasure but, by all accounts, he kept it to himself. But, shortly after he found the treasure, Esau developed the ability to talk to animals."

"I talk to animals all the time," Bones said, "but they never answer back."

"I think he means like a horse whisperer." Angel rolled her eyes.

Samuel nodded. "He could break a horse with the sound of his voice. He could catch a fish by whispering a few words and simply wait for it to swim into his hands."

"Forgive me, but it sounds like a fairly common legend," Angel said. "I'm sure I've heard a hundred similar tales from other families and certainly from other nations."

"Perhaps, but despite his reputation, everyone at the time seemed to take his power as a matter of fact. Many claim to have witnessed his abilities firsthand. According to my great-grandfather, the two of them once stumbled upon a mountain lion's den. Wanting to protect her cubs, the mother charged at them. Esau took one look at her, waved his hand, and said 'Shoo!'"

"And it worked?" Maddock asked.

"Yes." Samuel took another sip of coffee, closed his eyes, and smiled. "Excellent." He sat up a little straighter, as if the drink had fortified him, and went on. "When the War Between the States broke out, Esau left to join the Union army. He took his treasure with him for good luck. During the Chickamauga campaign, he and his unit found themselves separated from their main force. Trapped by the Confederates, they were slaughtered. Only Esau managed to stay alive by hiding in a cave behind a waterfall. He remained there, living off the raw fish he summoned, waiting for the enemy troops to leave the area. Finally, realizing he stood little chance of making his way through enemy lines and back to the Union forces, and not wanting to lose his treasure, he hid it in a crack in the cave wall, intending to return for it someday."

"I'm guessing he never went back?" Bones asked.

Samuel shook his head. "He was captured and spent the rest of the war wasting away in Andersonville."

Maddock let out a tiny whistle. Now a national historical site, Andersonville was a notorious Confederate prison camp. Captured Union soldiers were penned in an open stockade with no protection from the elements, and kept away from the shelter of the prison walls by the threat of the death line—an invisible line that marked out a buffer zone between the prisoners and the guards. A captive who stepped over it was shot immediately. Disease-ridden and malnourished, the prisoners who survived came out looking like the victims of the Nazi concentration camps in World War II. It was easily one of the most shameful chapters in the history of the so-called Civil War.

"He was never the same after that," Samuel said. "He was a broken man, half crippled and nearly mad. He lived out the remainder of his days in my great-grandfather's home. He eventually told the story to my grandfather, who passed it down to my father, who in turn told the story to me."

"Didn't anyone ever search for the treasure?" Angel

asked.

"Not as far as I know. Everyone believed Samuel owned something that he loved enough to call it a treasure, but they doubted it was anything of value. Besides, he had only a vague idea of where he had hidden it."

"The proverbial needle in a haystack," Bones said.

"But maybe not so impossible to find nowadays. We've got historical records to search through, topographical maps, and satellite imagery. It's possible." Maddock turned to Samuel. "Do you know any specifics about the place he hid the treasure? Landmarks? Nearby towns?"

"A few," Samuel said. "My grandfather wrote the story down." He turned to Miriam. "Would you please fetch me my Bible?"

Bones' mother hurried away and returned moments later with a battered old Bible. Its worn cover, cracked spine, and dog-eared pages said it had seen its share of use. Samuel took it from her with care, opened it, and thumbed through its yellowing pages until he found a single sheet of paper. He turned the Bible around so Bones and Maddock could see.

Maddock leaned in for a better look. Faded writing in a tight, neat hand filled the page. It recounted the story of the skirmish, Esau's escape, and his discovery of the cave. The details of the cave's location were few, but there were enough to give Maddock hope that, with help, they could find it. The final line caught his attention.

Blood is the key.

"Blood is the key. Any idea what that means?"

Samuel shook his head. "I can't say for certain, but since it is the story of a family treasure, I assume Esau was speaking of the importance of the family bloodline."

"We'll just have to figure it out. So," he said to Bones, "are we going to go for it?"

"That's sort of what we do, isn't it? But I don't want to leave Grandfather alone, not with those men still out there."

"He won't be alone." Crazy Charlie spoke for the first time. "I'll take him to my house and have my security men on guard twenty-four/seven." As the wealthiest man in the community, and a person who didn't mind skating around the gray areas of the law, he had a myriad of resources at his disposal.

"And he'll have me." Angel reached out and took her grandfather's hand. "I hope they come back. I'd love a shot at those assclowns." Her lovely face was suddenly filled with the dark ferocity usually reserved for her opponents in the cage.

"Easy there," Maddock said. "We'll just have to hope it doesn't come to that." He sat up straight. "It's settled, then. I say we send a copy of this to Jimmy and see what he can come up with." Jimmy Letson was an old friend and an accomplished hacker who had helped them on many treasure hunts in the past. If anyone could piece these clues together and come up with something useful, it was him.

Bones stood, cracked his knuckles, and smiled.

"Let's do it."

CHAPTER 5

"This looks like the place." Bones pointed at the weathered sign. Despite the faded letters, he could make out the words *National Park Service, Black Break, Georgia.* Jimmy's research had provided quick results. He'd entered all the details from the document and matched them up to survivor accounts of a modest-sized Civil War skirmish just south of Lookout Mountain. It didn't appear on any map, nor in any history book, but it existed nonetheless.

He guided the car up the cracked asphalt drive and parked in front of a shabby-looking office building. The brown paint was peeling off in patches the size of swim fins and seedling pines peeked over the edge of the gutter that ran along the front of the single-story building.

"Not too impressed, I have to say." Maddock shook his head as he took in the sight. "Definitely not ship-shape."

"It's not an episode of Cribs, and it sure as hell isn't the Navy," Bones said. "We just need directions to the battlefield." He cut the engine and pocketed the keys.

"What did you do that for? Springsteen's on."

"That's exactly why I did it. See you in a minute."

He bypassed the sagging stairs and stepped directly up onto the covered porch. A solitary rocking chair sat by the screen door. A discarded newspaper lay alongside it underneath a rusted JFG coffee can that had obviously been put to use as a spittoon at some point in the last century. Bones wrinkled his nose and the dried, brown gunk stuck to the inside of the can, and drew the door open. The hinges, much in need of oil, announced his arrival before he could step inside.

A wrinkled woman stood behind the counter, watching The Price is Right on a tiny color television. She wore a crisp tan uniform, with a tag that named her

Betty Tull. She initially spared him only a glance as he entered, then snapped her head around and gaped up at him. "My goodness."

"I know," Bones said with a grin. "I'm the tallest Indian you've ever seen." A six-foot-five Cherokee was not a common sight in any neck of the woods.

"You've heard that before, I reckon?" She kept staring at him, not the least bit embarrassed by her reaction of a moment before.

"A time or two. I was wondering if you could give me directions..." The sudden change in Betty's expression made him pause. Her eyes narrowed to slits, her lips pursed, and she directed her full attention to the door behind him. He spun around, his hand instinctively going to his hip where he had worn a sidearm for so many years in the service, and still wore it on occasion, but no one was there.

"Did you sit in that rocking chair, young man?" She sounded like a teacher scolding her pupil. He shook his head. "It's moving. Did you push it? Brush up against it? You look like you might be clumsy."

"I don't think so. Why? Is it an antique?"

"A bad omen," she muttered in a voice almost too soft to be heard. She bit her lip, and then returned her attention to him. "Anyhow, you were saying?"

"I was hoping you could give me directions. I understand there's a Civil War battlefield in this area. Is there a park map that might show it?"

"The battlefield." It was as if a shade had been drawn down across her face, all previous emotion gone. "You want to go there?"

"Yes," Bones said. "One of my ancestors fought in a battle somewhere near here back during the war. I was hoping to visit the site, maybe take a few pictures. Just have a look around." He gave her a congenial smile and leaned casually against the counter, trying to put her at ease.

"It's not technically part of the park."

"That's fine. Could you give me directions?"

"I'll help the gentleman, Betty." A keg of a man almost bursting out of his park ranger uniform stepped out from an office in the back. "Why don't you go on and take your lunch break?" Betty fixed Bones with an unreadable look and then headed into the office. When she was gone, the man smiled at Bones and offered his hand. "I'm Earl Eddings, the man who passes for ranger in these parts."

"Bones." He shook the ranger's strong, calloused hand. Clearly this Eddings fellow did more than sit behind a desk all day. "That's what they call me, anyway. My mother stuck me with a weird name I don't cop to if I can help it."

"Understood." Eddings grinned. "So, you say you're looking for Dark Entry?"

"I'm looking for the site of the Battle of Black Break. Is that the same place?"

"We don't call it that around here. Black Break's the Yankee name for it, you see."

"Oh, right. The North named battles after the closest town, and the South usually named them after landmarks, right?"

Eddings nodded. "A lot of the times that was the case. Anyhow, they won the war, so..." He threw out hands in a gesture of futility. "Dark Entry is the name of the stream that feeds the lake at the site of the battle. Of course, you can't properly call it a battlefield, since it was more of a skirmish in a mountain valley, but it's all we've got around here."

Bones' heart beat faster. A stream-fed lake in a mountain valley at the site of a Civil War skirmish. So, at least that part of the story was accurate, and if that part was true, why not the rest? Perhaps Esau really had hidden a treasure there.

"So what is it you say you're looking for up there?" Eddings' tone, a bit too casual, didn't match the suspicion in his eyes.

"Nothing. I was researching my family tree and this place came up as a likely spot for the battle my ancestor took part in. I figured if I was ever in the neighborhood I'd check it out. I've got business in Atlanta so I took a little spontaneous detour. Beats working."

Eddings smiled. "You don't have to tell me twice. I just have to warn off the people who go up there looking for artifacts, you understand. It's not government land but it's part of our history, and it's protected by county ordinance."

"Do you get many visitors up the battlefield?"

"Almost none. It's not very well-known. Locals might go up there for a picnic." Eddings paused and fixed Bones with an appraising look. "Which side did your ancestor fight for?"

"The Confederacy," Bones lied. He was in the heart of Dixie and figured he needed all the goodwill he could get. Eddings' smile told him that was the right answer.

"Good man. I used to be a reenactor."

"Really?" Bones didn't want to waste time with small talk but he supposed he wasn't truly in a hurry. "Me too. I've scalped General Custer, like, a thousand times."

Eddings gaped at him and then guffawed. "Good one." He took a deep breath and sighed. "I don't get many laughs around here. Betty's no Larry the Cable Guy."

"And you're no Red Skelton." Betty said, leaning through the doorway. "If you're planning on sending him up to the battlefield, are you going to tell him about the curse? All the disappearances? It's only right. You can't let him go up there and have Lord knows what happen to him."

"I will tell him. Thank you, Betty." Eddings kept his voice pleasant, though his eyes had gone flinty. "Sorry about that. It's a remote location, and the site has had its share of tragedies: drownings, fatal falls, hikers gone missing. Plus, there's a long-standing belief that the site is haunted. Kids go up there to party sometimes. They start drinking and smoking the marijuana and have fun scaring each other. Anyway, you can see why some people," he rolled his eyes toward the open office door, "let their superstitious beliefs get the better of them. There's no reason for concern as long as you use caution. Just watch your step, and keep an eye out for the bears and the snakes."

"Thank you for the warning. I'll be careful. Do you have a map that shows how to get there?"

"No, but I'll draw you one. It's not too difficult." Eddings took out a legal pad, tore off the faded top page, and sketched out a map. He jotted a few notes about landmarks along the way and emphasized what he said were the more confusing turns. When he finished, he passed the paper to Bones.

"You taking anyone up there with you?"

There was something about the way in which the Ranger asked the question that put Bones on his guard. "Nope. Just me. Like I said, I'm traveling for business and I made a side trip on a whim." For an instant, he feared the ranger was about to offer to accompany him, which would be entirely out of the question considering what Bones and Maddock planned to do. "It's kind of a personal journey for me. Trying to get in touch with the spirit of my ancestor, you know."

Eddings' smile did not reach his eyes, but he nodded and assured Bones that he understood completely. That was one of the advantages to being an Indian. You could heap a big, steaming pile of spiritual crap onto white people and they'd believe it every time.

"Just curious," Eddings said. "If you got in trouble up there I'd want the sheriff to know how many people to look for."

Bones shook Eddings' hand, called a thank-you to Betty, and slipped out the door. This time, he was extra careful to not touch the rocking chair.

Eddings watched the big Indian step down off the porch and disappear from sight. He listened as an engine roared to life and then receded as the man drove away. Only then did he head to the office.

"Betty, can I have the office for a minute? I need to

make a personal call."

"All right." Betty pushed back from the desk and wobbled to her feet. "It must be your mama because I know you don't have a girlfriend."

"Thanks so awful much, Betty." He closed the door behind her, moved to his desk, and sank heavily into the chair. Pushing aside Betty's tomato sandwich and bottle of water, he rested his elbows on the desk and buried his face in his hands. He hated what he was about to do, but he had no choice. He took out his cell phone and punched up the number.

"It's me," he said as soon as the party at the other end picked up. "We got a live one heading for the hills."

"You think we can do it clean?" the voice said.

"Should be all right. He said he was headed to Atlanta and came here on a lark. You can check his phone and see if he might have called someone to tell them where he was going, but even if he did, he wouldn't be the first to get lost in the woods."

"That's true. How about the other thing?"

Eddings bit his lip. The "other thing" was a mystery he hadn't yet been let in on, and it stuck in his craw that he wasn't in the know. "I can't say for sure, but it's doubtful. I tried to trip him up. He says he's just up here for ancestry research."

"He had an ancestor in the battle?"

"Yeah, but on our side."

"We'll interrogate him just to be sure. Anything else I should know?"

"He's big fellow. Looks like he can handle himself."

"That just makes it more fun."

The call ended and Eddings sat, staring at his phone. He didn't envy what was about to happen to that Indian.

CHAPTER 6

"So you think this is it?" Maddock took in the narrow valley. Mountain peaks cast long shadows, and the tall, dark pines that covered their slopes leaned in on all sides, as if daring anyone to try and climb out. A stream cascaded down moss-covered rocks into a tiny lake of deep green. In the distance, the open field that must have been the site of the battle gave way to a dense forest.

"It fits the description." Bones gazed out across the water. "If the story is true, the hidden cave should be somewhere in the area of that waterfall." He pointed to the falls.

"By the way, how did your great, great granduncle or whatever he was, come to be fighting for the Union in the first place? I would have thought the Indian Removal Act would have given your family ample reason to hate the federal government."

"They did," Bones said. "When Jackson sent the soldiers in, my family hid in the mountains. They hated living like refugees in land that was rightfully their own. But, like my grandfather said, my uncle was an odd sort of fellow, so fighting for the North was probably his way of messing with people." He flashed a bright smile. "Or, maybe he just hated rednecks as much as I do."

"Let's go over things one more time," Maddock said. "If I've got the story straight, by the time he came to this battle, he'd been carrying this family heirloom all throughout the war. And then, when he saw the battle was lost, he stashed it here, knowing he'd have a hard time making it back to Union lines."

"Yep. He dove into the lake, thinking he could swim away and find a place to hide." Bones moved closer to the water, his eyes locked on the far shore as if he could see right through the mountainside. "He had almost made it to the far shore when the Confederates spotted him and started shooting. He dove down as deep as he could and came across the entrance to the underwater cavern. I don't know what possessed him to swim into it, not knowing if there would be air pockets, but he did."

"I've noticed a certain recklessness in the generations of Bonebrakes."

"We call it 'balls.' You should consider growing some."

Maddock chuckled. "So, we're looking for an underwater cave, and then we have to make our way back into it until it's too narrow to go any farther, and that's where it will be hidden?"

Bones nodded. "That's the plan. Of course, I have no idea how big a dude he was. No telling how far back he was able to make it before the cave got too tight for him."

"We'll just have to take our chances." Maddock fished a quarter from his pocket. "Flip you to see who has to stay topside?"

"No need." Bones waved the coin away. "I told the ranger I'd be coming up here alone. I don't know why, but I just had a bad feeling about him. It wouldn't surprise me if he showed up to check on us, and if he sees you here with our car, he's going to want to know where I am and why I lied to him."

"We can't have that now, can we?" Maddock grinned. In general, he didn't care for fresh water dives, but if the choice was between a dive and standing around doing nothing for an hour, he'd take the fresh water.

"Besides," Bones said, "a shrimp like you will be able to push farther into the cave than I could. I guess there are advantages to being a dwarf."

Maddock could think of a dozen witty comebacks but he was eager to get out of the Georgia heat and into the cool water. In a matter of minutes, he was suited up and ready to dive.

"Don't fart around down there," Bones said. "I'll stick near the shore, look like a tourist, and keep an eye out for you. And try not to get tangled in anything. I really don't want to come in after you. Mountain lakes are cold."

"I'm definitely not looking forward to the shrinkage factor." Maddock grimaced.

"How can you tell the difference?" Bones took a quick step back. "Just kidding, bro. Have a good dive." He fished a small camera from his pocket and strolled away. "Oh, by the way!" he called as Maddock stepped into the water. "Watch out for snapping turtles! One of those gets you in the wrong place and no nieces or nephews for me."

Laughing, Maddock turned and gritted his teeth as he waded into the chilly lake. This was a far cry from the warm waters of Key West. His full suit would keep him fairly warm, but just knowing he was surrounded by all that cold water was enough to raise goosebumps all over his body. He was a Caribbean and Gulf of Mexico kind of guy, not a mountain man. He slipped beneath the dark water, wishing for sun, sea, and a Dos Equis with lime.

The sun's rays did not penetrate more than a few meters below the surface of the lake, but the beam of the dive light affixed to his forehead revealed boulders and sunken logs, all coated with slimy mud and decayed vegetation. He swam with care, not wanting to limit visibility by stirring up a cloud of debris. A few small fish darted past, but otherwise he saw few signs of life in this place.

Once he neared the waterfall there was no need to be concerned about stirring up silt. Water roiled and churned, bringing visibility down to a few feet. He had worried that the cave, if it truly existed, might have already been discovered. Now, seeing the murky cloud someone would have to penetrate in order to stumble across it, he felt hope rising. He dove down as far as he could, careful to watch for potential snares, and swam hard against the force of the surging water. He kicked harder, creeping inexorably toward his goal.

His hands met stone an instant before his face would have. He found an uneven rock edge and held on tight, his body buffeted by the force of the waterfall. Slowly and methodically, he searched the area below the waterfall. His gloved hands probed each crevice and recess, but to no avail.

Doubts arose anew. What if they were in the wrong place? What if Esau had gotten confused in the retelling, and conflated the memory of the battle with the memory of hiding his treasure in a cave somewhere else entirely? What if there was no treasure at all?

Too many questions. He was here to do a job, and he would do it thoroughly. No way would he go back and tell Bones he had failed unless he had first given it his full effort. Determined to do this right, he resumed the search.

After a few more passes turned up nothing, he was on the verge of declaring the cave a myth when his light fell on an odd rock formation just beyond the area he had been searching. Behind an upright stone formation lay a dark, vertical gash in the wall. His heart pounding, he slid behind the rock and into the crevasse. The way was narrow and his shoulders almost touched the sides, but after a few feet, the fissure opened up again and he came to a sheer wall. He changed direction, followed his bubbles upward, until at last he broke the surface inside a pitch-black cavern.

He had found it!

CHAPTER 7

Dima's office was small but today it felt like a prison cell. Ever since she'd begun working on Robert's mysterious document, she'd battled the overwhelming urge to go off on the sort of adventure she'd fantasized about since she was a child. If this document were the real thing, she might even do it. Leaning in closer to her computer monitor, she typed another term into the search engine.

"My, you look intense. Let me guess, updating your dating profile again?" Addie leaned in to look over Dima's shoulder. "Noah's Ark? That's not going to get you a guy. At least, not a hot guy."

"What are you talking about? Hot people can't like ancient mysteries?"

"Please, I've seen those shows. That guy with the alien theories? Where did he get that hairstyle?"

"If you say so." Dima kept her eyes locked on the screen.

What are you working on, exactly?" The perky redhead was Dima's assistant and the closest thing she had to a friend in Atlanta.

"It's sort of my hobby. Always has been." That was imprecise. Her interest lay not only in the Noah tale, but in all the various flood myths and legends throughout history. She'd been fascinated with them since childhood when she watched a rerun of "In Search Of." She'd only tuned in because Leonard Nimoy, aka Mr. Spock, was the host. By the time the show ended, she was hooked.

"I thought they found the ark years ago." Addie drew up a chair and sat down beside Dima. "You know, up on a mountain in Turkey? There's a formation of a fossilized boat, or something. I don't know. My knowledge of Noah is limited to Sunday School when I was a kid."

"You are thinking of the Durupinar Structure. It's probably the best-known site associated with the Noah myth, but it really is just a rock formation that happens to be vaguely shaped like a boat. There's another, similarly-shaped site on a mountain in the same region, but it's not the ark either."

"Bummer." Addie frowned, but her face brightened almost immediately. "That means it's still out there, and you could be the one to find it!"

Dima smiled. She had certainly entertained that fantasy enough times in her life. "Maybe."

"What did you mean by Noah 'myth'? Why are you looking for it if you don't think it's real?"

"A myth isn't necessarily untrue. It's what we call a traditional story, usually one about the early history of a people. Sometimes it explains a natural phenomenon, something about their culture, and it typically has a supernatural component."

Addie pursed her lips. "Okay, I think I remember something about that from high school English. So you think there really was a guy who built a boat during a big flood, but just without the God stuff?"

"I don't know what I think. I'm trying to have an open mind. I do believe there was some sort of event, and perhaps an individual, that inspired the flood stories, including that of Noah. Maybe it happened exactly like the Bible says, maybe not, but I believe there's something there worth exploring."

"So what's got you barking up the Noah tree today?"

Dima hesitated, but Addie was trustworthy, and she wanted to tell someone about this.

"Have you ever heard of the *Book of Noah*?"

"Never."

"It's a lost book. We know it existed because there are references made to it in extra-biblical texts, and it's even quoted in some of them." Dima paused to see if Addie scoffed at this proclamation. When her friend did not, she continued.

"Here," she clicked on a tab to open a browser

screen, "is a passage from the book of Enoch." She gave her friend a moment to read the passage. "A friend of mine, a guy I used to work with, sent me a fragment from an old manuscript that contains this material, but it also contains a reference to three stones. Aside from not being mentioned in the Bible, there's no reference to three stones in any of the known surviving bits of the *Book of Noah*. That tells me that the bit he sent to me pre-dates anything we have from that book."

"Maybe it's from the original?" Mischief twinkled in Addie's big, green eyes. "And then you'd be the most famous Noah researcher in the world. No more teaching history to spoiled college brats. Am I right?"

Dima smiled. She couldn't deny having entertained that fantasy once or twice since she'd made the connection to the *Book of Noah*, but what were the odds?

"Why don't you ask this friend of yours where he got the fragment? That would be a good place to start, wouldn't it?"

"I can't get in touch with him. What's more, the note he attached was…weird." She made a face, knowing she sounded like a drama queen or conspiracy theorist.

"I'll work on it for you." Addie took out her phone and opened the note-taking app. "Look for," she whispered as she typed, "Noah Stones and *Book of Noah*."

"You don't have to do that." Dima couldn't escape the uneasy feeling about the manuscript fragment, but what could the harm be if Addie did a bit of checking? People researched Noah all the time.

"I'm your grad assistant. I'm assisting you with a project related to world history. Besides, if you find anything, you'll publish, won't you? That makes it connected to your job."

"I guess so, just…" Dima was about to tell Addie to be careful, but that seemed a touch too dramatic. "Just don't feel like you have to make it a priority."

"No worries. There's a cute guy in the religious

studies department I've been wanting to meet. You've just given me an excuse." Addie sprang out of her seat and bounded to the door, her red curls bouncing as she walked.

"Of course I have," Dima mumbled. She returned to her work, searching through websites dedicated to the Noah legend. The deeper she probed, the crazier the sites became. After thirty minutes of searching culminated with an essay explaining that Noah was an alien and the Great Flood was responsible for the destruction of Atlantis, she decided to take a break. "I have officially entered the sketchy part of the internet." Staring at the screen as if it had given offense, she picked up her now-cold cup of coffee and took a sip.

A sharp knock at the door startled her, eliciting a yelp and causing her to slosh coffee on her lap. "Oh my…" she growled. "Unbelievable."

"I'm so sorry," came a deep voice with a pleasant Caribbean lilt. "I didn't intend to startle you."

"Forget about it." She grabbed a handful of tissues and dabbed at the wet spot on her thigh. At least her cup had been almost empty. "What can I do for you?" She turned and was surprised to see a tall man with a shaved head and umber skin standing in the doorway. He had an athletic build, friendly eyes, and an easy smile. Not bad. "If you're looking for Addie, she just left."

"Are you Dima Zafrini?"

Dima blinked twice and nodded. "Yes," she finally managed, lurching to her feet and rubbing her legs as if smoothing a skirt. Did she always have to make an ass of herself around good-looking guys?

"My name is Tyson." The man closed the distance between them in two long strides and handed her a business card that read, *Daniel Tyson, Purchasing Agent, Trident Antiquities, N'Djamena, Chad.*

"I'm Dima, but you already know that." They shook hands. His grip was strong but not forceful. "How can I help?"

"I'm trying to find someone, and I'm hoping you can

assist me. It's someone you know."

"Oh?"

"Robert Crane. I understand the two of you were colleagues."

Suddenly, Tyson's smile didn't seem so pleasant. Dima managed to keep her own grin firmly in place as she replied.

"Yes, but it's been a few years. What do you want with him?"

"I had negotiated on behalf of my company to buy something from him. He didn't show up for our meeting and hasn't returned my calls. I won't deny that my primary concern is to conclude our business, but I am worried about him. He's a good fellow."

"He is." Thoughts exploded in Dima's mind like fireworks. Robert wouldn't sell antiquities. Would he? Maybe he was desperate for money? In any case, why would anyone come to her for information about Robert? And then it hit her. Tyson was after the document. Why hadn't it occurred to her in the first place? She realized she'd been silent for far too long. Tyson continued to smile down at her. "Forgive me, but if you're looking for Robert, why come to me? We're friendly, but we aren't exactly close."

"He mentioned you. You have a pretty name, so it stuck in my mind. If you don't mind my saying, I think Robert might have a thing for you. His face lit up when he spoke of you. Said you were one of the best in the field of Middle Eastern history, and that you had an interest in ancient literature."

Well, that was interesting, since Robert was gay and the last time they'd spoken, he was planning to propose to his partner. Furthermore, Dima was hardly a leading expert in her field. Tyson was lying.

"Ancient literature? So it was a book you were going to buy from him?"

"I'm afraid I'm not at liberty to say. Confidentiality agreements and all that. You understand, of course."

"Certainly I do." Her heart hammered in her chest.

How hard would Tyson press her if he thought she had the Noah fragment? "Well, like I said, I haven't heard from Robert in some time. I have your number." She held up the business card he had provided. "I'll call you if I hear anything."

"Are you sure you haven't heard from Robert? Not even an email, text message, Christmas card?" Still smiling, Tyson took a step closer. "Think hard."

Now Dima was pissed. Bullying misogynists were one of the prime motivating factors behind her move to the States. She met his eyes with a hard stare. "I'm sure."

Footsteps padded in the hallway and Addie appeared in the doorway, followed by Wayne, a fellow grad student who often trailed along behind Addie like a lovesick puppy. Though he was a gentle soul, Wayne was a bodybuilder who looked like a young Mr. Clean. Dima was thankful for the backup.

"No luck. The cute guy isn't there today." Addie froze when her eyes fell on Tyson. "Hello there. I'm Addie." She swept over to Tyson's side and offered her hand.

"I'm Tyson. It's a pleasure to meet you." He gave her hand a gentle shake, stepped back, and turned to Dima. "Thank you very much for your time, Miss Zafrini. I'll be in touch."

Addie stared, a tiny smile playing across her lips, as Tyson strode from the room.

"Where," she said to Dima, "have you been hiding that? He's tall but it would totally be worth the climb."

"It was just business. I don't know the guy."

"Well you should get to know him. He gave you his number, didn't he?" She pointed to the card Dima still clutched. "I'll bet he did that for a reason."

"Trust me, that's *not* the reason." Dima turned to her desk, reached for the mouse, intending to shut down her computer, and froze. The browser window was still open to the wacky Noah's Ark theory site. There was no way Tyson could have missed it. She felt a heavy lump form in her stomach. If he had suspected her before, now he knew for certain. What was to stop him following her home, or accosting her somewhere?

Addie must have seen the look on her face. "Dima, what's wrong?"

"Nothing. I've just got a few things on my mind." Dima cleared her internet search history and shut down the computer. She turned to see Addie still staring at her with a look of deep concern painted across her face. Wayne still leaned in the doorway, looking forlorn. Dima had an idea.

"Let's go out tonight."

Addie blinked. "What?"

"You're always telling me I work too much. Let's go out, have a few drinks, act stupid."

"Seriously? Dima Zafrini is going out for a night on the town?"

"Nothing wild, but yes. Somewhere I can get a beer and a burger. Wayne can come too!" Dima hated crowds, noise, and drunk people, but it was worth it just to see the way Wayne's face brightened while Addie's fell. "Wayne, do you still have that king cab pickup truck with the shotgun rack in the back?"

Wayne nodded, apparently rendered mute by this turn of good fortune.

"Great. You drive." She glanced at her watch. It wasn't close to quitting time, but she wanted out of here. "Let's go early. Meet me around back. There's something I need to do before we go."

Addie fixed her with a quizzical look but didn't argue. "Okay, if you say so." She turned to Wayne. "You heard the lady. Let's go out on the town."

When the two had left, Dima opened her briefcase and removed the box that held the document Robert had sent her. She wanted to keep it with her, but she couldn't shake her bad feeling about Tyson and, should she run across him or someone else who wanted it, a briefcase or pocketbook would be too obvious a hiding place.

The document was still inside its protective envelope. Inventing wildly, she removed the document from its box, slipped it inside a padded envelope, sealed it, and tucked it in the waistband of her pants at the small of her back. Next, she removed everything she actually cared about from her briefcase and stuffed it all in a desk drawer along with the box.

She pulled an old book off the shelf—a volume of Mark Twain short stories printed in the early 1900s, tore out a page at random, shredded the edges a bit, and put it inside a protective sheet. Finally, she placed the decoy page inside her briefcase and locked it. It wouldn't stand up to any kind of scrutiny, but it might fool someone at first glance should they try and rob her.

"Dima," she said to herself as she stepped out of her office and headed for the emergency stairwell at the back of the building, "I really hope you're just being paranoid."

CHAPTER 8

Bones kept a close eye on the calm, dark lake. He tracked Maddock's progress by the bubbles rising to the otherwise smooth surface of the water until, finally, the turbulence around the waterfall hid all signs of his partner.

"Good luck, Maddock. And hurry in case Eddings shows up."

The roar of a vehicle speeding up the dirt road caught his ear. Was it the nosy ranger coming to check up on him? Bones turned his camera on and aimed it at the waterfall, trying to look like a sightseer. Since he'd already voiced his concern that Eddings might make in appearance, he had every confidence that Maddock would be cautious about his return to the surface. They didn't need the hassle.

The roar grew louder and Bones realized that, in fact, several vehicles were approaching. A keen sense of vulnerability pierced his heart and he suddenly wished he had not left his Glock in the car. Abandoning any pretense of casual sightseeing, he hurried back around the edge of the lake toward the place they had parked, but he had not gone more than twenty paces when a pickup barreled out of the woods. The truck shot out onto the grassy valley floor, fishtailed as it turned, and then headed straight for Bones.

An open-top jeep, its driver looking stern and the fellow in the passenger seat hooting like a hog caller, and two more pickups followed behind. The lead truck skidded to a halt right in front of Bones. The driver gave a friendly wave before climbing out of the cab. The jeep pulled up alongside the truck. The young man on the passenger side was smiling and waving as well.

Bones didn't relax one bit. Rednecks got on his nerves in the best of circumstances, and these circumstances were far from the best. He nodded politely to the first man, a broad-shouldered fellow of early middle years, whose flannel-covered paunch hung down over what Bones just knew was a big silver belt buckle.

The two in the jeep were ruddy-faced and flaxen-haired, clearly father and son. The driver's face was lined and his temples dusted with white. Were it not for the added years, the two could have been brothers, even twins. The hunting rifles they suddenly leveled at Bones, however, were identical.

"Hands behind your head, boy." The paunchy man who had arrived first drew an old Colt long barrel and leveled it at Bones' head. "You got any weapons on you?"

"No, but I'd sure love to shoot that revolver of yours." Though his thoughts were racing a mile a minute, years of training and experience in tight situations allowed him to remain calm. "What model is that?"

"U.S. Army 1903. But I don't let nobody shoot this 'cept me. Do I, Nathan?" The young man in the jeep shook his head. "Tell you what. We'll wait for the others to get here before I search you. You look like you might could give somebody a spot of trouble if you had a mind to."

"Yes he does, Carter." The driver of the jeep spoke in a deep, rich voice befitting a politician or a morning radio host. "He does indeed." Oddly, the man seemed to relish the thought.

"Not me," Bones said. "I'm a wuss. I take bubble baths and listen to Kenny what's-his-name. That curly-haired dude."

"Kenny Roberts?" Nathan pursed his lips. "Naw, that Footloose guy. Kenny Loggins!" His face lit up like he'd just guessed the answer to Final Jeopardy.

"He's a funny one," Carter said. Far behind him, the two pickup trucks had boxed in Bones' car, and their passengers had unloaded. There were four of them, all carrying rifles and looking decidedly inbred. Bones soon found himself surrounded by seven hillbillies, all of whom looked like they could handle their weapons. What was going on?

"You gonna' search him, Carter?" Nathan could not keep a tremor of excitement from his voice. "Search him quick so we can get started."

Carter silenced Nathan with a glance before holstering his pistol and approaching Bones with cautious steps.

"I'm going to search you, boy. You try anything funny, I promise you'll be dead in the time it takes these fellows to pull the trigger. You understand me?"

"Do you mind if I asked what I'm supposed to have done? I checked in with the local ranger and told him I was doing some sightseeing. That's not illegal, is it?"

"How about you just shut your mouth until I'm ready to tell you what happens next?"

Bones nodded. He had no doubt he could kill Carter, and perhaps a second man, but seven was far too many to take on single-handed, not to mention unarmed. Even if Maddock were to show up right now, he had no weapon, and thus would be able to do little, if anything, to help. Bones' best hope was to remain alive and hope Maddock would return, realize what was going on and, come up with one of his patented plans. He waited impatiently while Carter patted him down and relieved him of his watch, wallet, keys, and camera.

"Tell me, boy. What are you looking for up here?"

"Nothing. Just taking pictures. Check my camera."

"What did your ancestor lose up here?" Carter asked sharply.

Had Bones not received extensive training in how to deal with interrogation, that question might have drawn a reaction, but he kept up his confused facade. "I don't get it."

"You told Eddings you had an ancestor who fought here. Did he lose something?"

"Only his freedom. He was captured and taken to Andersonville."

"So he was a Yankee!" Nathan exclaimed.

Bones shrugged. "Look, this place was a turning point in my great granduncle's life. I just wanted to see it. I don't think I'm trespassing or anything, but if you want me to leave, I will."

"You're going to leave, all right, but not the way you think," Nathan said.

"Shut up, Nathan," Carter said. "Here's how this is going to work." He stepped back as he spoke, pocketing Bones' possessions before drawing his pistol again. "You are going to run thataway." He nodded in the direction of the forest. "In five minutes, Kevin here is going to fire his rifle." One of the late arrivals, a moon-faced young man with a wispy mustache and his cheek bulging from what must have been a plum-sized wad of chewing tobacco, nodded. "That'll let you know we're coming for you. We want to make it all sportsmanlike, you know." Carter grinned.

"What the hell are you talking about?" Bones kept his voice level, but his insides were ice. The man couldn't be serious.

"Just a little game we like to play. It's much more entertaining than deer hunting, and sometimes more challenging."

"Is this a joke?"

Carter shook his head.

"In that case, if you want to give me a sporting chance, shouldn't I get a rifle too?"

Carter glanced at his wristwatch. "You should get moving. You've already wasted ten seconds."

"And you ain't got that many left to live. Run boy!" Nathan fired off a shot near Bones' feet.

Still unable to believe what was happening, Bones dashed toward the forest, wondering all the while how he was going to get out of this alive.

CHAPTER 9

Maddock shone his light around the cavern. It was very much like what he had pictured in his mind: a wedge-shaped passageway leading back into the darkness. He slipped out of his mask, tank, and fins, and began to explore. The walls grew narrower the deeper he went. It was far from the tightest space he had ever been in, but he was well aware of the need for caution. It would be all too easy to get stuck in a place like this if one was not careful, and he had no one to pull him free should he get stuck.

The unyielding stone of the cave was virtually without feature, save the occasional fissure, each of which he inspected with care. The walls closed tighter around him with every step and soon he was forced to turn sideways in order to keep moving. He wondered if Esau Bonebrake had been a skinnier man than himself. If so, Maddock might not be able to penetrate deep enough into the cramped passage to find the hiding place.

There you go again, Maddock. Borrowing trouble.

Finally, the way grew too narrow for him to proceed. He shone his light up and down the walls of unrelenting gray stone. Nothing. He did not want to risk getting stuck, but what if it the hiding place was only a bit farther away? Perhaps just beyond his reach. He couldn't go back and tell Bones he had failed unless he was certain the thing was not here. He had to try. He bent his knees, lowering his torso down to where the way wasn't so tight, gaining himself bit of space. He squeezed forward one small step, then another. The cold stone pressed into his chest and shoulder blades. Much more of this and he would no longer be able to breathe, much less move.

And then he saw it.

Just a few feet ahead, something darker than the

natural rock was wedged inside a head-high crack in the wall. He could not switch his flashlight to his right hand, so he stuck it in his mouth, holding it with his teeth, and reached out. His outstretched fingers met smooth stone. He was tantalizingly close—only an inch, to go if that. He took two shallow breaths, forced all the air from his lungs, relaxing as he exhaled, and slipped deeper down the passageway. Stretching... reaching... until his hand closed around the object and he slid it free.

It was a triangle, almost like a dull spear point about the size of his palm. It was carved from some sort of shiny black stone he did not immediately recognize and was surprisingly heavy. A meteorite, perhaps? He and Bones would give it a closer examination once he got it out into daylight. But first, he had to get out of this cave.

The tight walls were constricting his chest, making breathing almost impossible. He was conditioned to holding his breath for extended periods of time, but his body was beginning to complain about the lack of oxygen. His lungs burned, craving more air.

He tried to move back toward the entrance, but could not. He was stuck.

Someone with less experience caving might have panicked in this situation and inadvertently gasped for breath. Maddock remained calm, adjusted his position, and relaxed. With a supreme effort of will, he coaxed the last remnants of air from his lungs, and pushed.

He did not budge an inch.

I should have skipped breakfast this morning.

He continued to lean in his intended direction, careful not to push too hard and perhaps wedge himself too tightly to escape. Spots danced in front of his eyes, and his lungs now screamed for air. He felt along the wall with his right hand and found an inch-wide crack into which he was able to work his index and middle fingers. He was unable to bend his elbow in these tight quarters, but he flexed his fingers, pulling with all the strength he had in his hand. Fire coursed down his arm, and his legs trembled.

After all my close calls, I'm going to die stuck in a freaking tunnel. All for a freaking rock. Thanks, Bones.

And then he moved. It was only a centimeter, if that, but he had definitely moved. His fingers flexed, his chest slid along the cold stone. He moved an inch...then another...and another.

And then he was free.

With agonizing slowness he continued to move forward, resisting the urge to take more than tiny sips of air and thus risk getting himself stuck again. It was only a matter of seconds, but it felt like a week before he could breathe freely again, filling his lungs deeply. It was better than a kiss. Well, almost.

No longer fearing for his life, he allowed himself a moment to take a closer look at what he had found.

Upon closer inspection, the spear point theory was a definite possibility, though the edge wasn't as sharp as one made of flint. He turned the black triangle over in his hands. If it wasn't a meteorite, it was crafted of some other unearthly stone. A few years ago, that would have seemed unlikely to him, but recent events had opened his mind to such possibilities. It seemed too substantial for mere stone, yet the substance was not quite metal. What was more, a virtual field guide to the fauna of the eastern United States was etched all across its surface: bears, cougars, wolves, coyotes, birds of prey, snakes, stags, alligators, even bison, and what looked like a woolly mammoth. He couldn't see anything especially mysterious about it, but it was a fine piece, and Bones would be stoked that they had solved the old family mystery.

Of course, he would have to mess with Bones' head first. Maddock would tell him that, upon finding the cave, he'd discovered signs that it was no longer a secret location. Rednecks had found the place first and trashed it, leaving behind Bud Light cans, Marlboro butts, and Copenhagen tins. *One of them must have found the treasure first, Bones. Sorry about that. I guess we'll never know what it was.* Grinning at the thought of his friend's reaction, he stashed the stone in his mesh dive bag and donned his dive gear.

He had just put the regulator between his teeth and slid beneath the surface of the icy lake when he heard a muffled crack like a gunshot. He paused, straining to make out further sounds above the subdued rush of the waterfall, but he could hear nothing else. He was sure it had been a gunshot. Water was an excellent conductor of sound and Maddock had been under fire more times than he could count.

An icy ball formed in the pit of his stomach. He and Bones had stashed their side arms in the car in order to avoid raising unnecessary suspicion should the ranger pay them a visit. What reason would Bones have to retrieve his Glock, much less fire it? Certain he was not going to like what he found outside, Maddock drew his dive knife and began to swim.

He exited the cavern and surfaced beneath the waterfall. Careful to avoid notice until he knew what was going on, he pushed back his mask and inched out until he could see through the hazy mist kicked up by the churning water.

Seven armed men stood off to the side of the lake, pointing at something in the distance and laughing. Down on the far end, where the dirt road opened onto the battlefield, two pickup trucks had his and Bones' vehicle blocked in. Something serious was going on, but what?

He weighed his options. He could swim to the far end of the lake, try to slip out unnoticed, and retrieve their weapons from the car. Problem was, Bones had the keys and Maddock had no idea if they had left the vehicle unlocked. If these men intended to do them harm, and he had a strong feeling they did, there was no way Maddock could sneak to the car, break a window, retrieve his Walther, and take out seven armed men before at least one of them got him. But he couldn't take out that many armed men with only a knife. In any case, he supposed he ought to make completely certain that these men intended him and Bones harm before he mapped out a battle plan. Of course, all signs pointed to that conclusion.

He would have to get closer in order to hear what they were saying, and he'd have to do it without being spotted. It was easily done—he'd had plenty such training, but in those cases he'd always been outfitted in something less conspicuous than a blue neoprene suit. He dove down deep, staying as close as he dared to the lake bed as he approached his target. Finally, he surfaced in silence among the thick reeds at the water's edge.

"Has it been five minutes yet?" a young man asked, tapping his booted foot on the soft earth.

"Hold your horses. It's almost time." The speaker looked like an older, more sober version of the young man. "I want you to stay close to me. This one looks like he might actually give us a challenge." The young man started to object, but the older man talked over him. "This is not deer hunting. A man, even an unarmed one, is an infinitely more dangerous quarry. That's what makes this the greatest sport in the world, and the true test of a man."

Maddock tensed. Was he serious? The pieces fell into place quickly. Bones was alive, unarmed, and in the woods somewhere in the direction in which the men were staring. And these men intended to kill him. The only positive of which Maddock could think was that these yokels didn't seem to know Bones was not alone. What Maddock could do about it remained to be seen.

"I reckon it's been long enough." One of the men checked his watch. "Yep. That'll do." He turned to another of his party. "Bevel, it's your turn to guard the vehicles."

"Aww! C'mon Carter." Bevel took off his camouflage NASCAR number three hat and fanned his face. "The kid's the new one in the group. Let him take the first shift."

Carter shook his head. "No. He at least deserves a chance to draw first blood. If we haven't made the kill in an hour, you'll rotate in. Same as always."

Bevel cursed and spat on the ground.

"Don't get your shorts in a bunch," Carter said. "If this one's as resourceful as he looks, it'll be a long hunt. You'll get your shot at him."

"If you get to him first, remember I want one of his ears for my collection."

Maddock's stomach twisted and he fought the urge to spring. This was as sick a collection of not-quite-humans as he'd ever come across.

The others fanned out, leaving Bevel alone. This was Maddock's chance. He slithered forward like a cottonmouth in the mud, careful not to make a sound. He was grateful for the rush of the waterfall that helped to mask any sound he might make.

Bevel watched the men go, muttered a curse, and then sat down on a stone near the water's edge. He laid his rifle across his lap and fished into his shirt pocket for a cigarette and a lighter. Maddock tensed. At the instant the man's hands were fully occupied, his attention focused on lighting his smoke, Maddock pounced.

He covered the space between them in less than a second. By the time Bevel realized someone else was there, Maddock had his gloved hand clamped firmly over the man's mouth, the keen blade of his knife pressing down hard on the exposed flesh of his neck.

"You make a single loud sound or try to fight me, and I open your throat," he whispered. "Don't doubt me. I've killed better men than you. Blink once if you understand." Bevel blinked one time, and rolled his wide eyes back, trying to catch a glimpse of Maddock. "I'm going to uncover your mouth so you can answer my questions. If you, move, cry out, or even talk too loudly, I'll gag you, cut your Achilles tendons so you can't run, and kill you as painfully as possible." Privately, Maddock doubted he could bring himself to torture someone, but Bevel didn't know that. "Blink once if you understand me." The man blinked, still trying to see who held him from behind, and Maddock removed his hand. "Are you hunting my friend?"

"N-no."

Maddock pressed the knife harder against the man's neck.

"Yes. Don't cut me. Please." Bevel's voice was a desperate whisper and his entire body trembled.

"Why are you doing this?"

"It's j-jist what we do. All we got around here are deer, maybe a bear or a mountain lion sometimes. It ain't no challenge. People are more fun."

"You've done this before?" Maddock's stomach clenched and it was all he could do not to open the idiot's throat right then. "How many times?"

"A bunch. It's sort of a… tradition in these parts for generations. Nowadays the ranger is the point man. He lets Carter know when someone's going to be up here and he tells us. When we get the word, we drop everything and come quick."

Maddock couldn't believe what he was hearing. "That's the only reason? Some sick hillbilly tradition?"

Bevel's eyes narrowed at that, but he seemed to lack the courage to retort. "Carter's got a special interest in this place. He always asks them questions before he hunts them. It's like he thinks one of them has information he needs."

"What sorts of questions?"

Bevel considered this. "He always wants to know if they're looking for something. I think somebody wants Carter to find something up here but he can't. He's been all around with a metal detector."

That was interesting. Was this related to the search for Esau's treasure? That was a subject for another time. "Are you telling me the police haven't investigated all these missing people?"

Bevel barked a short laugh. "Nothing to investigate. Eddings drives up here, takes a look around, and tells the authorities a story. They always chalk it up to lost hikers, careless folk killed by animals, or bad falls."

"No one's ever gotten away to tell what the hell

you're doing up here?"

"Not a one. We always get 'em." Bevel managed a smirk, unapologetic in the face of death. "They'll get you too if you try anything."

Maddock's blood ran hot. "You've never hunted a SEAL before, have you?"

"A seal? We ain't got no seals around here. Maybe some otters. What do you think this is, California?"

"A Navy SEAL, you idiot. My friend was one, and so was I. You have no idea what you've gotten yourself into."

If Bevel had been pale before, his face went snow white at this new piece of information.

Maddock's thoughts raced. Should he just kill the man now? No. He would tie him up with his own shoelaces, gag him with his socks, and stow him in the back of the truck. Then he would take the rifle and go after Bones.

"I'm going to remove this knife from your throat. When I do, I want you to very slowly get face-down on the ground. No noise, no sudden movements. You get me?"

"I hear you."

Maddock released his grip on Bevel but kept his knife at the ready. He moved around in front of Bevel and prompted him to get down on the ground. Bevel complied, sinking to his knees.

And that was when he made a fatal mistake.

Bevel lurched to one side, rolling over and coming up with a .22 caliber pistol. Maddock was on him before he could pull the trigger, pinning his gun hand to the ground and burying his knife in Bevel's heart. Just to be safe, he covered Bevel's mouth and nose, and waited for him to expire. It was a grisly kill, but one Maddock had tried to avoid. When he was sure the man was dead, Maddock relieved him of his pistol and his ammunition belt, which held spare bullets both for the hunting rifle and the pistol.

He dragged Bevel's body into the reeds and hastily

covered it over with mud and debris. When the next man came to take his turn at guard duty, hopefully that person would assume Bevel had grown impatient and joined the hunt early, and therefore not grow suspicious. Maddock and Bones were going to need every advantage they could get.

His pulse pounding, he slipped on the ammunition belt, tucked the pistol inside his suit, hefted the rifle, and set out on a little hunting expedition of his own.

CHAPTER 10

Dry leaves crackled underfoot as Bones ran. Dark green foliage flashed by in his peripheral vision. Low hanging branches swatted him and undergrowth snatched at his ankles.

When you're waiting in a doctor's office, five minutes takes freaking forever. When you're being hunted by a bunch of inbreeders, it flies by.

Strangely, Bones was not frightened. Perhaps it was due to the surreal nature of the situation in which he found himself. Of course, this was far from the first time his life had been in danger, and he'd always come out alive. Deep inside, he always assumed things would somehow turn out all right.

Now he kept his eyes peeled as he dashed through the woods, looking for something that could give him an advantage. He stopped to pick up a few fist-sized stones and stuff them into his pockets. He kept moving, and soon he found himself running along the base of a twenty-foot rock wall. This could be it.

He hastily spied out cracks and outcroppings that would serve as handholds, and clambered up. It wasn't an easy climb, but scaling rock walls was one of his specialties. Aside from Maddock, few could keep up with him on a free climb. Bones could scale a wall that others would consider impossible to climb. His pursuers would never look for him up here. In short order, he was at the top and hidden in a thicket of hemlock. He waited, all his senses alive and attuned to every sound, every motion in the forest.

He was rewarded in a matter of minutes. A bearded man in a John Deere cap came trotting along the base of the cliff. It was one of those who had arrived last. Bones did not know his name and didn't care. As the man passed below him, Bones rose up and flung one of the stones he had picked up as hard as he could down onto the passer-by.

The missile struck the man on the crown of his head, and with a surprised grunt, he crumpled to the ground. After looking around for other hunters and seeing none, Bones climbed back down to where the man lay. He rolled the fellow over onto his back and removed his cap to reveal a split scalp and a deep indentation that indicated a fractured skull. The wound was probably fatal, but Bones couldn't take the chance that the man would come after him. After all, this guy had been hunting him like an animal and would have shot him for the sheer pleasure of it if he'd gotten the chance.

Bones growled at the memory of the men taunting him, laughing as they sent him running into the woods. He dragged the dying man off the trail and bound him to a tree with his own belt. The man would probably die there very soon, but Bones didn't care. These were no longer human beings to him. They were targets to be eliminated.

One down.

The man up ahead of Maddock was making far too much noise, carelessly crushing dry leaves and twigs underfoot. Either he was a complete idiot or he didn't suspect danger lurked anywhere nearby. Probably a bit of both.

With so many threats out there, Maddock needed to dispatch the hunter in front of him as quietly as possible. He didn't want to use the rifle unless there was no alternative. Even if the other hunters heard the shot and believed it was one of their own firing at Bones, it would still draw them toward the sound and they would be wary.

Careful to remain silent, Maddock slid the rifle beneath a thick mountain laurel and placed the ammunition belt atop it. He tucked the dive bag holding the stone inside his suit, drew his knife and Bevel's pistol, and silently crept up on the unsuspecting hunter. Much more cautious than the lummox he stalked, he moved with catlike grace, choosing his footfalls with care. He was keenly aware of the danger he was in as he closed the distance between them. There was no cover along the last intervening twenty paces. If the man heard or sensed his approach, well, Maddock would probably get him first with the .22, but unless he managed a head shot, the fellow just might manage to put a round or two into Maddock with his Remington. Furthermore, the gunfire would be a call to the other hunters. Finally, a voice inside Maddock's head pointed out that he had never fired this particular pistol, so he had no idea of its accuracy or firing tendencies. He shut the voice up, since the point was now moot. He'd make it work.

Fifteen feet...

Ten feet...

Five feet...

The man finally realized someone was coming and whirled around. He was too late to bring his rifle to bear, but the barrel smashed into Maddock's left hand, knocking the .22 free. Maddock lashed out with his knife, catching the man across the throat, but it was a shallow slice, barely worse than a cut from shaving. His opponent instinctively drew back, but before Maddock could stab him in the gut, the man struck at Maddock with the butt of his rifle. Maddock took the blow on the back of his left shoulder, turning with it. He spun, brought the knife around in a wide arc, and drove it backhanded into the man's neck just above his right shoulder. The man roared in pain and panic.

In his death throes, he pulled the trigger, firing wildly into the air. Maddock silenced him with a hard left to the temple that sent him crumpling to the ground. The neck wound was a death sentence, but Maddock didn't want the others to hear any more sounds from the dying man.

Too late.

Feet crashed through the undergrowth. Gunfire rang out and a bullet flew past his head and clipped a bough from the pine tree behind him. At least one of the others had been much closer than he expected! He took off back the way he had come, weaving between any bits of cover he could find. A moving target was difficult to hit. A moving target behind cover was even more so.

"He got Jason!" The cry was punctuated with another shot that barely missed. He dodged to his right into a dense stand of pines. Limbs struck his face and pine cones pierced his bare feet as he ran. In the stillness of the forest he could hear the men's voices as plain as day.

"How do you think he got behind us, Pa?"

"He's an Indian. I suppose they have some tricks up his sleeve. I told you he would be a tough one. We'll just have to be extra careful."

"Bevel will get him if he heads back to the clearing. I'm going to go after him!"

Maddock spotted a low-growing patch of rhododendron and dove beneath it. He wormed his way in as far as he could go and waited. The footsteps came closer and two sets of booted feet trotted past his hiding place. They would figure out soon enough that Bevel wouldn't be getting anyone ever again. He gave them time to get out of earshot and then headed back toward the place where he'd hidden the rifle. He had not made it far when he heard more voices.

"He's dead," said a calm, confident voice.

"Who do you think done it, Carter? Was it the Indian?"

"Obviously, unless you think someone else is out here. But why didn't he take Jason's rifle when he killed him? It's strange. And whose pistol is this?"

Maddock crept silently away. Now he had two men on either side of him, and only his knife for a weapon. On a positive note, he could now account for the locations of six of the seven men, two of them were permanently accounted for. Even better, it seemed that none of them had gotten Bones. At least, not yet.

He moved into deeper cover among the trees that

lined the sloping valley wall. When he was far enough away to feel safe stopping for a few moments, he took time to rub dirt on his face, and did his best to blacken his dive suit with more of the rich, dark earth before moving on. He soon came to a spot where time and weather had eroded a deep, winding channel up the side of the mountain. It would likely provide an easy passageway to the top, but he hesitated, fearing he might stumble upon the seventh hunter coming around a blind curve. Instead, he chose a more difficult route up the slope, keeping in sight of the channel, but remaining behind cover as much as he could.

The sound of the waterfall grew louder as he climbed and he emerged on a ledge overlooking the lake and valley below. The two men who had shot at him were standing alongside the vehicles. The older of the two was speaking, waving his hands and emphasizing his points by poking the younger man in the chest. If either were to look this way, they would spot Maddock in an instant. That gave him an idea. But how best to put it into effect?

CHAPTER 11

The dense tangle of trees seemed to reach out to grab Bones as he dashed through the forest. Breaking into a clearing, he had to watch his step as the holes of long ago rotted stumps made his path a veritable minefield. He leaped across a deep gap where the game trail he followed had eroded into one of the holes, and landed on an uneven patch of ground. His ankle rolled and hot pain coursed through his leg.

He had caught a glimpse of two men who were pursuing him. He had a good lead on them, but they definitely had his trail. He'd tried to hide signs of his passing as much as he could, considering the rapidity of his flight, but it had not thrown them off. It galled him that he could not shake the hunters.

He caught a glimpse of sunlight and blue sky up ahead. The forest was thinning out. Perhaps there was an end to this valley, maybe even a road or some other sign of civilization.

He burst through the undergrowth and came skidding to a halt. The tips of his booted feet slid over the edge of a sheer cliff. The drop was hundreds of feet to the rocks below. No wonder his pursuers had no fear of him escaping. The wooded area through which he ran had neatly funneled him to this dead end. Could he double back and work his way past them or at least get back to high ground? They would expect him to end up here, so they would be moving this way. How could he use that to his advantage? Keenly aware that the sand was running out of the hourglass, he concentrated. What could he do? A thought struck him and he hurried back to the clearing.

He had done this many times before, so the task was a simple one. In less than a minute he had scooped heaps of crumbling earth out of the hole in the trail until it was a good three feet deep. He'd then covered it over with twigs, leaves, and soil. Ideally, he'd have dug a deep pit and placed sharpened stakes at the bottom, but he lacked the time or tools to create such a trap. When the Viet Cong had made pits like this one, they smeared the sharpened stakes with their own feces in order to give the victim a septic infection. He grinned at the thought of one of these inbreeders impaled on a sharpened crap stick. Too bad he couldn't go that route. In this case, he just needed to distract his pursuers long enough for him to get away.

He melted into the brush near the cliff and began working his way back in the direction of the battlefield. In a matter of seconds he heard the stealthy approach of his stalkers. He froze, knowing that any movement could give him away. He watched as the men, the younger one in the lead, followed by Carter, the big, paunchy guy who seemed to be in charge of the group, moved along the path. They were quiet, at least, quiet for white guys, and moved well in the woods; he'd give them that much. Thirty yards from where he watched, the young man stepped right into Bones' trap, gave a yelp of surprise, and fell face-first onto the trail.

Bones fired off two quick shots at Carter, but the man had reacted the moment the ground gave way beneath his companion's feet. Moving faster than Bones would have believed possible for a man of his bulk and girth, he dived to the ground and rolled behind a tree. Bones' shots sizzled through empty air. He flattened out behind a stump, cursing his luck.

Now up on all fours, the younger man scrambled for his rifle. Bones squeezed off a carefully aimed shot that took his target in the head. Carter cried out in anger at the sight of his fallen comrade. Bones snapped off another shot in the direction of the cry and then ran as fast as his injured ankle would permit.

Bullets shredded the greenery around him. He dodged to his right, trying to put an oak tree between himself and his attacker, but just before he moved behind the tree, fire lanced across his chest, and he heard the rifle's report. He knew immediately he had been shot.

There wasn't time to do more than glance at the bloody streak across his pectoral muscle, but he could tell it was not a serious wound—little more than a scratch. He paused behind the tree long enough to fire off another shot in the direction of his attacker before taking off again. He wondered if the gunfire would draw the other hunters. He assumed it would, but at least he had taken care of another one of them. But could he really expect to take out all of them? His luck couldn't hold that long.

Somehow, he had to find Maddock and get the hell out of here.

Maddock pressed his body into the hollow of an old oak tree. The earthy smells of the forest surrounded him. A gentle breeze swayed the treetops. It should have been a peaceful moment, but the perverse juxtaposition of tranquility and his life-and-death struggle turned his stomach. He gripped the strange black stone he had found in the cave, finding comfort in its weight. It would make for a decent weapon in a pinch.

Shielded on his other side by a fir tree, he would be nigh invisible to anyone headed up the wash, and he had reason to believe someone would be coming soon. He had prepared his trap and then let himself be spotted crossing the top of the ridge. He had been certain to look like he was on the move, in hopes the men who saw him would not expect an ambush. Now he waited.

Soon, he heard the faint scuff of a booted foot on stone. Whoever was climbing the wash was being careless. Maddock prayed the man was equally unobservant. His prayer was answered moments later with a loud thwack and a shout of surprise and pain and the sound of something metal clattering to the ground. Maddock sprang from his hiding place and leaped into the wash, the sharp stone upraised, but when his eyes fell on the man, he realized immediately that there was no need for the weapon.

It was Nathan, the youngest of the hunters. His eyes were wide in death, surprised at what had befallen him, and his mouth hung open, a string of spittle dripping from his lower lip. His first blood had been his own.

Maddock had found a springy sapling growing chest-high out of a crack in the stone just beyond a sharp bend in the rock, tied his dive knife to it, bent it back and fixed it in place. He then set a trip line made of vine. It was one of the many tricks he'd picked up during his time as a SEAL. He had expected it to distract and hopefully injure his enemy, but he was gratified to see that the knife had found the young man's heart. Perhaps he should feel bad about taking the life of a youth of no more than twenty, but he could muster no sympathy for one who would hunt down another man like an animal.

One less murderer walking among us.

He listened for any sound that would indicate the approach of another hunter. Hearing none, he set to work. He took Nathan's rifle and a few spare rounds. Next, he freed his knife from the makeshift trap and cleaned the blade on the dead man's shirt. Another one down, but how many more to go?

If only he could find Bones, they could get out of this mess. Of course, he had heard shouts and gunfire somewhere down below. He hoped that meant Bones was taking care of business. Bones had to be all right.

He spotted a flash of movement in the undergrowth below. It was barely more than a momentary glimpse. He froze, looking and listening, but he neither saw nor heard anything else. He knew only one person who could move like that in the forest.

"Bones?" In the quiet, his whisper sounded louder than any gunshot.

"Maddock?" Bones melted out of the nearby trees. Blood soaked one side of his shirt, but he otherwise looked strong. "About time you showed up. How many did you get?"

"Three."

"You suck. I've only gotten two. The next one is mine, and we can flip for the last." He looked around and caught sight of Nathan's body. He spotted the vine tied to the sapling and nodded.

"Nice booby trap, Maddock. You keep hanging around with us natives and we'll turn you into a real woodsman. I guess you used your knife?" Maddock nodded. "Good job. I didn't like that kid. Didn't have proper respect for his elders."

As they moved on up the mountain, each filled the other in on the events that had brought them to this point. Bones cursed when Maddock told him what he had learned from Bevel about the corrupt park ranger and the self-styled hunters of men.

"They asked me some weird questions, too. It's almost as if they've got some connection to the people who came after Grandfather."

"I think Carter does," Maddock said, remembering Bevel's words.

Suddenly, a bestial cry of pain and rage shattered the silence. Maddock immediately dropped to his belly and pointed his rifle in the direction of the cry. From his hiding place, he could see that Nathan's father had found his son's body. Maddock inched forward, looking for a clear shot. Bones wormed his way up alongside him.

"My turn," Bones whispered.

But there was no need for either of them to take the shot, though. Letting loose an anguished wail, Nathan's father let his rifle fall to the ground. He dropped to his knees and drew a pistol from his belt. With trembling hands, he reversed the weapon and put it in his mouth.

Maddock closed his eyes as the sound of the shot echoed through the canyon.

"You're such a wimp." Bones face split in a wicked grin. "It's not like it's the first death you've ever seen, and that guy totally deserved it. He's the one who brought his son into this, and turned him into a wannabe killer just like his old man."

"I know." Maddock grimaced at the thought of what

had just transpired. "Suicide just seems like it should be a... private thing." Nathan's father deserved no sympathy. In fact, Maddock would have killed him without remorse, yet he took no pleasure from witnessing death. Sometimes, killing needed to be done, but there was always a part of him that found it regrettable.

"We can talk philosophy later. Let's get on to the important subject. Did you find it?"

It took Maddock a moment to realize Bones was asking about the stone. "Oh, sorry dude. All I found was one of those rubber-tipped spears like you guys sell to little kids at your trading posts. Oh, and an Indian taco. I ate that."

Bones' eyes, which had fallen at the word "sorry," widened as he realized Maddock was messing with him. "Hand it over, bro. Now!"

Maddock drew the stone from his bag and held it out.

Bones gasped. He took it in trembling hands and held it up. His eyes glowed, and his grin was almost beatific as he gazed on his ancestor's treasure.

"This is really it," he whispered. "A part of me thought Esau was full of crap and maybe he'd made it all up. But it's real."

"So what do you think it is?" Maddock thought it was a fine example of craftsmanship, but apparently there was much more to the artifact.

"It looks kind of like a spear point, but I don't think it's a Native American artifact. The shape is too...refined, I guess. And there's something about the stone itself that makes it seem..."

Ancient? Otherworldly? Alien?"

"Yeah, all that crap and more." He lowered his hands and his eyes met Maddock's. "Thanks, bro. You don't know what this means to me."

"No worries. Hopefully this is the first step to getting those guys off your grandfather's back."

"For sure." Bones continued to examine the stone.

"All these carvings of animals. They're rough, like they were scratched on long after this was made. It's weird, but when I look at them, I'm sure this thing has power."

"You think it'll let you talk to animals?"

"Maybe." Bones admired the stone for a moment longer before tucking it into his belt and rising to his feet. "There'll be time to look at it later. It occurs to me there's only one man left. Let's find our friend Carter and show him what it's like to be hunted."

They made their way to the cliff that overlooked the battlefield, lake, and vehicles. "We're almost too late." Maddock pointed to the spot where a figure had just broken from the cover of the forest and was lumbering toward the parked trucks and jeeps. Carter.

"We can't let him get away," Bones said. "If this place has a tradition of hunting outsiders, they'll want to cover it up. No way we'd get a fair trial around here."

Maddock sighed. "Do what you've got to do."

Bones smiled and raised his rifle.

"That's a long shot." Maddock arched an eyebrow. "Think you can make it?"

Bones only grinned more broadly as he gently squeezed the trigger. Far below them, Carter fell flat on his face. "Dinner's on you for doubting me."

"Are you kidding me? You can even think about eating after all this?" Maddock rubbed his temples. "We need to get out of here, and fast. Like you said, even though we're in the right, if we're caught, what chance would we have of getting any kind of justice around here? Hell, in a town like this, the judge, jury, and victims are probably all first cousins. I think we need to dispose of the bodies, pitch the rifles into the lake, and get the hell out of Dodge."

"You're right." Bones drew the stone from where he had tucked it into his belt. "But if what Grandfather said about this thing is true, we won't have any trouble dealing with the bodies. After that, we've got one more loose end I'm going to tie up."

"What are you going to do?" Maddock took a step

back.

"I'm not sure." Bones held the stone in the flat of his palm, staring hard at it. A minute passed in silence. Bones shook his head. "Either Esau was full of crap or we're missing the key to unlock this thing."

Maddock frowned. The key to unlock the stone. The key…

"Blood is the key! Remember the last line of the story.

"Maddock, you're a freaking genius." Bones pressed the stone against his still dripping chest wound, and closed his eyes. "Dude, I can feel it."

"Feel what?"

"I can't explain it but… holy crap, they're coming."

"Who is coming?" As if in reply, a loud rustling sound filled the forest. What Maddock saw momentarily took his breath. "Unbelievable."

CHAPTER 12

Words failed Maddock as they drove away from the battlefield. What he had seen was burned in his mind. The power of the stone was real, and it just might have been their salvation.

They had wiped and disposed of all the rifles and pistols, tossing them into the lake. Bones wanted to save Carter's antique Colt, but Maddock put his foot down.

"Something that could be evidence at your murder trial doesn't make for a good souvenir," he said for what felt like the hundredth time.

"I know, but that was a sweet piece. He didn't deserve it."

"For what it's worth, I think you covered our tracks nicely. I doubt anyone will find the bodies, and if they do..."

"Eaten by bears," Bones said. "This stone is something else. You'll have to try it sometime."

"Sure. Next time we need to make it look like seven dead men were victims of animal attacks, I'll use it."

He had a feeling the names of the seven dead men would simply be added to the list of strange disappearances in Dark Entry. Maddock had seen and experienced some strange things in the time he and Bones had known one another, but what Bones had done with that stone was near the top of the list. The bears emerging silently from the trees and dragging away the bodies. The coyotes lapping up the blood. He shuddered at the memory. He supposed he would never grow fully accustomed to the idea that there were forces in this world that defied understanding.

When they were a quarter of a mile from the ranger station, he pulled the car off the shoulder of the road and cut the engine.

Bones grabbed his arm before he could open the

door and get out. "You sure you want to be a part of this? I can take care of it myself."

"They were hunting both of us." Maddock felt the heat rising inside of him as he thought about what the men had tried to do to them. The way he saw it, justice had been meted out, but there was one more person who needed to pay. There was no telling how many murders could be laid at the man's feet.

"I know." Bones looked up at the night sky. "It's just that you and I are different, Maddock. You're... better than me. You've always killed in combat or self-defense."

"And you haven't?"

"Well, still. I don't want you to..."

"Don't worry about it. My conscience is clear on this one. Besides, *we're* not going to do anything to the man. At least, not if your plan works."

Bones gingerly drew his backpack from the back seat and held it at arm's length. He clutched the stone in his other hand. He and Maddock had washed up in the lake and changed into clean clothes, but Maddock thought he could see a darkness in Bones' face that wouldn't soon wash away.

"It will work. It worked back at Dark Entry, didn't it?"

Maddock grimaced at the memory and nodded. It certainly had worked and he would never forget it. "Let's get on with it then."

Earl Eddings checked his watch for what must have been the twentieth time. He should have heard from Carter by now. He wanted to call and make sure everything was all right, but that was strictly forbidden. Their connection had to be carefully hidden. Carter had already let too many people in on their little game. Perhaps it was time to put an end to it. He'd made a nice chunk of change out of the deal, Carter and his friends had their fun, and together they'd made sure the deaths were always written off as missing persons or tragic accidents. Perhaps they were tempting fate by keeping things going. Of course, getting out of the arrangement would be neither simple nor easy.

He propped his feet up on the desk and reached for his coffee. It had gone cold, but he didn't feel like brewing another pot. Besides, once he heard from Carter, he'd close the office and retire to his apartment in the back. He'd heat up a frozen pizza, watch a movie, maybe Smokey and the Bandit, and hit the sack. He swished the bitter drink around in his mouth and closed his eyes, trying to coax a bit of flavor from it. Paul Revere and the Raiders were on the radio. It was a good song, one of his favorites.

"I hope I'm not interrupting anything."

Eddings' eyes snapped open as the coffee cup fell from his limp fingers. It was the Indian from earlier today. How could he be here? He got a grip on himself and forced a smile.

"Not at all, you just gave me a start, that's all." He sat up, letting his feet fall to the floor. "Did you find the battlefield all right?" The Indian didn't appear to have a gun, just a backpack. Still smiling, Eddings let his hand drift toward the bottom drawer of his desk where he kept his .38 revolver.

"Keep your hands where we can see them." Another man had slipped through the door while Eddings' eyes were on the Indian. He was shorter than the Indian, not quite six feet, with close-cropped blond hair, blue-gray eyes, and a calm demeanor that was somehow even more intimidating than the seething rage that boiled behind the Indian's eyes. He held a pistol trained on Eddings, and it was readily apparent that the man had both the ability and inclination to use it if he so desired.

Eddings recognized the gun. "So your plan is to kill me with Carter's gun and hope it gets pinned on him?" He forced a laugh. "You two don't understand. This is bigger than me. Bigger than this town, even. The Trident will come after you."

"Who the hell is the Trident?"

"A group of powerful men who are very interested in

the battlefield. Carter works for them."

"You mean 'worked' for them." The big Indian grinned.

Eddings' heart raced. "If you kill me, you'll just be sticking your hand into the viper's nest."

"Funny you should mention snakes." The Indian deftly unzipped his backpack and upended it, spilling two twisting, black-banded forms onto the desk. Timber rattlers! They were each a good four feet long, and they both immediately coiled as if to strike, rattles buzzing, and eyes locked on Eddings.

"What is this?" Eddings tried to keep his voice calm, but it came out as a hoarse whisper. "Do you think you can make these things do your bidding?" The thought was absurd but, seeing the way these snakes kept their eyes trained on him, he believed, against all rational thought, the Indian could do exactly that.

"Oh, you wouldn't believe what I can do." The Indian pulled a black stone from his belt and slowly drew the blade across his palm. He squeezed his fist and let the blood drip down onto the triangular stone, which seemed to sparkle as if shooting stars whirled inside it. The Indian's eyes remained locked on Eddings as he raised the stone to his lips and whispered a single word.

The snakes struck as one. Eddings screamed as the fangs bit into him again and again, hot pain searing his body, burning through the numbing disbelief that clouded his senses. The agony seemed to go on forever. And then it stopped.

He watched through cloudy eyes as the rattlesnakes slithered off his desk, dropped to the floor, and disappeared. As light and life fled, he saw the Indian make a mocking bow, turn, and walk away.

CHAPTER 13

Maddock turned the triangular stone over in his hands, examining the carvings etched in its surface. Despite the warmth of the day, it sent a chill through him. It was difficult to believe that through it, one could indeed control animal behavior, but he'd witnessed it first-hand. Besides, he had to admit, it wasn't the craziest thing he and Bones had experienced.

"The animal carvings are shallow, like whoever carved it barely managed to etch them in." He held the stone out so Bones could take a closer look. They sat on a sagging picnic table in a small campground somewhere in the mountains of North Georgia. They'd wanted somewhere off the beaten path to lie low and plan their next move, and this place, little more than a gravel drive running alongside a mountain stream, with a few turnouts for parking, fit the bill. They didn't even have to provide names or an electronic form of payment—only a few dollars stuffed in an envelope and dropped into the payment box. Even better, they were the campground's only visitors.

"I wonder what this thing is made of." Bones took it and swung it back and forth in half-speed cuts. "It's heavy as hell. Almost like a meteorite or something. And even though it looks kind of like flint, it doesn't seem brittle."

"I had the same thought. It's very strange stone."

Without warning, Bones raised the stone, point down.

"Bones, wait!" Maddock shouted as his friend drove the point of the stone into one of the warped boards of the table top. It bit deeply into the wood and stuck there.

"Dude, you have got to chill." Bones waved away Maddock's concern. "I'm conducting an experiment here. You know, science?"

"What if it had broken?" Maddock pulled it free and returned to scrutinizing its surface.

"Then we'd have known for sure that it really was brittle. I was testing my hypothesis." Bones stood and stretched, his back popping loudly. "Sleeping on the ground sucks. My back is one giant mass of knots. You think they've got a massage parlor in that town we passed through last night?"

"Maybe, but do you really want to get a massage from one of the locals? This place has got a Deliverance vibe to it."

Bones shuddered. "You're right. It's probably like that topless place south of Cheyenne I stopped at that one time. I will never, ever unsee that. Stretch marks for miles."

"You stopped during the lunch shift. What did you expect?"

Bones grimaced and shook his head. "Let's get back to a happier topic."

"You mean like, 'Why is someone willing to hurt your grandfather just to obtain this artifact?'"

"Yeah, that." Bones did a few toe touches and then returned to his seat. "Where do we go from here? The only way to get the Trident, whoever they are, off my grandfather's back, would be to either give them the stone, or let it be known that we've found it."

Maddock nodded. "Obviously, we can't hand it over. Its power is incredible and we don't know its limits. We have no understanding of what this thing is or what else it can do. Nor do we have any idea who the Trident is and what they want with it. Bossing around animals can't be the full extent of it." He couldn't shake the feeling that he'd heard the name "Trident" before.

"In a perfect world," Bones said, "we'd learn its origin and give it over to the tribe that has the best claim on it, assuming it's a Native American artifact. But if we do that, I'm sure the Trident will just steal it."

"Agreed." Maddock had contemplated that very thing. "Obviously, we should try to learn all we can about this thing before we make any firm decisions."

"Obviously," Bones said. "We'd do that regardless."

"Right. Second, we need to find out who the Trident is. If we've got another Dominion on our hands, I want to know about it." The Dominion was an extremist religious group of whom Maddock and Bones had run afoul many times. "We also need to know if Tyson and Ahmed are connected to that group or if they're free agents. It would be one heck of a coincidence if they're unrelated."

"Should we check with Tam Broderick? She's a Fed who deals with this kind of stuff. Maybe she's heard of the Trident."

"I don't know." Maddock scratched his chin, eyes still fixed on the stone. "We just got out from under her thumb. I'm not sure I want to go to that well unless we absolutely have to." Tam was on the right side, but she always had her own agenda and she seldom shared it with anyone else. She also never failed to call in a favor owed.

"Your sister still works for her, doesn't she?"

"Good idea. If the Myrmidon files contain something about the Trident, she'll hopefully be able to access it."

"That's a plan," Bone said. "Now, how do we get the heat off of Grandfather?"

"Unfortunately, I think we need to let it be known that we've found Esau's treasure. It's possible that Eddings really did get the word out about us, but we should make our own efforts in that regard. We'll be the rabbit the Trident is chasing."

"Holy crap." Bones buried his face in his hands. "We spent enough time yesterday being chased. It's already getting old, but I think you're right."

Maddock couldn't disagree. "Maybe a rabbit is a bad analogy. We'll be the bait in the trap."

Bones eyed him, a curious look in his eyes. "I guess that's a little bit better, but you realize, even when the trap works, the bait tends to get eaten."

CHAPTER 14

The vibrating phone rattled on the desk, breaking Avery Halsey's contemplative silence. She sat alone in her tiny office at Myrmidon headquarters beneath the Truman White House in Key West. Tam had loaded her down with work and she really didn't have time for a personal call. She reached over to tap the Decline button, but then she saw the name on the caller ID.

"What's up?" she said by way of greeting. "I haven't heard from you since you called to tell me you're engaged. You haven't already gotten cold feet have you?"

"No, it's still a go," said the familiar voice on the other end. *"So, how's it going, Sis?"*

"Maddock, do you really think I don't notice when you do that?" He was so predictable.

"What's that?"

"You only call me 'Sis' when you want something." She grinned at the sudden pause on the other end of the line. She and Maddock had only known one another for a short while, and she enjoyed ribbing him.

"No, it's not like that. I'm trying to be more personable, that's all. You're always telling me how distant I am."

"So you *don't* want anything?" Another pause.

"Well…"

"What is it? I'm glad to help if I can, but Tam's got me working on something she says is urgent and the last thing I need is her catching me taking a personal call, particularly if it involved doing you a favor while I'm on the clock."

"Are you ever really off the clock when you work for Tam?"

"Good point," she admitted. "What do you need?"

"Bones and I have made some new friends."

Avery sighed. "Of course you have. I thought you left

the Myrmidons because you wanted a quieter life with your new fiancée. By the way, tell her no pink or yellow for the bridesmaids' dresses. I look hideous in both."

"I'll try and remember to tell her that. I'm actually avoiding the whole wedding topic. No hurry."

"Oh, Maddock. You're a mess." Avery rubbed her temples. What was it about her brother that every time they talked he managed to stress her out. "Tell you what, I'll call Angel myself. We'll get these wedding plans moving."

"Gee, thanks." Maddock cleared his throat. "Anyway, these guys showed up out of the blue and they came after Bones' grandfather."

Avery sat up a little straighter. "That's terrible. Why would they do that?"

"It's a long story. I'll tell you all about it when we both have more time. Anyway, we're wondering if the Myrmidons have run across a group called the Trident."

"The Trident." Her heart skipped a beat. She knew that name very well.

"Yes. And I've got two names which might be connected: Tyson and Ahmed."

"Maddock, you've heard of both the Trident and Tyson. When Tam and I went to the Jefferson Memorial, Tyson is the guy who tried to trap us down there. He works for them. He said so."

"You're right. I should have remembered. I've been distracted for a while now." Maddock pause. *"So, have you guys got anything on them?"*

"I'm not sure. Tam said she'd put out some feelers but it's not a priority. We're all about the Dominion, as you well know."

"Feel free to keep them off of our backs. I've had enough of those guys to last a lifetime."

Avery managed a small laugh. "Maddock, this sounds serious. You really ought to talk to Tam. If anybody knows about them, she does."

"I'll think about it."

"She's not one of the bad guys. You just don't like

dealing with someone who's as stubborn as you are."

"I deal with you, don't I?"

"You're such a jerk. But even if that's true, you're stuck with me. I'm your sister."

"Tam never does a favor without expecting something in return. I know that from experience." She heard a muffled voice in the background. She couldn't make out the words, but she recognized Bones' voice. "All right," Maddock finally said. *"We'll touch base with her when we know a little more about what's going on. In the meantime, see what you can find out, okay?"*

Avery sighed. "All right, but promise me you'll be careful."

"When have I not been careful?"

"Not funny. I'll talk to you soon."

The call ended and she sat staring at the phone. Sometimes she wondered if having a brother was worth the worry.

CHAPTER 15

"You do realize the guy is going to think we're nuts, don't you?" Bones asked as they entered the New Echota visitor center. Formerly the capital of the Cherokee nation and the place where the "Trail of Tears" officially began, New Echota was now an official historic site. Off the beaten path, it drew few visitors to its cluster of historic buildings, and today seemed to be no exception. Maddock had noticed only a handful of cars in the parking lot and no one was in sight on the grounds.

A young woman with curly, red hair and blue eyes stood behind the counter. When she heard them enter, she looked up from the book she was reading and smiled brightly.

"Welcome to New Echota! How can I help you?"

Bones immediately strode to the counter, leaned against it, and smiled. "As a matter of fact," he paused to glance at her name tag, "Teagan, I have a big problem that I know you can help me with."

Teagan adopted an appropriately concerned expression. "Really? What's that?"

"I've looked and I've looked, and I can't seem to find your number anywhere."

She looked surprised, but then let out a small laugh. "You're funny."

"It's not funny; it's tragic."

Teagan tilted her head and gazed up at him, lips pursed. "No offense, but how old are you? Aren't you, like, thirty?"

Bones' jaw dropped and he stood there blinking, temporarily rendered speechless.

Though he was tempted to let his friend twist in the wind, Maddock stepped in. "We have an appointment with Ben. Is he here?"

"Sure. I'll get him for you." She disappeared down a

narrow hallway at the end of the counter and returned a minute later, followed by a short, stocky man with blue eyes who introduced himself as Ben.

"I assume you're Bonebrake?" he said as he shook hands with Bones.

"Guilty."

"I've come across that name many times in my studies." He turned to Maddock. "And that makes you Maddock. Come on back to my office."

He led them to a small room crowded with shelves crammed full of books, and boxes of papers and magazines. A bulky desktop computer and monitor sat atop a coffee-stained calendar on the small, metal desk. Ben took a pair of folding chairs from the corner behind the door and handed them to Maddock and Bones.

"Make yourself as at home as you can in here. Sorry about the clutter. I'd make an excuse, but I'm an unrepentant slob."

"I would be too if the Navy hadn't drilled it out of me," Bones said, gingerly easing himself into the chair until he was certain it would support his weight.

"Thanks for meeting with us on such short notice," Maddock said.

"I'm happy to. The lore of the Southeastern tribes is my specialty. I'm part Cherokee, you know."

Maddock took in the man's fair skin, round face, and light-colored eyes, and managed to nod gravely.

"But the Irish in me is winning, as you can see," Ben added. "Sorry, just a little joke. My wife says it wasn't funny the first thousand times I told it, but I'm hoping it will age like wine."

"Keep hoping," Bones said, adding a wink.

"Will do." Ben sat down behind the desk, folded his hands, and adopted a businesslike manner. "You said you had some questions about an artifact?"

"Correct," Maddock said. He and Bones had debated about how much to tell the man beforehand. They wanted word to get out that they'd located the artifact, but they didn't know what sort of resources the Trident had at their disposal, nor how quickly the organization could act. Consequently, they'd decided to meet with Ben first and try to get the jump on their enemies before spreading the word of their discovery. "Are you familiar with any legends about men who are able to control animals?"

"That's a pretty common theme, actually," Ben said. "Well, not exactly *controlling* animals, but native lore is filled with stories of people who can talk with them."

"Not talking," Bones said. "We're looking specifically for stories about men who can control their behavior." He glanced at Maddock. "Or legends about an object that gives a person that kind of control."

Ben's eyes widened. "Funny you should ask. I know of exactly one such story. It's not commonly known. I actually collected that story myself from an elder of the Chicora tribe during my grad school days."

"Chicora?" Bones asked. "I'm not familiar with them."

"A small coastal tribe down in South Carolina. They're considered Catawban. What remains of them are petitioning for recognition. They don't have an official reservation, but I found a cluster of them living in a rural area not far from Myrtle Beach. Hold on a minute." He rolled his chair into the corner, took a box from a bottom shelf, and began rummaging through it. "Believe it or not," he said as he shuffled through old papers, "I have an organizational system. It just isn't readily apparent to anyone but me. Ah, here it is." He took out an old composition book, replaced the box, and rolled back to the desk. "Let me find it." He thumbed through the notebook. "Got it."

"The Chicora tell of a white man dressed all in white who swam to shore on the coast of South Carolina many years ago. He said he had come from across the sea along with others of his like, and their numbers were seven, seven, and seven."

"So, like seven hundred seventy-seven?" Bones asked. "Or twenty-one?"

"I can't say for certain, and the storyteller didn't know either," Ben said. "But, if we assume the story is based in fact, we can assume twenty-one men would be a better fit for an old sailing vessel." He returned to his notes.

"The man carried with him a stone which he said wielded great power and that its sister stones had been lost. To prove his claim, he raised the stone and called out to the creatures of the forest. One by one, two by two, and seven by seven they came and circled around. The bear and the rabbit, the cougar and the deer all sat calmly and waited to do his bidding. The man called again and birds settled on his shoulders, the eagle on one and the dove on the other.

"When all had seen that he spoke the truth, the man dismissed the animals and made a gift of the stone to the chief in exchange for his life. From then on, the tribe was always blessed with good hunting.

"The chief sought to carve it into a pleasing shape but found it to be the hardest stone he had ever encountered. Every night he worked at it, but managed only to make etchings upon its surface."

"What sort of etchings?" Bones asked.

Ben shrugged. "No one knows."

Maddock and Bones exchanged a quick glance. They thought they knew what the etchings were.

Ben returned to his notes.

"When the chief died, his sons contended for possession of the stone. The eldest son wished to use it as a weapon of war. He vowed to command the fierce creatures of the forest to do his bidding, and would thus destroy his enemies. The second son sought to control the people through use of the stone."

"You can control people with it?" Bones interrupted.

Ben shook his head. "He figured with the stone he could drive away all the game or call it to him. Controlling a large portion of the food supply is an effective way to control a population." He glanced back down at his notebook.

"To save her people from the inevitable conflict, the chief's daughter stole the stone and made away with it. From that day, the tribe has prayed for its return." Ben closed the notebook. "Not exactly poetic language but that's pretty much the size of it."

"Are there any other legends about the stone?" Maddock asked.

"A few, but this," he tapped the notebook, "is what I believe to be the source of all those stories. I spent a lot of time tracing it back. All the elders I spoke with told the same tale in the same way. The elder with whom I spoke insisted that the tribe still possesses some of the white man's belongings. He wouldn't show them to me so who knows?"

"The story mentions sister stones," Maddock said. "Any idea about them? What they were, what they could do?"

Ben shook his head. "No clue, sorry."

"No problem. We'd love to talk with the elder if he'd be willing to meet with us. Could we trouble you to give us his name?" Maddock asked.

"Sure thing. It's Archer. I don't know if that's a first name or a last name, and as far as I know, he's never shot a bow and arrow. He did, however, give me permission to share his information. He's the oldest of the bunch and highly respected in his community. He knows his stuff." Ben consulted his address book and then jotted down a name and address on a legal pad, tore off the sheet, and handed it to Maddock.

Maddock thanked him, pocketed the paper, and rose to leave.

"You know, it's weird," Ben said. "I don't think anyone's ever asked me about the legend of the stone and then I hear from two people in the same day."

Maddock froze. Had the Trident gotten ahead of them? "Really? Who else is interested? Maybe it's someone we know." He hoped he sounded casual.

"A professor from Atlanta. Dima Zafrini is her name. I only spoke to her on the phone but she sounded hot." Ben flashed a lopsided grin at Bones who returned the smile.

"Maybe we'll cross paths with her," Bones said. "Always happy to make a hot new friend."

"May I ask why you're interested in the legend? It's not a well-known story."

Maddock tensed. He and Bones made a practice of keeping their secrets close, but they needed to get the Trident away from Bones' family, and maybe Ben could unwittingly help them do that.

"I know it's hard to believe, but we think we found the stone in question."

"You're kidding." Ben gaped at him.

"I'm serious. We don't know much about it, which is why we wanted to speak with an expert such as yourself. It's an interesting find, but has potential to be a controversial one, as I'm sure you can imagine. We don't want to publish until we know more about it."

"Can I see it?" Hunger burned in Ben's eyes.

"I'm afraid we don't have it with us. We're keeping it somewhere safe for now." Actually, somewhere safe was a pocket inside Bones' leather jacket, but no one needed to know that. "We will definitely give you a call when we're ready to publish our findings. You've been very helpful." He extended his hand to shake.

"Wait a minute." Then sprang to his feet. "How did you find it? Where? What makes you think it's the stone?"

Maddock glanced at his watch and made a face. "I'm afraid that's a much longer story than we have time for. We're going to be traveling but we really want to follow up with this contact you gave us before then."

"How about we buy you a beer and tell you the story once we get back into the country?" Bones asked.

"Of course," Ben said. "It's probably overly dramatic to call the stone my life's work, but it certainly a passion. I'd like to be involved in any way I can."

He had taken the bait. Now it was up to Maddock to set the hook. "There is actually something you can do to help. We're going to be working on a different project for a few weeks but we'd like for someone to lay the groundwork for a documentary were going to film about the stone. If you could put out feelers for people who have any knowledge about the stone or similar legends that would be great."

Ben nodded eagerly. "I'll hit a couple of the message boards that I frequent and also touch base with some of my colleagues. Is it okay if I tell them someone has found the stone?"

Maddock and Bones pretended to consider this. "I think so," Maddock finally said. "Well, we really do have to be going but we really appreciate your help. Will be in touch soon."

"By the way, I forgot to tell you what the Chicora tribe calls the stone," Ben said. "It's a goofy name but you'll want to use it or else Archer will think you don't know what you're talking about."

"Great. What's the name?" Maddock asked.

"They call it the Noah Stone."

CHAPTER 16

The CRV bounced and jostled along the rutted dirt road. Dima's GPS had lost its signal about a mile back. As far as she knew, she was in the right place. Archer's house should be somewhere close by.

Her cell phone vibrated, making her jump. "Sure. Now you get a signal." She glanced at the caller ID. It was Addie.

"Hey, what's up?"

"What's up?" Addie scolded. *"Seriously? You leave me a message telling me I have to take over all your classes for the rest of the semester and you want to know what's up?"*

"The semester's over in two weeks, Addie. I've already made up the exams. You can handle it."

Addie let out an exasperated sigh. *"That's not what I'm trying to say. I'm worried about you, you idiot. You've never taken a day off of work, and now you take an indefinite leave? What's going on?"*

Dima bit her lip. She wanted to explain to Addie, but she couldn't bring herself to do it. Suddenly this trip to meet Archer felt foolish in the extreme. She was freaked out, to be sure, but the stronger motivating factor was her desire to follow the clue Robert had sent her. Her fascination with Noah and the flood myths had taken hold, and this legend of a Noah Stone seemed the best way to start, at least until Robert showed up again. If he showed up again.

"I'm okay, I just need some time to myself," she lied. "It's a long story and I promise I'll tell you as soon as I can, but it's not a phone conversation."

The silence on the other end of the line lasted so long that she thought the call had dropped.

"Addie, are you there?"

"I'm here. I just wish you'd tell me what's wrong."

"Don't worry about me. I promise I'll be okay. I just need a long-overdue vacation. When I'm back in the swing of things we'll have another night out and I'll tell you all about it."

Up ahead, the drive opened up into a clearing. A tiny, well-kept house stood on the other side. This must be the place.

"All right," Addie said. *"Stay safe and keep in touch."*

"I will." She was about to end the call when a sudden thought occurred to her. "Say, do you remember that Tyson guy that stopped by the office?"

"Tall, dark, and handsome? Of course I do."

"That's him. Listen. If he shows up again, be wary of him."

"Really? Why?"

"I can't explain. Just trust me."

Addie didn't like it but she agreed with just a hint of reluctance. Dima pocketed her phone, pulled up close to the house, and stopped. She took a deep breath. Archer wasn't expecting her, and she wondered if he'd consider her sudden appearance an intrusion. It suddenly occurred to her that the man might not even be home. If not, she'd just have to wait for him. She had to see this thing through.

She cut the engine and stepped out into the humid South Carolina day. It wasn't as bad as Atlanta, but still the damp air felt like a steam room after the blast of her car's air conditioning. The scent of pine hung heavy in the air and it made her nose itch. Just her luck to discover she had a pine allergy only after moving to the Southeast.

Footsteps from somewhere nearby caught her attention and she turned, expecting to see Archer. Instead, her eyes fell on a hook-nosed man, a Saudi by the look of him, striding toward her. She wondered where he'd come from, but the question was answered when she spotted a white Toyota 4Runner parked in the shelter of a leafy dogwood. She'd been so immersed in her conversation with Addie that she hadn't even notice.

"Dima Zafrini?"

Alarm bells rang in her mind. Who was he? How did he know her name? How did he know he would find her here? This was all wrong. She was halfway back into her car when a hand clamped over her mouth and a strong arm snaked around her waist.

"I need you to come with me." The man's breath smelled of clove cigarettes and his oily tone soured her stomach.

She tried to scream but managed only a muffled groan. Her hands grabbed for the steering wheel, but he yanked her out of the cab and dragged her, thrashing wildly, toward his waiting vehicle. She fought like a cornered cat, kicking and scratching for all she was worth. She jerked her head to the side and managed to utter a weak, "Help" before he muffled her again. She bit down on his finger and heard a satisfying curse, but her efforts were too little. Dima knew how to defend herself, but the man was too strong.

"We want the three stones, and I think you know where to find them," the man snarled.

Somewhere within the terror coursing through her, she became aware of the crunch of tires on the drive. Her captor released her just as a silver Hyundai Santa Fe skidded to a halt. The doors flew open, and two men leaped out.

Everything happened in a flash. Shots rang out, an engine roared to life, more shots, and then a crash as the Toyota driven by the man who had just attempted to capture her clipped the back of the Hyundai. By the time the dust settled and Dima regained her composure, the man was gone.

She looked at her rescuers, if that was, indeed, what they were. One was a stocky blond man of above-average height. The other was a huge Native American with a ponytail. Both held handguns at their sides and stared in the direction where the Toyota had gone.

"Unbelievable," the blond man said as he kicked the rear passenger-side tire. He clipped us just right and knocked it off the rim."

"That was one of the guys, wasn't it?" his friend asked. "Ahmed."

"Looked like him. The nose." The blond man holstered his pistol and turned, his eyes falling on Dima. "Are you all right?"

Adrenaline coursing through her, all her fight or flight responses firing at once, Dima managed only three clipped words. "Who are you?"

"I'm Maddock. This is Bones." Maddock paused, as if she was supposed to recognize the names. "Look, I know you've got to be freaked out about what just happened, but I promise you're safe now. We've already had one run-in with that guy."

Dima bit her lip. If these two were planning on hurting her, there was nothing she could do. For the first time since moving to Atlanta she wished she'd allowed herself to get caught up in the Southern gun culture.

"I just want to leave." She hated the quaver in her voice.

"We won't stop you," the big guy, Bones, said. "But if he's lying in wait somewhere down the road, you might find yourself in another hard place. You want to call the cops?"

That eased her concerns a bit, though she was still on her guard. "You said you've met him before. Have you had dealings with Trident?"

The way their jaws dropped, almost in unison, would have elicited a giggle from her in almost any other circumstance.

"You know about the Trident?" Maddock asked.

"I don't know about *the* Trident, but I know about a company called Trident that deals in antiquities. I've got a card from a guy named Tyson." She returned to her CRV, fished around in her purse until she found the card, and brought it back to show them.

Maddock glanced at it and passed it over to Bones. "Tyson and the guy who tried to kidnap you work together. They attacked Bones' grandfather trying to get information."

"Are you serious? What kind of information?"

"The same information you're looking for—the Noah Stone."

She saw sincerity in Maddock's eyes and knew he was telling the truth. She wasn't completely comfortable with these two just yet, but she was beginning to think maybe she could trust them.

"Everything calming down out here?" said a gruff voice from the direction of the house.

She turned to see a wizened old man standing on the front porch, aiming a rifle in their direction. This must be Archer.

"We're fine," she said. "Someone tried to kidnap me and these men chased him off."

"I saw the end of it," the man said. "I watched long enough to make sure these two didn't try anything. I would've shot you both if you had."

"I don't blame you," Bones said. "Are you Archer?"

"How about we continue this conversation after you fellows have handed your guns to the young lady?"

"No problem," Bones said. Slowly, he and Maddock reversed their pistols and handed them to Dima.

"Are the safeties on?" She hoped the answer was "yes." She didn't actually know where the safety was on either of these weapons, though she could probably figure it out.

"Mine's a Glock," Bones said, as if that answered the question.

"No external safety on that one," Archer called, apparently seeing her bemusement. "Lock them in your car for now."

She complied, and the three of them slowly approached the house.

Archer let his rifle dip, but didn't lower it completely.

"I appreciate the trigger discipline," Maddock said.

"I'm a veteran," Archer said simply.

Dima had no idea what they were talking about, and

it pissed her off. She made a quick mental note to fill in this gaping hole in her knowledge base, and then interrupted the budding boys' club. "Mister Archer, we're here about the Noah Stone. We didn't come together, but that's what all three of us are researching. Ben Street from New Echota said you might be willing to talk to us about it."

"Ordinarily I would be, but this is hardly an ordinary circumstance. You need to convince me real quick why I should talk to you."

"How about we show you?" Bones slowly opened his leather jacket, reached inside, and withdrew an oddly-shaped black object. "We found the stone."

CHAPTER 17

Archer invited them inside and offered them coffee. The last thing Maddock wanted on this humid afternoon was a hot drink, but he and the others accepted out of courtesy. After the way they'd started off, manners were essential. If Archer had anything of interest to tell them, they didn't want to give offense. While the old man busied himself in the kitchen, Maddock, Bones, and Dima made small talk. She was clearly frightened, but seemed to be warming to them. The revelation that he and Bones possessed the Noah Stone, had gone a long way toward convincing her they were legit. By the time Archer served the coffee, she seemed eager to hear their story.

Archer pulled up a rickety kitchen chair and faced his three guests who sat arrayed on a sagging, overstuffed sofa. He took a sip of his coffee, grimaced, and sat it down on the coffee table that stood between them. "Mixed it too strong. That's the problem with instant. Hard to get it right." A fat, gray cat hopped onto his lap, turned, and cast suspicious eyes on Maddock.

"All right, you two. "How about you explain yourselves?"

Bones quickly recounted the events of the past few days, emphasizing the attack on his grandfather and their desire to get to the bottom of the mystery behind the Noah Stone, not for their own gain, but to hopefully foil whatever plan the Trident might have and to protect his family.

Archer listened intently, nodding his head at appropriate times. Dima stared at Bones, her expression unreadable. When Bones finished telling the story, Archer gazed at the ceiling for several moments before speaking.

"How do you know the stone is real?"

Maddock looked at Bones and waved his hand in a "go ahead" gesture. They had agreed to keep the circumstances surrounding the recovery of the stone a secret, but otherwise to be open about things. Besides, even if Archer repeated the tale, who would believe him?

"Because it works." Bones took out the Noah Stone, pressed the sharp edge to his palm, and dragged it across his flesh.

Dima let out a little gasp, but Archer's expression remained stolid as Bones let a few drops of blood trickled onto the stone. He then looked at the cat and said, "Jump."

The cat immediately sprang off of the old man's lap and onto the coffee table.

"Sit."

The cat sat down and stared expectantly at Bones.

"Roll over."

Maddock snatched up his coffee cup just in time to keep the enraptured feline from upending it.

"I don't believe it." Awe and wonder filled Dima's soft voice. Then her eyes narrowed and she looked at Archer. "Your cat doesn't know any tricks, does she?"

Archer chuckled. "She's never followed an order in her life until just now."

"Would it work on wild animals?" she said to Bones.

"It already has. I've done it." Bones handed the stone to Maddock. "Your turn. I don't feel like cutting myself any deeper. Besides, this is the hand I use to brush a lady's hair back before kiss her." He flashed a smile at Dima.

"I just narrowly avoided being kidnaped and you choose now to hit on me?" She folded her arms and gave him a stare like a disapproving schoolteacher.

"Sorry. I can't always turn it off. There's something about an intelligent woman."

Dima smiled, or perhaps it was a smirk, but that ended the exchange and everyone turned their attention to Maddock.

He hadn't tried using the stone yet, but he'd watched

Bones do it a few times, and his friend had described how it worked. He took a deep breath and pressed the stone into his hand. The moment his blood oozed onto the stone, his flesh began to tingle. The air around him seemed to crackle as if an aura of energy surrounded him. He sensed life all around him. Something moved in the forest close to the house and he called out to it with his mind. After a moment's hesitation, he felt it approach. Something clattered outside the front door. Moments later, Archer let out a surprised curse followed by a chortle.

Maddock turned to see a doe peering in the window. Their eyes met, and then he felt the connection break. In that instant, the deer darted away.

"Well, I'll be damned. Can I see that?" Archer held out his callused hand.

Maddock passed the stone to the old man, who turned it over and over, examining every detail. "I always believed the stories were true, but to actually see it for myself, that's truly something." He smiled and handed the stone back to Maddock. "Needless to say, I believe you boys."

"It's amazing," Dima said, "but my interest is in the Noah's Ark story. Other than the nickname 'Noah Stone' there's not really any connection to the Biblical Noah."

"I think there might be." Archer stood, retrieved his rifle and headed for the door. "You three come with me. There's something I have to show you."

They piled into Archer's battered pickup. Dima rode in the cab while Maddock and Bones sat in the back. Now satisfied that they meant him no harm, the old man had told Dima to return their weapons, and now the two of them were on high alert, wondering if the Trident would make another appearance.

After a short drive down a rutted dirt road, they pulled over to the side in the middle of the forest. Archer led the way, changing directions seemingly at random. Ordinarily Maddock would have enjoyed the lush greenery, cool air, earthy aroma, and the soft ground beneath his feet, but after the incident at Dark Entry, he found no comfort in the woods. The way grew more difficult as they picked their way through rocky terrain choked with brush and brambles. Finally, Archer called a halt.

"There's a sinkhole up here. Be careful on the way down."

The hole was large enough to swallow a small house, and filled with more of the tangled undergrowth they'd fought their way through. A stand of trees grew out of the center, a testament to the years that had passed since the ground in this spot had collapsed. Inside, only thin slivers of sunlight filtered in, and Maddock felt they were walking at twilight. When they came to a halt at the far end of the hole, Dima put her hands on her hips and frowned. "You brought us to see a hole?"

Archer smiled, pushed aside a tangle of vines, then slipped his hand into a crack in the rock face, and pulled. He skipped to the side with surprising agility for a man of his apparent age as a tall, flat chunk of stone teetered and fell with a muffled thump. Where it had leaned against the rocky face, a two-foot wide crack split the rock.

"In here," he said. "It isn't far." He turned, scooted sideways into the passageway, and disappeared from sight.

Bones tilted his head and pursed his lips. "I suppose I'll go next. If I can make it through, you two definitely will.

"And if you get stuck, I'll be here to pull you out," Maddock added.

"Thanks for that." Bones exhaled loudly and slid into the passage. He needn't have worried—there was plenty of clearance and he too quickly disappeared into the darkness. Dima followed behind him with Maddock bringing up the rear.

There was a dank, musty air about the place. This close to the coastline, Maddock was surprised to find an underground space completely free of groundwater. The Chicora had chosen a good place to hide whatever it was they kept down here.

About ten meters back, they found themselves in a tiny cave. The old flashlight Archer carried cast a faint yellow light. Probably needed fresh batteries. When Maddock and Bones added the beams of their mini Maglites, the cave lit up. They found themselves facing a stout metal door set in the rock. Archer produced a key and unlocked the padlock that held it closed.

"We don't let many people in here," he said, pushing the door open. "Don't touch anything."

Beyond the door lay another, even smaller cave. Rusted metal shelves stood to their left and right, all piled with Native American artifacts, but it was what lay before them that caught his eye.

A rectangular stone box set against the far wall. Maddock knew immediately what it was.

"The man who brought us the stone was real. We know it to be true because this is his final resting place." Archer moved to the crypt, grabbed hold of the lid, and slid it to the side. A low grinding sound and a fine cloud of dust rose around them.

Bones leaned down and shone his light into the stone coffin and cursed.

"What's the matter?" Maddock asked. "This is hardly your first dead body."

"You need to see what he's buried with." Bones glanced at Archer. "I know were not supposed to touch anything but would it be all right if we remove the lid?"

Archer stared at him, chewing his cheek, before finally nodding.

"We'll be careful," Maddock reassured. "We've done this before." Carefully, he and Bones lifted the stone lid and set it gently on the ground. Maddock shone his light inside the coffin and immediately understood Bones' reaction.

The skeleton that grinned up at them was clad in what had once been a white cloak. In his hand he clutched a dagger with a familiar symbol on the pommel—a red cross.

"He was a Templar," Dima whispered.

Maddock and Bones nodded.

"I've never seen anything like this," she said.

"We have, but it's been a while." Maddock ran the beam of his light all around the coffin and immediately spotted a wooden cylinder. "What's inside there?"

"He recorded his story before he died, at least as much of a as he could remember." Archer held up a hand. "No, you can't open it, and there's no need. I know the story verbatim. It's been handed down from generation to generation. I'll write it down for you. But the short story is, he and his companions came over the ocean in a ship carrying items they wanted to keep away from the Saracens. The items he treasured the most were a pair of sacred stones."

"A pair?" Dima asked. "Not three?"

Archer shook his head. "Only two, but that doesn't mean they weren't part of a trio. Anyway, their ship went down in a storm just off the shore of Bowhead Island. The only thing he saved was the single stone—the one you have now."

"If you have an idea where the ship went down, why hasn't anyone tried to recover it?" Bones asked.

"People try from time to time, but they've never succeeded."

They stood there in silence, gazing at the knight's remains.

"You're right," Dima finally said. "If a Templar brought the stone here, that makes it much easier to believe that the stone came from the Holy Land."

"Do you think this," Bones patted his chest pocket where he held the stone, "might be what Noah used to bring the animals onto the ark?"

"I'm starting to think so," Dima said. "The fragment of the *Book of Noah* mentions stones, a Templar brings your stone to the New World, and it holds a power that could fit in with the Noah story."

"It's just so hard to believe," Archer said.

Bones looked at the man and grinned. "Trust me, in our line of work, it's not that far-fetched."

CHAPTER 18

The heat struck him as soon as he emerged from the underground chamber. Maddock mopped his brow and tried to process what he'd just learned. The stone that had belonged to Bones' ancestor had been brought to the New World by a Templar, which meant there was a good chance it was, indeed, an artifact from the Holy Land. Another stone had been lost in a shipwreck somewhere off the coast of South Carolina. When he considered Dima's evidence that Noah possessed three stones that were at least special enough to merit a mention in the *Book of Noah*, the objective seemed clear to him. He was about to share his thoughts with Bones when he saw movement up ahead.

"Hold on." He held out his hand and motioned for the others to stop.

Bones didn't need him to explain. His friend spotted the movement as well and rested his hand on his Glock.

A short, stout young man, Native American by the looks of him, emerged from the trees and stopped at the edge of the sinkhole. He was clad in a police uniform.

"Is that you Archer?"

Archer moved to the front of the group. "Yep, it's me. What are you doing out here Carl?"

"We got a report of shots fired in the area around your house. I stopped by there and all I saw was an unfamiliar vehicle that had obviously been in some kind of accident, and your truck was gone. When you didn't answer the door I feared the worst so I came looking for you."

"Well, thank you for looking out for me." Archer said. "How did you know to check for me here?"

Maddock watched Carl closely. Archer's question echoed his own thoughts. Maddock and the others had not been here very long. For Carl to have stopped by

Archer's house, determine that he wasn't home, and then arrive at this spot so quickly was suspicious to say the least.

Carl hesitated only a moment before replying.

"Just a lucky guess. If I hadn't found you quickly I would've put out an APB." He frowned as his eyes passed over Maddock, Bones, and Dima. "Now, why don't you all come up out of there and you can introduce me to your friends?"

When they exited the sinkhole, Archer introduced the group. Carl shook hands with each of them in turn. Maddock sized him up in an instant. He was broad of shoulder but thick around the middle, clearly out of shape, and his grip was weak. Furthermore, he was reluctant to meet anyone's eye for more than a brief instant. He was no threat.

"Well, I guess we'd better be going," Archer said. "Thanks again for checking on me." He headed back toward the spot where they parked the truck but Carl moved to block his way.

"Wait a minute. Can I talk to you in private?"

"Why private?" Archer asked. "There's no problem here. These are good folks."

Carl cast a sour frown in their direction and then nodded. "I just want to know why you would bring them out here, that's all. This isn't a place we show to just anybody."

"They aren't just anybody. They have a good reason to be here."

"And that reason would be?" Carl put his hands on his hips and puffed out his chest, failing miserably to look tough.

"They have the stone that…" Archer froze, anger burning in his eyes. He winced and gritted his teeth. Obviously, he knew he had made a misstep.

Maddock expected Carl to appear surprised or skeptical, but instead a look of keen interest filled his eyes. "Really?" He said softly. "*The* stone? How is that possible?"

"Well, we have *a* stone," Maddock said. "It belongs to my friend's family." He inclined his head toward Bones. "In the process of doing some research, we learned about the stone that was once here and we wondered if they might be one and the same. Archer was kind enough to show us around."

"We're archaeologists," Bones added. "So we've got an interest in history and artifacts."

"Can I see it?" Carl said, a bit too quickly for Maddock's liking.

"We don't keep it with us," Bones said. "It's in a safe deposit box at our family's bank. We know it's probably not worth much but it special to us."

"Really? Which bank?"

Maddock almost laughed. The man had no subtlety.

"Cherokee Community, close to the reservation." Because Maddock knew Bones so well, he saw the tiny glint in his friend's eye. "We bring it out for family reunions. I was telling Archer that if he wants to check it out, he should come up for the next one on the Fourth of July. You can come to if you like."

"Thanks. I just might." Carl looked around. "I guess I'd better go. Glad you're okay," he said Archer. He turned on his heel and hurried off.

"That's an odd fellow," Dima observed.

"That's a bought fellow," Maddock said.

Dima frowned. What do you mean?

"If I don't miss my guess, our friend Carl is about to make a phone call to someone who is very interested in the stone."

"Carl?" Archer asked. "The boy's an idiot. How could he be in league with anyone of consequence?"

"It seems to be part of the Trident's practice to buy off low-level functionaries," Bones said. "We ran across a couple recently."

"Archer, I think you should consider getting away for a while," Maddock said. "Is there anywhere you can go? Someone you can stay with where the Trident wouldn't easily find you?"

"Do you really think that's necessary? Carl knows the story just as well as I do. If he's in league with this Trident group, he's told them all about the stone and about this place." He gestured back toward the passageway.

"Maddock's right," Bones said. "It's not worth the risk. Even if Carl tells them the story, there's no guarantee they won't come after you just to cover their bases. They might not trust him to have told them the whole story. Like you said, the guy's an idiot. Besides, Dima's presence here proves that you're a person of interest in this whole thing."

Archer considered this for a few moments and then side. "All right. I'll do it. I've got a few places to choose from."

"Don't tell anyone where you're going. Not even us," Maddock said. He doubted Carl was hiding nearby eavesdropping but it wasn't worth the risk.

"You're good boys, but you sure do know how to complicate a man's life."

"Sorry about that," Maddock said, and he meant it. Archer seemed like a good fellow.

"So what do we do now?" Dima asked. She raised her hand before either of them could protest. "It seems like there's a chance we are after the same thing, so it only makes sense to combine our resources. If yours truly is a Noah stone, you need me. I'm something of an expert in that area. And don't say it's too dangerous. The Trident is already after me and I have a feeling you two can protect me better than I can protect myself."

Maddock and Bones looked at one another and Maddock nodded.

"Good. That's settled then." Dima folded her arms. "So I ask again. What do we do now?"

"Bones and I are going to call our crew," Maddock said. "I want to go after the second stone."

CHAPTER 19

Tyson wanted to break something. He sat in a coffeehouse in Augusta, Georgia, near the South Carolina line, listening to Ahmed's story. Tyson had set Ahmed to go after Zafrini while he paid a visit to New Echota. It had seemed an efficient plan, but Ahmed had botched it.

"You let her get away? And you didn't get the document?" Tyson threw his hands in the air. "I knew I shouldn't have let you go alone."

"It's not my fault. Two men showed up. Both were armed." Ahmed shifted nervously in his chair.

"They just showed up? Pure coincidence?" Tyson wasn't buying it.

"I don't think it was a coincidence at all." Ahmed paused and looked down at the floor as if he were considering his words carefully. "I'm almost certain they were the same men who stopped us from questioning old man Bonebrake."

"*Almost* certain?" Tyson asked.

"Well, the blond haired man didn't ring any bells for me, but how many Indians do you know who are that big?"

It was a fair point. The man they had encountered in North Carolina cut and imposing figure, and a memorable one.

Tyson had thought it wise for the two of them to follow up on different leads. Ahmed was to keep an eye on Archer's place in case Dima showed up there. Meanwhile Tyson had continued to survey the woman's home and office.

"If those two showed up at Archer's house, that means they're following the same trail we are. Obviously, old man Bonebrake told him something."

"So, do we go back after him?" Ahmed asked.

Tyson began pacing back and forth across the room. "Possibly, but we won't be able to take him by surprise. Perhaps there's another way of finding out what he knows."

His cell phone rang, interrupting his thoughts.

"Mr. Tyson? This is Carly with the Horry County Sheriff's department. You asked me to call you if anyone else came around asking about the... you know."

"Let me guess," Tyson said. "It was a tall, Native American man and a blond man."

"How did you know? Carl stammered.

Tyson rolled his eyes. The gods save him from insufferable fools. "Never mind that. Can you tell me anything about them? Did you speak with them?"

"Oh yes." Carl's voice suddenly rang with enthusiasm.

Tyson had offered him compensation for useful information. He'd offered a paltry sum, in fact, but the man did not appear to be wealthy by any stretch of the imagination.

"They were asking about the Noah Stone."

Tyson's chest constricted. It was as he had feared. These men, whoever they were, were following the same trail. "Anything else?" He snapped a bit too harshly.

"Yeah, but it was kind of ridiculous. They claim they have a stone of their own. Or, at least, something similar."

Tyson froze. Ahmed, seeing the expression on his face, rose halfway out of his seat but Tyson waved him away. "Do you think they were telling the truth?"

"Well, that I can't say, but they seemed sincere. It's not like they were boasting or anything."

"Did they show you their stone?"

"No, but they told me where they're keeping it. In the Cherokee Community bank up in North Carolina."

A broad grin spread across Tyson's face. "Carl, tell me everything they said. Don't leave out a single detail."

CHAPTER 20

The sun beat down on the white sands of Bowhead Island. The tiny island off the shore of South Carolina was home to no one, save the birds and squirrels high in the lush, green trees and the snakes and rodents that slithered beneath the palmettos. It was a fine day at sea, but Maddock wasn't feeling it.

"I don't think you know where to look." Willis Sanders leaned over Maddock's shoulder to look at the map where Maddock had marked the most likely spot where the wreck would be found. Willis was a former comrade in the SEALs and now a member of Maddock's crew. The other crew members, Matt Barnaby and Corey Dean, were busy at the helm of their boat, *Sea Foam*. Bones was elsewhere, presumably watching Dima soak up the sun in her bikini.

"Of course I don't know where it is," Maddock said. "We're working from a five hundred year-old story. That's why they call it an educated guess."

"Man, don't even try to get all pedantic on me. I just don't want to spend any more time in this sun than I have to." Willis had slathered his dark brown skin with sunblock, giving his face an odd, grayish tinge where he hadn't rubbed it in thoroughly.

"What is it with you and the sun lately? You've never been this uptight about it."

"Skin cancer. It's the silent killer."

Maddock scratched his head. "I thought that was carbon monoxide."

"You die your way, I'll die mine."

Maddock rolled his eyes and returned his attention to the map. "We know the Templar, whoever he was, came ashore in this area." He tapped a spot on the map. "Working backward, he was probably carried past the northern tip of Bowhead Island. Considering the way the currents run in this area, it's most likely the ship went down somewhere along this path." He traced a fishhook-shaped line he'd drawn on the map.

"Hopefully it wasn't too close to land." If the wreck lay too close to shore, it risked being broken up by the ebb and flow of the tides. In deeper water it could lie untouched for centuries.

"We know he caught sight of the island just before the ship went down, so it can't have been too far away. We'll keep our fingers crossed."

"We've got a hit, Maddock." Corey, the tech guy of the crew, sat watching the sonar readouts on a digital display. The fair-skinned redhead preferred the shelter of the cabin to exposure to the elements.

"Already?" Their luck couldn't be that good.

"Wait. It's looking like...yeah, never mind. It can't be what we're looking for. False alarm."

Maddock didn't bother checking. They'd done this sort of thing for years and Corey knew what he was doing.

"I'm going to stretch my legs. Let me know if you find anything promising."

"A stretch sounds good," Matt agreed. "Willis, take the helm?" The stocky, brown-haired man gave up the wheel and sidled up to Maddock. "Spending a little time with our new friend also sounds good."

"She's our colleague. Be professional," Maddock said without a trace of sincerity.

"Seriously? And how long did it take you to hook up with Jade when she was working with us?"

Maddock grimaced. "Fine. Knock yourself out."

They headed out onto the deck and back to the stern where Bones and Dima stood gazing out at the white ribbon of wake that trailed behind them.

"Are we there yet?" Bones asked.

"Yeah. Get out." Maddock sat down on the deck with his back against the rail. "What's going on out here?"

"Not much. Just getting ready to soak up some rays."

He flashed a smile at Dima, who returned a frown.

"Yes," she said, "I'm wearing a swimsuit under my clothes and I wanted to work on my tan, but now you've made it weird."

"No skin for you," Matt jibed.

"Fine. Never let it be said I stood between a lovely lady and her quest for the perfect tan." Bones stood and stripped off his t-shirt. "Okay, now I'm topless too."

This elicited the tiniest of laughs from Dima, and Maddock didn't miss the way she eyed Bones' muscular frame. "All right, when in Rome, I suppose." She gracefully slipped out of her shorts and shirt. Her bright, yellow bikini perfectly offset her deeply tanned skin.

"Do you need someone to lotion your back?" Bones asked.

"As a matter of fact, I do. Matt, will you do the honors?"

The former Army Ranger played it cool, accepting the bottle of suntan lotion and giving it a shake, but as soon as Dima turned around, he pumped his fist in triumph.

Maddock looked on with a touch of envy as his crew mate attended to the attractive woman.

"Good thing my sister can't see you looking at her like that." Bones arched an eyebrow at Maddock.

"What? No, I wasn't looking." Maddock had to laugh. "Okay, busted. But your sister doesn't get too terribly jealous."

"Angel doesn't get jealous? Are we talking about the same person?"

"Well, not compared to some women I've dated."

Bones nodded sagely.

"I've been thinking," Maddock said a bit too loudly, trying to redirect the conversation, "about our next move once we find the second stone."

"Find the third one?" Matt said, not looking up from the task at hand.

"Yeah, but how?" Bones asked. "We've got no clues."

"Not yet, but I think the next step is to follow up on

Dima's *Book of Noah*. As far as we know, it's the only text in history that mentions the stones. Right?"

"As far as I know," Dima said from her position on the deck. She lay face-down on a towel, the sun glinting off her oiled back. "I've been studying Noah's ark for years and never heard of the Noah Stones until my friend Robert sent me the fragment. I was a little skeptical at first, but now that we know they're real, I think we should try to find it."

"This is kind of premature, don't you think?" Bones said. "Even if we find the wreck, and the stone really was on the ship, there's no guarantee the stone is still there."

"Aren't you the optimist? What's up with you?"

"Nothing."

Maddock didn't miss the scowl Bones directed at Matt, who was now working on Dima's legs, and he understood. "First the girl at the museum and now her. You're striking out all over the place, aren't you?"

"It's not that. Well, it's mostly not that. My dry spells tend to be shorter than your…" Bones glanced down and cleared his throat. "Never mind. Anyway, it's knowing what those guys did to my grandfather, and facing the fact that they got away from us twice. I want to hit someone, Maddock. Hard. In the face."

"I'm sure you'll get the chance before this is all over."

The boat slowed and the whine of the engine lowered in pitch. "Looks like they found something," Maddock said. "Let's check it out."

The stop turned out to be for nothing. Under closer scrutiny, the wreck Corey had spotted turned out to be too recent. Three hours and two more false alarms later, Maddock was ready to pop open a Dos Equis and call it a day. He was about to suggest the same to his crew when Corey got another hit on sonar.

"I'm not getting my hopes up," Corey said, "but this one looks promising."

"Let's send Uma down to check it out." Uma was the nickname of their underwater miniature submersible camera. The robotic device could get an up close look at a wreck without stirring up too much silt and could safely go in and out of narrow spaces.

They hastily readied the device and sent it down. The crew huddled around the screen that displayed the images Uma sent back. Soon the image of a sunken ship filled the screen. Maddock had to admit it did look promising. It was a wooden ship, mostly buried in the sand.

Corey guided the submersible up and down the length of the ship. They couldn't make out many details from the exposed portion of the wreck so next they had Uma scan the seabed around the wreck, looking for objects that might have spilled out.

Maddock watched, hoping for some clue that would tell them they were on the right track. Finally, he spotted something.

"Stop. Over there." He tapped the top right corner of the screen.

Corey brought Uma to a halt, rotated her a few degrees, and panned out. A dark, cylindrical object lay in a rocky section of the sea floor. He had almost missed it.

"Bring her in close."

Corey complied, and as the object grew larger, Maddock's heart fell. Even in its current condition, he could tell they had missed their mark.

"What is that?" Dima leaned in for a closer look.

"It's a cannon," he said.

"Is that a bad thing?" she asked.

"In this case it is," Bones said. "Its way to modern. Probably Civil War." He turned to Maddock. "I could go down for a closer look just to be sure."

Maddock shook his head. "There's no need. This isn't the wreck we're looking for."

"But are they the droids we're looking for?" Bones made a face. "Sorry, just trying to lighten the mood."

"Nice try," Maddock said. "Right now, I think a beer is the only thing that will do the trick."

CHAPTER 21

Maddock rose early the next morning and sat down on the deck with a strong cup of coffee and waited to watch the sunrise. He took a sip of the hot, bitter brew and gazed out at the horizon. A thin gray line painted across the ocean portended the sun's arrival. Any day at sea was a good day for him, but mornings were special. He closed his eyes and allowed the cool breeze to wash over him. He was a patient man, especially compared to Bones, but he couldn't deny his eagerness to find the sunken ship and its lost cargo. He wanted to solve the mystery. The thought of locating these so-called Noah Stones and perhaps the legendary ark itself set his heart racing, but the real drive was to make sure Bones' family, and Angel in particular, was safe. Though she was not the target of the Trident, he knew she would not hesitate to put herself in harm's way to protect her grandfather, should the men come after him again.

"That smells good. Have you got a cup for me?" Dima, clad in track pants and a tight-fitting tank top, padded up on bare feet and sat down beside him.

"No, but you're welcome to share this one if you take it black." He handed her the mug.

"It's coffee. I take it any way it comes." She raised the mug to her lips, took a sip, and grimaced. "My God, that is strong." She took another sip and handed it back.

"You're up early," Maddock said.

"I'm a light sleeper. It's gotten even worse since Robert sent me that document. I just can't slow my mind down and I imagine I see those guys around every corner, coming after me."

"I hope you feel safe with us," he said.

"I do. At least, as safe as I'm capable of feeling. I grew up in the Middle East so I've always walked on eggshells." She let out a small sigh. "So, what is the deal with you and Bones? You two make an odd pair."

"He's my best friend. It wasn't always that way. We hated each other at first, but we got over it. I guess you could say we are yen and yang."

"I can believe that. You definitely seem like opposites." She tilted her head and looked at him thoughtfully. "Are you as big a ladies man as he seems to be?"

Maddock grinned and shook his head. "Not me. I'm engaged. To his sister, in fact." He felt a touch of amusement as the lines creasing Dima's face betrayed the same confusion so many others had felt when trying to picture Bones' sister. "Don't worry. She's not his twin or anything." He took out his phone and showed her a picture of Angel.

"She's beautiful. Is she a model or an actress, something like that?"

"Professional fighter." He said, pocketing the phone.

"A fighter. Are you winding me up?"

Maddock shook his head. "Dead serious. She's one-of-a-kind. Kind of like Bones in that way."

"He is unique." Dima bit her lip. "So, what is his deal? I mean, is he in a relationship? Does he even have relationships?"

Maddock always found these questions awkward. The truth was, Bones had never stayed with one woman for any length of time, but there were reasons for that. Reasons his friend would not want shared. "Sure he does. It's just taking him longer to find the right girl." Maddock looked her in the eye. "But I can tell you he's a good man. Maybe the best I've ever known."

Dima turned and looked thoughtfully out at the water. The morning breeze ruffled her long, dark hair, and she brushed a strand from her face. Maddock decided he liked her— she was smart, sincere, and lovely. Bones could do much worse. They sat there in contemplative silence until she spoke again.

"What if Bones is right? What if the wreck really isn't here? Or what if something did happen to it?"

"Doubtful. I did a lot of research and I haven't found any accounts of a Templar ship being found anywhere in this area."

"What if... I don't know, what if it washed away or something? Could that happen?"

Maddock froze. Something had just clicked into place.

"If you'll excuse me," he said, climbing to his feet, "you just reminded me of something I need to check out. You want the rest of this?" He handed her the coffee and hurried back into the cabin. He hoped his hunch was right.

"So, explain to us again this hunch of yours." Willis stood, leaning against the cabin wall, with his muscular arms folded across his chest. The man was a top-notch soldier when he believed in what he was doing, but he always required convincing first.

"It's pretty simple, actually," Maddock said. "The water here is shallower than we had hoped, so the wreck is more likely to have been affected by tides and the like than would a wreck in deeper water. This area has been hit by some major hurricanes and all of them have followed the same path." He traced the point of a pencil in a line running north by northwest. "The prevailing currents run the same way. Since we believe the ship went down southeast of the island, it's possible that the wreckage was pushed ashore."

"The island is boomerang-shaped." Corey took up the explanation. "The wreckage could have been driven right into the center of the V, if you will, and trapped there. The Templar's story indicated that the ship foundered very close to the island so it's possible that we'll find its cargo somewhere in this area. That's one of the pluses of this being a deserted island. No one's been around to stumble upon any wreckage."

"And there are no records of any such cargo being recovered in the vicinity of the island," Maddock added. "At least, not that I could find."

The others appear doubtful. "What if it's buried in the sand?" Matt asked.

"Then we'll find it with metal detectors," Maddock said. "But I doubt that's the case." He took out another chart. "Right here, just offshore of the island, is a deep hole. It's not as large as the blue holes you find in other parts of the world, but it's large enough to suck in a sailing ship."

Bones raised his eyebrows. "That could explain why the wreckage has never been discovered."

"My thoughts exactly." Maddock knew that if he won Bones over, the others would follow suit. "I know the dive could be dangerous but you can't tell me it's not worth a try."

"Come on, Maddock. You think we're scared of a dangerous dive?" Willis asked. "I'll race you to the bottom."

"Excellent." Maddock smiled and nodded. "Let's do it."

CHAPTER 22

"There's something down there." Corey's outward calm could not mask the tremor of excitement in his voice. As Uma descended into the sinkhole, her lights gradually illuminated the bottom. There amongst the rocks and sand lay the unmistakable remains of a shipwreck.

"Come on, baby," Willis whispered. By his side, Bones and Dima stood shoulder to shoulder, both watching in tense anticipation. As they stared at the monitor, Dima absently took Bones' hand and laced her fingers between his. Maddock couldn't help but smile.

"It's definitely a wooden ship," Corey said. "But I don't think I will be able to tell much more with Uma. You guys are going to have to check it out up close and personal."

"We'll take it in shifts," Maddock said. "Bones and I will go first."

"Aw, come on man, let's at least flip for it," Willis protested.

"It's okay, Maddock," Bones said. "Why don't we let the second string have the first crack at it? Save the big guns for last."

It was a measure of how badly Willis and Matt wanted to dive the wreck that neither of them responded to the second string comment. Maddock wasn't fooled. Bones hated hanging out on deck when there was diving to be done. Clearly, his friend wanted to spend time with Dima.

"All right," Maddock agreed. "One hour and not a minute more. If you get into any kind of trouble, come back up. "

"Yes, mom," Matt said. "Would you like to dress us, maybe tie our shoes for us too?"

"Just be careful."

Fifty minutes into the dive, Matt and Willis high-fived, then turned and gave the thumbs-up to the crew via Uma's underwater camera through which those on board *Sea Foam* had been following the divers' progress. They began working at something in the midst of the wreckage, stirring up a cloud of silt. Moments later, they emerged. Willis swam toward the camera and held up a long, narrow object. Maddock recognized it immediately.

"A short sword." The blade was dark and pitted, but the image on the hilt was clear—a Templar cross!

"Yes!" Bones shouted. "You did it, Maddock."

"We're not there yet. Let's get ready to take our turn."

Matt and Willis surfaced, grinning broadly. "Jackpot!" Willis exclaimed as Maddock hauled him out of the water.

"Good work." Maddock accepted the sword from Willis and held it out in the bright morning sun. Time and salt water had done its work on the blade, but it was still a fine piece.

"You know, this here dive could make us some serious change, stone or no stone," Willis said. "I think there's a lot more down toward the back of the sinkhole. We were picking up a lot of hits with the detector, but you know how that thing works. Can't tell treasure from junk. Lots of metal down there."

Maddock had been so immersed in the search for the stone that he hadn't even considered that this was what they did for a living. "That would be a nice bonus, wouldn't it?" He handed the sword back to Willis. "You guys can make sure this is properly cared for."

"I've never seen a Templar sword up close before." Dima gazed in admiration at the aged weapon. "It's really something."

"Maddock, we should get going." Bones tone was brusque and his countenance dark.

Dima frowned at the big native but didn't ask what was on his mind.

Maddock thought he knew—early on in their days in

the SEALs they had been called on to find another Templar treasure, and Bones had lost someone dear to him. He supposed wounds like that never truly healed.

"Ready when you are," Maddock said. They finished their prep, secured their masks, and slid into the cool water.

Maddock descended slowly, savoring the way the cool, dark water enveloped him. The sea felt like home. Down below, the dark circle of the sinkhole loomed large in his vision. He was about to turn on his dive light when something moved off to the side. A quick glance told him it was a shark—a Great White if he was not mistaken. He motioned to Bones, who spotted it immediately and nodded. No need to panic. Sharks typically kept to themselves unless given good reason to attack. Still, he kept an eye on it as they continued their descent into the darkness.

By the time they reached the bottom of the sinkhole, all thoughts of the marine predator were forgotten. Here they were, diving on a five hundred-year-old wreck. He couldn't wait to begin the search.

Bones operated the pulse induction underwater metal detector while Maddock swam at his side, eyes scanning the wreck. Several times, they stopped when Bones got a strong hit. They sorted through many bits that held no value, but they did find a number of gold coins and a few carved pieces. Maddock secured them in the mesh bag at his waist and continued searching.

As the minutes slipped past, they added a few more items to the dive bag, but nothing that looked like a Noah Stone. Maddock was beginning to think this was going to be an even bigger endeavor than he had feared, when he felt a warm sensation against his leg. He looked down for the source, absently wondering if something had stung him, and realized it was coming from the thigh pocket where he'd secured the pointed stone—the first Noah Stone. He wasn't sure why he'd brought it with him. Something had told him not to leave it unattended. He quickly realized the stone itself was heating up. It had never done that before. Perhaps…

He took the stone from his pocket and began moving it in a broad arc. Nearby, Bones cocked his head and held up a hand in confusion. Maddock continued to sweep the stone around until he felt it grow warmer. He continued this game of "Cold, Warm, Hot" until he found himself at the very back of the sinkhole. Letting the stone be his guide, he pushed aside a chunk of decking and brushed away the sand beneath it. His fingers found something solid…and warm. Heart racing, he once again pocketed the Noah Stone and dug with both hands until he had freed a second shiny stone. It too was triangular and roughly the size of his fist. Aside from being a dark shade of gray instead of black, it was nearly the twin of the first stone, and it burned with the same heat. This was it!

He turned toward Bones, held the stone up, and gave the thumbs-up. Bones returned the gesture emphatically. They moved to the center of the sinkhole, where Maddock secured the mesh bag containing the items they'd recovered to a large lift bag, and proceeded to fill the lift bag with air from his scuba tank. Once filled, it slowly began to rise, and Maddock and Bones swam alongside it.

As they exited the deep hole into open water, Maddock again spotted movement nearby. He turned, expecting to see the shark, and was forced to dodge to the side as something small and fast-moving sliced through the water where his head had been an instant before. A diver, armed with a harpoon gun, had been lying in wait for them. Another harpoon whizzed past them, this one from the other direction. Maddock and Bones released the bag, letting it fly free, and dove for the sinkhole. There wasn't much safety to be found there, but they'd be sitting ducks if they swam for the boat right now.

They were in trouble. Neither he nor Bones carried a weapon other than a dive knife. He considered his options. There were no good hiding places inside of the sinkhole, no spot from which they could ambush the attackers. If the crew, watching through Uma, didn't see what was going on and send help in time, they were done for. Or were they?

He reached into his thigh pocket and pulled out the first Noah Stone. He had no idea if it would work underwater but it was worth a try.

He dragged the blade across his forearm, cutting deeper than he had when he had used the stone previously. A cloud of blood swirled up and he concentrated. It was working! He could feel the mysterious bond between him and the stone forming.

He reached out with his mind, just as he had at Archer's house, and his thoughts connected with the shark, which still lurked nearby. He called out to it, at least that was the best way he could think of to describe what he was doing. As if on command, it turned and made a beeline for the attackers.

One of the newcomers had broken off the attack and was swimming for the lift bag containing the items they had recovered from the wreck. The other was closing in on Maddock and Bones, his harpoon gun loaded and held out in front of him, ready to fire.

Maddock focused his thoughts on this man and tensed. Would it work?

In a flash of gray and white, the shark appeared in the circle of light at the top of the sinkhole. The diver with the harpoon gun had only an instant to turn and fire a shot that went wild before the shark was on him. Its jaws closed on the diver's leg. The surprised man dropped his harpoon gun and began beating ineffectually on the shark's snout. A few moments of violent thrashing and then the shark swam away with his prey in tow, leaving a thin cloud of blood trailing behind.

Bones turned to look at Maddock, saw the Noah Stone, and nodded. Without wasting another second, they swam for the boat.

When they reached open water, there was no sign of either diver. How had the second man gotten away so fast? That question was answered when they broke the surface and found their friends waiting for them.

"What happened down there?" Matt asked. "A diver surfaced holding the lift bag. About the time we realized it wasn't you, another guy came zipping by on a Sea Doo, fired a few shots across our bow, picked up the other fellow, and was gone."

"We wanted to chase them, but we didn't know what had happened to you. Matt and I were about to come in after you." Willis' tall, muscular frame quaked with suppressed rage.

"They took the lift bag?" Bones asked. "Holy crap. They got the stone."

"No they didn't." Maddock reached into his thigh pocket and pulled out the second Noah Stone. "There's no way I was letting either of these babies out of my sight for a second." He took a moment to enjoy the surprised grins of his crew mates. "Now let's get out of here before they realize they failed and come back with bigger guns."

CHAPTER 23

Dima turned the stone over in her hands, her fingers tracing it smooth surface. She held it up to the light, transfixed by the sparkles that seemed to emanate from beneath the surface of the glossy black stone. It was all almost too much to believe.

She looked out the cabin window at the darkening sky. They were headed south, eager to put as much distance between themselves and the Trident, if that's who, in fact, they had encountered earlier, as possible. Their destination was Key West, where Maddock and his crew made their home. She considered how odd it was that she had so quickly and completely put her trust in these men but instincts told her it was the right decision.

She glanced up as Maddock and Bones entered the cabin.

"Are you enjoying your pleasure cruise?" Bones asked.

"Oh, yes. Getting shot at today was a high point."

"Stick with us. You'll get used to it."

She frowned. "You say that like it's a good thing."

"That's just the way it is." Bones pulled up a chair and sat down beside her.

"You're confident this is the second Noah Stone?" she asked, looking at the artifact they'd brought up from the sinkhole. "I mean, it certainly looks the part."

"Absolutely." Maddock reached into his pocket, pulled out the triangle-shaped stone that had belonged to Bones' family, and handed it to her. "They're the same size and shape, the color is slightly different but both appear to be formed of the same stone—a stone the likes of which we've never seen. But the clincher is the way they react to one another. Try bringing them close together."

Dima had already noticed the strange warmth in the

stones but as she brought them closer to one another the heat intensified. "This is impossible. Stones don't work this way."

"Don't be so sure," Bones said. "We've seen some very strange phenomena from unusual stones. It just might surprise you to find out what all is possible."

"You've seen stones that grow hot when they come close to one another, even without an energy source?"

"The heat is a new thing, but we've seen stones that absorb and amplify light, stones that pass energy from one to the other, and much crazier stuff."

Dima looked him in the eye, searching for signs of deception, and found none. "You two are either full of crap or you have led a very interesting life."

"A little of both." Maddock said.

"You said our next move would be to search for the book of Noah. Any idea how and where, exactly, you want to start? I was hanging my hopes on the Native American legend, but it seems like we've hit the end of the line on that score."

"I'm thinking we need to follow your friend Robert's trail. Clearly he was on to something. Do you have any idea where he was when he sent you the document? That could at least give us a starting point while a friend of mine does some checking of his own."

Dima wondered exactly what sort of checking Maddock's friend might be doing but that wasn't important right now.

"I'm not sure. There was no return address on the package and the note was cryptic."

"What about the postmark?" Maddock pressed. "Where was it from?"

Dima felt like an idiot. She hadn't even looked at the postmark. From the moment she had laid eyes on the fragment she could think of little else. The book of Noah had consumed her. "I don't know," she confessed. She hated making the admission. Maddock and Bones were so…competent, and she wanted them to respect her as well. And then she had an idea. "But I know somebody who can find out for us."

It felt like an eternity as she waited for Addie's reply. Dima had left the box in which the document had been shipped, inside her desk at work. She had texted her assistant, asking her to locate the package. Finally, two hours later, her phone rang.

"Hey Dima, it's Addie. So sorry for the delay. I'm a little bit busy since I took over your job for you." Addie's tone held only a touch of chastisement.

"I know, and I really appreciate it. I promise I'll explain when I can, but right now things are…weird."

"Does it at least involve a good-looking guy?"

"Yes," she said, glancing at Bones. "Several, in fact."

"Ooh! Do tell."

"I will next time I see you. I'll even bring a few pics. These guys spent a lot of time with their shirts off." She winked at Bones who was grinning broadly. "Did you find the shipping box I asked you about?"

"I did, but I totally can't read this postmark. It's 'dog' something."

Dima frowned. "Did you say dog?"

"Yeah. Tell you what. I'll snap a picture and text it to you. How's that?"

"Perfect." Dima hesitated. "Addie, has everything been all right there? I mean, nobody's given you a hard time or anything have they?" She hoped that, with the Trident apparently on their trail, Addie and her colleagues were safe, but she still worried.

"They're college students and I'm a teaching assistant who suddenly responsible for their final grades. They all give me a hard time."

"That's not what I mean. Are you safe?" She tried to ignore the sick feeling in the pit of her stomach. She just hoped Addie wouldn't get caught up in all of this.

"Safe?" Addie asked. *"Yeah, I'm good. Dima, I wish you would tell me what this is all about."*

"Trust me. It's better that you don't know. Just keep your eyes open, okay?"

"Okay." Addie stretched the word out in true Southern fashion.

"I gotta go. Send me that picture, okay?"

"Will do. Love you."

"Love you too." Dima ended the call and waited. Moments later, a text message came through. It was a snapshot of the postmark on the package.

Bones moved to her side and looked as she zoomed in on the image. "Dogub... what the hell is that? Greek?"

"No. It's Turkish." She sprang to her feet, wrapped her arms around his neck, and gave him a squeeze. "I know exactly where Robert was."

CHAPTER 24

The tour van bounced along the rough dirt road. Up ahead the snow-capped peak of Mount Ararat towered above them. The higher peak of the dormant compound volcano stood nearly seventeen thousand feet, dwarfing the four-thousand-foot high cone of Lesser Ararat. Maddock felt a sudden surge of adrenaline as he looked up at the fabled mountain. He couldn't believe he was here.

Dima had immediately recognized the name Dogubeyazit as a small city in eastern Turkey, near the borders of Iran and Armenia. It was, she said, a place name any true Noah's Ark aficionado would know, as it was the closest town to Mount Ararat.

"I'm a little confused," Bones said. "Haven't researchers pretty much debunked the theory that the Ararat anomaly is Noah's Ark?"

The Ararat Anomaly was a vaguely boat-shaped formation located on the northwestern corner of Ararat's Western plateau. First photographed in 1949 by a United States Air Force reconnaissance mission, the locale had gained fame through various television shows and other media that focused on the search for the ark. The presence of another reputed ark location close by, the Durupinar Structure, only added to the region's notoriety.

"It has been dismissed as the ark. At least, for the most part," Dima said. "It's not easily studied. It's pretty much buried in ice and the government restricts access to it, but the size of it alone makes it a poor candidate for Noah's Ark. It's about as big as a modern aircraft carrier. Still, people persist in believing the legends."

"Well, the Bible does say it came to rest on Mount Ararat, doesn't it?" Maddock asked.

"Technically, it was the 'mountains' of Ararat, but

the translation is far from certain. It could be another place with a similar name. Ancient Hebrew contained no vowels so many of the words in the older portions of the Bible, particularly proper nouns, require a certain amount of guesswork. That's why God's name, for example, isn't certain."

"His name isn't God?" Bones asked.

"Some say it's Yahweh, others say it's Jehovah."

"Actually, I knew that. I just like listening to you lecture. You do this tilt of your head that's kind of hot. I'll bet you have a lot of male students in your courses, don't you?" Bones winked at her.

"You are a mess." Dima smiled shyly. "But yes, I do." She was obviously warming up to Bones.

"So why do so many people persist in believing the ark is here if the site is such a bad match?" Maddock asked.

"Like Bones said, part of it is the name Ararat. That's a strong connection to Scripture. Also, the rumors of the ark being located here are quite old. Marco Polo even wrote about it in his travels. He spoke of a mountain in the heart of Armenia where the summit is perpetually covered in snow, and said that this was the place where the ark was reputed to have come to rest. The ark is so imbued in local legend that it's hard to shake it. Plus, I imagine it's good for tourism. You know, like the Loch Ness Monster."

"Hey! That thing is real," Bones said.

"If you say so." Dima gave him a patronizing pat on the thigh.

"What do you think Robert was doing here if this probably isn't the location of the ark?" Bones asked.

"Obviously he was doing related research. And there just happens to be a well-known ark researcher working the mountain right now. I think it likely that Robert spoke to him."

"Crap. And here I thought we were going to get to do some climbing." Bones turned an accusing frown at Maddock. "Why did you let me think we were going to climb the mountain to look at the anomaly?"

"Because I knew that, if I told you the truth, you'd complain the whole way over, just like you're doing now."

"Fair enough. But I still say we should sneak up there and take a look around. If the third stone is up there, maybe the other two will react to it." He put a hand to his pocket, where he carried Esau's stone, and then eyed the small backpack where Maddock carried the Templar's stone.

"Let's hope it doesn't come to that," Maddock said. "That would be one heck of an undertaking, but we will do it if we have to."

The Jeep slowed and came to a halt.

"We are here," their guide announced. Faruk was a slightly built man in his late twenties with sharp brown eyes and a mustache which he had allowed to grow wild, perhaps to compensate for his receding hairline. "This is not one of the usual stops. I can take you to places with better views of the mountain if you like."

"Not right now," Dima said. "We are meeting someone at the camp. If you wouldn't mind waiting here?"

Faruk nodded, turned, and cranked up the radio. Loud music, an odd form of hip-hop with distinct Arabian strains, filled the van.

Maddock and the others climbed out and follow Dima over a low rise. Down below they spotted a small campsite. Several tents were arrayed in a circle around a cold campfire. In the distance, a man pushed a four-wheeled object that resembled a lawn mower.

"Ground penetrating radar," Maddock said. "We've used that a few times."

"What you mean we, white man?" Bones said. "You make me and Willis push the thing around while you sit back and drink mint juleps."

Before Maddock could correct him, someone called out from the bottom of the rise.

"Can I help you?"

The speaker was a bear of a man, broad shouldered and even bigger around the middle, with a silver-streaked black beard and mustache that obscured most of his face. He wore a pith helmet pushed down over his flyaway gray hair that seemed to stick out in every direction.

"Are you Henderson Bentley?" Dima asked.

The man might have frowned, but it was hard to tell behind the mass of facial hair. Only a furrowing of his brow afforded any hint to his mood.

"Who's asking?"

"My name is Dima Zafrini. I'm a professor from the United States." She hesitated. "I tried to contact you but I was unsuccessful."

"That's because I don't want to be contacted." Bentley folded his massive arms and glowered. "What do you people want?"

Maddock was quickly losing patience. "Were looking for a missing person. We have reason to believe he visited your camp recently."

Bentley tilted his head. "We haven't had many visitors. As you can see, I'm not the sociable type."

"His name is Robert Crane," Dima said.

The lines on Bentley's forehead smoothed and straight white teeth appeared in the gap between mustache and beard. "All right, then. Come on down."

The made their way down the slope and fell in alongside Bentley as they walked back toward camp. Dima introduced Maddock and Bones. At the mention of Maddock's name, Bentley stopped.

"Dane Maddock? I've heard that name before." His fingers vanished into his facial hair as he scratched his chin. Then his eyes brightened. "I remember. You know Jade Ihara, don't you?"

Maddock nodded. Jade was a former girlfriend with whom he was on the outs since he and Angel had gotten engaged.

Bentley threw back his head and laughed. "I tell you what. That girl can't decide if she loves you or hates you."

"You two have worked together?" Maddock asked as they resumed the track toward the camp.

"We attended the same seminar last summer. Didn't take too many drinks before the two of us started swapping stories of the lovers who have done us wrong. I gotta tell you, my ex is a vindictive little thing. Took off and stole my dog. But the memory of her doesn't raise half the ire in me that the thought of you does for Jade."

"She has…a bit of a temper."

"That she does. Anyway, I'm sorry about the way I acted. We get all sorts of crazies here: amateur archaeologists, conspiracy theorists, religious nuts. Try to do any kind of surveying, much less excavating, out here and people start thinking you've found Noah's Ark."

"Have you?" Bones asked.

"That's not what we're looking for. Not exactly. We are searching for signs of an ancient settlement that might have sprung up in the wake of the Great Flood."

"You believe there was a flood?" Maddock asked.

"I'm open to the possibility. I know the evidence is stacked against me but I still think it's not out of the question. I'm a true believer and I don't apologize for that."

"So, have you found anything promising?" Dima asked as they entered the circle of tents.

"Nothing like what we're looking for, but we did find something interesting. Remnants of an old monastery. Matter of fact, that's what your friend Robert came here to ask about.

"That's surprising," Dima said.

"He said he was following up on an old story and he just wanted to confirm it could be true. He seemed really pleased to learn that there had been a monastery here. He said it, what was the word, 'dovetailed' nicely with his research."

"Did he say if his research pertained to Noah's Ark?" Dima asked.

"No, he didn't. He said it was a story about a wandering monk. He also said that he had just come from the Ishak Pasha Palace down the road a ways. That's all I know. He looked around for a little while, had a cup of coffee, and went on his way."

"Did he say where he was going next?" Maddock asked.

Bentley looked up at the sky. "I believe he did. Let me think." He took off his pith helmet and ran a hand through his shaggy hair. "I remember. He said he was going to the ice cave."

CHAPTER 25

The tiny town of Halac lay deep in the shadow of Mount Ararat. Faruk steered the jeep along the narrow dirt street that ran between the mud and stone huts. Few passers-by looked up as they passed. Tourists were, according to Faruk, not uncommon here. People came to see Ararat or Durupinar, but the ice cave drew its share of interest.

"What do you think he was looking for in the ice cave?" Bones asked, keeping his voice low.

"Difficult to say," Maddock said.

"The cave is part of a massive system of lava tubes," Dima said. "Maybe he was looking for a passageway leading to…I don't know, maybe up to the anomaly?"

"It's possible," Maddock agreed. "Or maybe something connected to the monastery, since that's what he was interested in, according to Bentley."

They spent the remainder of the short ride exchanging ideas. They quickly ran out of realistic scenarios and soon delved into the absurd, each idea more ridiculous than the one before, until they had one another in stitches. By the time Faruk stopped the jeep, the three were in high spirits.

Maddock stepped out into the hot afternoon sun and looked around. "I don't see a cave."

"It's down in the hole." Faruk pointed to a spot in the distance. "We will have to walk the rest of the way."

"You can wait for us," Maddock said. "No need to exert yourself unnecessarily on our account," he added, seeing the hurt on their driver's face. "We've already taken you out of your way with this side-trip."

"It is no trouble. I would also like to visit the cave," Faruk said. "It would get me out of the heat."

Maddock couldn't think of a believable reason the man should remain behind, so he acquiesced and they followed the guide to a deep hole at the foot of the mountain.

"You can't see the cave from here," Faruk said. "It's at the bottom. We must be careful on the way down. The way is, how do you say it, steep?"

Maddock and Bones exchanged amused smiles.

"We've made our way down a steep hill or two in our time," Bones said.

"Very good." Faruk bobbed his head, smiled, and beckoned for them to follow him into the hole.

They worked their way down the steep slope until they reached the bottom. Here, the ground was flat but cluttered with undergrowth, boulders, and sharp, broken rocks. On the far side of the pit a dark shadow beckoned.

"That is the way in," Faruk said. He led the way toward the entrance, which was partially obscured by fallen stones from the ceiling of the cave entrance.

The moment Maddock set a foot inside the cave, the cool air raised goose bumps on his flesh. The difference in temperature from outside was remarkable.

The fifty foot descent to the main chamber, over slick, mud-covered rocks, proved to be much more challenging than their climb down into the pit, and by the time they reached the bottom they found themselves in deep darkness, with only faint light from the entrance to show the way.

"Looks like admission is free," Bones said. "At least there's no security guard or guides to avoid." He turned and looked at the slope down which they had just come. "Weird. Look at the entrance." He pointed up at the source of the light.

"I'm not seeing anything," Dima said.

"The way it's shaped. It looks like the Rolling Stones logo."

Maddock couldn't deny that the opening resembled a mouth with plump lips. What he didn't like was that the jagged rocks at the bottom reminded him of fangs.

"It looks more like a vampire's mouth to me," he said.

"That's what I love about you, Maddock. You find a way to take the fun out of everything."

Dima made a face and turned away, her shoulders quaking in silent laughter.

"I will wait here. I have seen the cave before." Faruk plopped down on a flat stone, pulled his knees to his chest, and wrapped his arms around his legs. "I am happy just to cool off."

"I don't know how long we will be," Maddock said.

Faruk made a small wave. "You hired me for the day. If I get cold I will go back to the Jeep. Take your time."

They thanked him, turned, and made their way into the cave. Maddock and Bones took out their Maglites and turn them on. As the bright, narrow beams sliced through the darkness, Dima let out a tiny gasp.

"This place is beautiful."

Up ahead, the cave sparkled with refracted light. All around stood tiny ice formations like crystalline sculptures. Most were transparent and the light shone through them, spreading out to illuminate deeper parts of the cave. Others were a cloudy white and glowed like low-wattage light bulbs.

"This is pretty cool," Bones said. "Weird we've never heard of it before."

"With all the traveling we've done," Maddock said, "I kind of like knowing the world still has plenty of surprises in store for us."

"You mean like stones that can let you boss animals around?" Bones asked.

"Exactly like that. Let's go."

They plunged on into the darkness, Maddock navigating the maze of ice. Here and there they passed frozen stalagmites and in a few spots Bones had to duck beneath the stalactites that hung like giant icicles from the cave ceiling. All around them lay natural wonders— frozen works wrought by nature's hands.

"You see that one, Maddock?" Bones asked, pointing at a frozen shape off to the right. "It looks like the sheep you took to prom."

"Yeah? Well, I would say this one," he pointed off to the left, "looks like your mom, but unlike you, your mom and sister are attractive."

"Maddock, I knew you're into my sister but I didn't know you liked mothers." Bones shook his head. "Man, you think you know a guy…"

Dima laughed out loud. "Are you sure you guys aren't brothers? You act like you grew up together."

They continued to explore, first following the well-worn paths, and then moving into the side chambers, all of which proved to be small and, though beautiful, not containing anything of interest.

"For the life of me, I can't figure out what Robert was doing here," Dima said. "Do you think he was just doing the tourist thing?"

Maddock checked his watch. They'd spent the better part of an hour investigating the cave. "Could be, but I'd like to keep looking. I want to make sure we didn't miss something."

"Let's make it quick," Bones said. "If we stay in this refrigerator much longer I'm gonna start craving coffee instead of beer. And that would be a crime."

"Turkish coffee is excellent," Dima said. She reached up and playfully tugged his ponytail. "We're going to have to break you of some bad habits."

"If you succeed, you'll be the first." Maddock turned and shone his light toward the back of the cave. "Let's go as deep as we possibly can and see if we missed anything." They kept exploring. It didn't take Maddock long to find what he was looking for.

"Check this out." At the base of the cave wall, where the ceiling dropped down to a height of no more than four feet, lay a jumble of broken stones.

"It's a pile of rocks. So?" Bones asked.

"Look at the other rock falls around here. They're all coated in ice. On these, the ice is on the underside."

"Right. Like somebody stacked them up here. I should've noticed that, but I'm distracted by the hot chick."

"What do you think is back there?" Dima asked.

"We're about to find out." Bones began moving the rocks aside, quickly revealing a hole in the wall. He knelt and shone his light into the opening. "There's a passageway back there. I can't tell how far it goes but it's worth checking out." Without waiting for a reply from the others he dropped down on all fours and squeezed his bulk into the narrow space. "It opens up back here." His voice sounded hollow to Maddock's ears. "Come on in. You'll have to crawl but if it's wide enough for me you definitely won't get stuck."

"You next," Maddock said to Dima.

"Promise you won't be checking me out from behind?" She batted her eyelashes and Maddock wasn't quite certain if she was teasing.

"I promise to try. That's the best you'll ever get from either one of us."

"That's the best you'll get from *him*," Bones shouted back. "I wouldn't even try."

Dima chuckled, dropped to the ground, and crawled into the passageway. When she vanished into the darkness, Maddock followed along. He held his Maglite in his teeth so as to keep his hands free. This was his least favorite part of caving. He had finally reached an age where his back and knees complained constantly when he crawled through low spaces, but he never complained. If he did, Bones and his crew mates would never let him live it down.

The farther they crawled, the more the cold stone sapped the warmth from his hands and knees. At least the numbness served to minimize the scrapes and bruises he was rapidly accumulating. He knew better than to go caving without gloves, kneepads, and a helmet, but sometimes the situation didn't allow for it. Furthermore, there was nothing to look at in this dark tunnel, except for Dima, and he was steadfastly trying to avoid ogling her. The monotony was becoming seriously annoying when Bones announced that he had found a chamber up ahead.

"Just a few more feet and you can stand up," he said. "Just don't impale yourself on the ice spikes."

Maddock breathed a sigh of relief when he was finally able to rise and stretch.

"Did that crawl get to you, old man?" Bones asked.

"Now, I'm good. I just…" Maddock paused in mid-sentence. The tiny cave was magnificent. Ice hung from the ceiling like chandeliers and protruded from the floor in thick spikes. "It's like being inside an iron maiden," he said.

Bones immediately began headbanging, thrashing his long hair back and forth, while playing an air guitar.

"Is this really the time?" Dima asked.

Bones straightened, put his hands on his hips, and looked down at her. "There's always time for metal."

"Let's check this place out," Maddock said. "I'm sure Faruk is getting tired of waiting on us."

They began a careful inspection of the cave, Bones and Maddock shining their lights into every recess and a crevice, Dima using the flashlight on her phone to inspect the floor. After a brief search Bones found something.

"There's a crack in the wall. It's pretty narrow, but if we can squeeze through here, it looks like there's another room we can check out."

Maddock and Dima joined him and inspected the opening. Maddock shone his light up and down, frowning.

"I think I can get through. Not sure about you, though."

"Let me try. I'm smallest." Dima's face was pale but resolve firmed her tone. "I'll slip in and see if there's anything back there."

"If you're sure," Maddock said.

She looked at the opening, swallowed hard, and nodded. "May I borrow someone's flashlight?"

Bones handed her his. "Don't worry. We'll call the fire department if you get stuck."

"Nice." She took a deep breath, exhaled, and slid

sideways into the passageway.

She needn't have worried. Her lithe form slipped through with ease. As soon as she had entered the next chamber she let out a cry.

"Oh my God. You guys have got to see this."

"You go, Maddock. If I get stuck in there we're screwed."

Maddock didn't have quite as easy a time as Dima had, but with only a little more effort he soon found himself standing beside her in the next chamber. He didn't need her to point out what it was she wanted him to see.

The frozen body of a man clad in a brown habit lay curled up in the fetal position. He was remarkably well-preserved, so well, in fact, that it was difficult to guess how long he had lain here. He had light colored skin, dark brown hair, and a bushy unibrow. His frozen lips were drawn back in a deathly rictus, revealing yellow teeth.

"This must be the monk Robert was searching for," Maddock said. He knelt beside the body and ran his light up and down it.

"Do you think he found the fragment of the book of Noah here?" Dima asked.

"Definitely. Look at the monk's hand." Maddock trained the beam of his light onto the monk's clenched fist. Ragged shards of paper stuck out where the man's fingertips met his palm.

Dima sucked in her breath. "Do you think we can get the rest of the fragment?"

"Maybe. Robert must have tried and failed."

"True, but you don't know Robert. He would've found a frozen body unnerving. I imagine he didn't try very hard before he took what he could and left."

"I'll see what I can do." Maddock tugged the frozen fingers, trying to pull them apart. They didn't budge.

"Too bad there's nothing here we could use to start a fire," Dima said. "Maybe we could thaw him out."

"Seriously?" Maddock cocked his head and

appraised her. "You're lot more hard-core than I gave you credit for."

She shrugged. "Just trying to solve the problem."

"What's going on in there?" Bones asked through the narrow opening.

"Not much. Just trying to pry something from a dude's cold, dead hands."

"Just break the fingers."

Maddock slapped himself on the forehead. "Bones, sometimes you're a genius."

"I don't think I can watch this." Dima turned her back on Maddock.

Forcing down the revulsion that was already rising within him, Maddock set his jaw, took hold of one finger, and began to pull. With a sharp crack, the finger snapped.

"Gross," Dima groaned.

"Only three to go." Maddock continued the grisly work until he had bent back all four fingers, revealing the monk's frozen palm. There lay the remainder of the document. He took hold of one corner and gently tugged. It was frozen solid.

"Bad news. It's stuck."

"You've got to be kidding me." Dima whirled around, eyes alight with anger. "All that work for nothing?"

"Maybe not." Maddock took out his phone and snapped a couple of pictures of the exposed portion of the document. "Maybe you can make something of that."

A dull, distant popping sound reverberated through the passageway. And then another.

"What is that?" Dima asked.

Maddock came to his feet slowly. They were in serious trouble.

"Hey Maddock," Bones said, "do you think I can fit through there?"

"I think you'd better find a way," Maddock said. He turned to Dima. "Those were gunshots."

CHAPTER 26

"Come on, Bones. You can make it," Maddock urged.

"If I get stuck in here and get shot in the butt, I'm going to haunt you in the next life." Bones turned sideways and forced his bulk into the crevice. Slowly he inched forward, grunting with the effort.

"Maybe if you sucked in your gut?" Dima asked.

"I… don't… have… a… gut." Bones said through gritted teeth. He stopped and for a moment Maddock feared his friend was indeed trapped in the narrow passage. "I'm okay," Bones said. He then closed his eyes and slowly exhaled with a hiss like the last dregs of air leaving a deflating tire. He reached out his hand and Maddock took it.

"On three. One… two…" Voices rose in the distance, coming closer. "Three!" Maddock heaved with all his might. For a moment, Bones didn't move. But then, with agonizing slowness, his body slid forward. Maddock braced a foot against the cavern wall and pushed. Like a cork out of a champagne bottle, Bones suddenly flew out and landed in a heap on top of Maddock. Maddock's head hit the cavern floor with a crack and red light flashed across his vision.

"We have got to stop meeting like this," Bones said. He clambered to his feet and hauled Maddock up. "Now what?"

"We go deeper," Maddock said, pointing to the back of the cavern where he had spotted another small passageway. "You go first," he said to Bones.

"No way. If I get stuck, the two of you are dead."

"Trust me. I have a plan." He fixed Bones with a determined look. His friend knew right away that Maddock would not be moved. As Bones and Dima rushed to the back of the cavern, Maddock took hold of a frozen stalagmite and wrestled with it until it broke free with a sharp crack. Holding it like a baseball bat, he moved to the edge of the narrow opening that led back to the ice cave.

He listened intently as the voices drew closer. He could make out only snatches of conversation, enough to know for certain that there were at least two men out there and they were looking for someone. He stood there, body coiled like a spring, waiting. The icy stalagmite sapped the warmth from his hands. *You idiots need to get here before my fingers grow numb,* he thought.

He got his wish. He heard a scuffling sound and then a grunt as one of the pursuers began to work his way toward the small cave where Maddock waited. Seconds seemed to stretch into hours, and then a hand holding a gun appeared.

Like a man splitting wood, Maddock brought the stalagmite down onto the exposed wrist. The man cried out in pain as bone and ice shattered and his pistol went clattering to the cave floor. Maddock sprang out in front of the opening and raised the remnants of the stalagmite. He had a moment to take in the sight of a man with dark skin and amber eyes wide with shock, before he brought his makeshift weapon down on the man's head. The man slumped, his limp body now firmly wedged in the rock.

"Good luck getting him out anytime soon," Maddock said. He snatched up the fallen pistol, a Glock similar to the one Bones usually carried, and headed for the back passageway.

He dropped to his knees and plunged into the low, narrow lava tube. After a few minutes of rapid and sometimes painful crawling, he heard Bones and Dima up ahead. He called out to let them know he was all right and they waited for him to catch up.

"Wonder how far this goes?" Bones said. "If there's no way out, we could be in trouble."

"At least we have a fighting chance now." Maddock held up the Glock and Bones grinned.

"Nice job."

They continued on in the darkness. There was such a regularity to the passageway that Maddock found himself wondering if they were moving forward at all. Finally, the way began to open up. The tunnel grew wider and taller until they could walk hunched over and then, finally, stand up straight.

"Holy crap, that sucked." Bones turned to Dima. "Hey, are you any good at deep tissue massage?"

"I am, but don't count on getting one for me. I don't know you that well. At least, not yet." She grimaced and stretched. "I guess we have a decision to make."

"What do you mean?" Maddock asked.

Dima pointed down the passageway. About twenty meters up ahead, another lava tube intersected the one in which they walked. "Left, right, or straight ahead?"

"Let's check it out." Maddock strode quickly down the passageway, invigorated by the open space and the chance to actually walk upright on two legs. When he reached the intersection he stopped and shone his light down each tunnel in turn.

"What do you see?" Bones asked.

"There's a lot of rubble in the tunnel to the left," he said. "Makes me think the ceiling is unstable. The one to the right," he turned and shone his light in that direction, "narrows pretty quickly. I say we go straight ahead."

"You're the boss. How about you take the lead for a while? Give me the gun and I'll bring up the rear."

"You just want to do some shooting," he said, handing the Glock to Bones.

"You bet I do, and if you don't hurry, I'll be forced to start with you. Let's move."

Maddock chuckled, turned, and moved on ahead. The tiny, narrow beam of his Maglite danced off the shiny surface of the lava tube. There was no more ice here, only black rock, and as they walked, the air grew warmer and drier.

"I wonder where we're headed," Dima said.

"Worst case, into the heart of a volcano," Bones

replied. "I hope you brought the marshmallows."

"I can't decide if you are funny or annoying."

"Join the club," Maddock said. "I've felt the same way for as long as I've known him."

"Haters," Bones said. "You just…" He paused. "Hold on a second. Everybody quiet down."

Maddock stopped and turned. Bones stood, lips pursed, eyes narrowed, head cocked to the side, listening intently.

"Someone's coming," he whispered.

"I don't hear anything," Dima said.

"That's because you don't know what to listen for. We need to get a move on." Bones put a big hand on the small of Dima's back and gave her a gentle push to get her moving.

Maddock didn't ask how Bones knew what was coming. His friend had sharp ears and good instincts in situations like these. He set a faster pace, a slow jog which he knew he and Bones could keep up with ease for a long time. "Let me know if you need to rest," he said softly to Dima.

"I ran a 10K two weeks ago. I think I'm good."

At this, Maddock picked up the pace a little more. He kept his eyes glued to the floor in front of them, not wanting to risk tripping or stepping into a crack. A twisted ankle could spell doom for all of them.

After an hour of steady running, Maddock called a halt. They were all breathing heavily, but no one was yet spent. That was good.

"Don't stop on my account," Dima huffed. "I can go on, especially since there are armed men behind us."

"I like this girl. We should keep her around." Bones winked at her and she made a face that wasn't quite a frown.

"I wonder if we put much distance between us and them," Dima said.

As if in reply, a distant voice sounded in the darkness. And then another.

"You have got to be freaking kidding me." Bones

turned and raised the Glock. "I almost wish they'd catch up."

"Let's go." Maddock took off, this time at a run. His light bounced up and down in front of him, revealing the unrelenting black rock and darkness up ahead. His legs soon began to burn and his chest tightened from exertion. Just as he was contemplating calling a halt so they could turn and fight, his eyes fell upon an unexpected sight.

"Handholds! Look." He stopped and Bones and Dima skidded to a halt behind him. There was no mistaking it. Someone had carved a series of hand and footholds in the rock. He played his beam up the wall and saw that, about five meters above their heads, a section of the ceiling had given way and the handholds led through the small opening and into the darkness above. With no time to waste, he stuck his Maglite in his mouth, clamping down with his front teeth, and began to climb. With any luck, they would be out of here long before their pursuers reached this spot. And if the men who followed them didn't have sharp eyes, they just might continue on down the passageway, not knowing where Maddock and his friends had gone.

The climb would have been easier had he not been running for a couple of hours, but at least he had plenty of strength remaining in his shoulders and arms. He clambered up the steep face and out of the lava tube. Here, the stone was dark red in color and he realized they were now climbing through a natural fissure in the native rock.

He quickly reached the top and climbed out onto a rock strewn-ledge. He clambered over the rubble, turned, and waited for Dima to catch up. He helped her over and then offered Bones a hand, which was ignored.

"Just keep moving," Bones grunted.

There wasn't far to move. Ten paces ahead they hit a wall.

"So I guess we sit here and Bones shoots people as they climb up?" Dima asked.

"I don't think so. Someone carved those handholds, which means they must lead somewhere, or they did at one time. Look around."

They began a thorough inspection of the wall. Minutes later, Dima found something.

"Look at this. I think it's a dove."

Maddock and Bones shone their lights on the spot she indicated. The image was faint, as if someone had hurriedly scratched it, but the shape was unmistakable.

"What does it mean?" Bones asked.

"The dove is a symbol associated with the Noah story," she said.

Maddock nodded. "It could be our frozen monk scratched the symbol here so he could find his way out again. But how to actually get out?" He looked closer and noticed that the tiny oval that marked the eye of the dove was not scratched out like the rest of the image, but was in fact a small indentation in the stone.

He pressed his finger against it.

Nothing.

He pressed harder, and with an audible click, a meter wide section of wall descended into the bedrock.

"No way," Dima breathed. "I thought this sort of thing only happens in movies."

"If only." Maddock stepped over the descending wall and took a few steps. Up ahead, bars blocked their way.

"What is this? Where are we?" Dima asked.

"It looks like a dungeon," Maddock said. They were in a small cell hewn from the bedrock. Off to one side, a stone bench ran along the wall. There were no windows, only three stone walls, and floor to ceiling iron bars where the fourth wall should be.

"I think I know where we are," Dima said, looking around. "This is the Pasha Palace."

"Maddock, I think we have a problem," Bones said. "The trapdoor isn't going back up and I think I hear the bad guys coming."

"Are we stuck?" Dima asked.

"I don't think so." Maddock reached for the cell door

and pushed. It squealed open, assaulting his ears with the sound of rusted metal on metal. "It's not like they use this place for prisoners anymore, and they wouldn't want a tourist locking himself in. Come on out."

When Bones and Dima had exited the cell, Maddock knelt, pried up a floor tile, and shoved it into the small space beneath the cell door. He gave it a few kicks to wedge it in firmly, and grinned.

"That'll slow them a bit. Now, how about we get out of here?"

CHAPTER 27

The Ishak Pasha Palace sat perched atop a mountain ledge overlooking the town of Doğubeyazıt. Located only a few miles from the town, the historical site combined features of Ottoman, Seljuk, Persian, Armenian, and Georgian architecture, reflecting the many changes that had been made to it over the years. Under a different set of circumstances, Maddock would have loved to explore the place, but right now they needed to get away as fast as they could.

"Man, I can't believe you didn't at least let us check out the harem room," Bones said, as they exited the palace and strode out into the late afternoon sun. "I'm all about that."

"It's not like there are any women there," Maddock said.

"Shut it, dude. You're spoiling my fantasy."

"We need to find a driver and negotiate a ride back to town," Dima said. "Tourists will usually arrange for the driver to hang around, but it's such a short distance we can probably find someone to run us there and then come back for their regular fare."

"All right. Let's make it happen. I'd like to get out of here without any shooting," Maddock said. He turned his head away from the stiff wind that blew in from the East, carrying dust and sand with it. Behind them, the sun shone on the golden brown rocks of the palace, setting the spires, arches, and domes aglow in golden light. "Keep an eye out for anyone who looks like they're following us," he said to Bones.

"Already on it." Bones had the Glock tucked into his waistband, hidden beneath his shirt, and he kept his hand close by it, ready to draw and fire.

"Do you think they killed Faruk?" An icy ball of dread formed in Maddock's gut as he uttered the words.

"Maybe. I don't know who else they would've been shooting at. Hopefully they just chased him away, but who really knows?"

Maddock hated that an innocent person had gotten caught up in this, but he knew there was nothing to be gained from dwelling on it.

Up ahead, Dima was handing a few bills to a man who sat in an idling van.

"Come on," she said. "I found us a ride."

They climbed into the battered van, seated themselves, and engaged in a brief, fruitless search for seatbelts. Dima and Maddock braced themselves in time, but Bones managed to bang his head on the roof as the van lurched into motion.

"Such fun," he growled, casting a baleful look at the back of the driver's head.

Maddock's phone rang and he was pleased to see that his friend Jimmy Letson was on the other end of the line. Jimmy was a journalist and an accomplished hacker who had helped Maddock more times than he could count.

"Hey Maddock," came Jimmy's nasal voice, *"what's up?"*

"Not much. Just got chased by armed men through a hidden passageway, found a secret trapdoor, and escaped through a dungeon," Maddock deadpanned.

"Cool," Jimmy said, as if this happened every day. *"I've done some checking for you, and I'm sorry to say you probably don't owe me a bottle of scotch this time."*

"Struck out?" Maddock asked.

"On the Trident, yes. I couldn't really confirm anything you don't already know. They're an antiquities company, at least that's their front."

"Are you sure they're a front?"

"Considering I have had zero success hacking into their system, yes. Why would antiquities dealers need a firewall that would put the federal government to shame?"

"Fair enough. Did you learn anything?"

"Not really. I got the file on Daniel Tyson, but it's just his service record in the government. We already knew he used to work with Tam Broderick back in the day and then moved on the park service. One thing weird about the Trident—nothing about their corporate structure is publicly available, not even the name of their CEO."

"That *is* weird."

"I already said that. Anyway, I worked my magic and I came up with the name of the man who might be their leader." In true Jimmy fashion, he paused for dramatic effect.

"Just tell me," Maddock said as their driver turned a sharp right that sent him banging into the side of the van.

"Ibrahim Shawa. He's a guy who presents himself as a religious guru and claims descent from Noah's son, Ham. He lives high on the hog and, rumor has it, he's a powerful man who has connection to Boko Haram.

"Great. A jihadist." Maddock grimaced. "Anything else?"

"Not about the Trident, but I did manage to hack Robert's credit card account, and I know where he was going next." Another pause.

"Jimmy, you know it drives me nuts when you keep making me ask for information."

"Why do you think I do it? Anyway, when he left Turkey, he was planning to fly on to Rome."

"Great, because that's not a big city or anything," Maddock said.

"Somebody's grumpy today," Jimmy chastised. *"Think about it. He's looking for some kind of Noah's Ark crap. There's only one place in Rome he was likely to visit. The place where the most secret records of Christendom are supposedly kept."*

"The Vatican. That narrows it down but it also complicates things. If we're talking about the Secret Archives I don't think there's any way we will be able to get inside, much less find what we're looking for."

Located in Vatican City, the Vatican's secret archives was the central repository for all papal records. The archives were officially owned by the Pope until his death, at which time ownership was passed to his successor. The archives also contained account books, correspondence, and a myriad of documents the church had collected over the centuries. While the archives were not secret in the sense that they were hidden, they were deemed private and only a handful of researchers were given access to them each year. No one outside the highest levels of the Catholic Church truly knew the full extent of its holdings.

"This is where you are going to want to thank me," Jimmy said. *"I'm thinking at least a pint bottle of Wild Turkey will be in order."*

"Let's hear what you've got. If it's no good, you're getting Boone's Farm."

"I also hacked his email and I can't find any record of Robert seeking access to the secret archives, but he did have somewhere specific he wanted to go. In addition to the plane ticket, he booked a spot on a very special tour—a tour where there's really only one thing to see."

Maddock listened as Jimmy gave him the specifics. He thanked his friend and ended the call, his mind racing.

"What is it?" Bones asked.

"I know where we have to go next, and we're going to need some help to get there."

CHAPTER 28

The chairs in the waiting area outside the office of the Director of the CIA reminded Tam Broderick of the suits worn by its agents: simple, elegant, and uncomfortable. She shifted her weight, trying not to appear restless in front of the others who waited along with her. *Always look like you're in control,* she reminded herself. A woman, and a woman of color at that, didn't climb high in any federal agency if she didn't give off an air of supreme confidence and borderline disdain at all times.

Her phone rang. She took it out and scowled at it. More specifically, at the name on the display. For a moment, she contemplated letting it go to voicemail, but then she remembered her grandmother's words.

Only small people take pleasure in small insults. Don't be petty, Tamara.

Letting out a deep sigh, she accepted the call.

"Dane Maddock. You finally decided to stop bypassing the chain of command and talk to me directly?"

"Come on," came the voice on the other end, *"I'm not allowed to call my sister from time to time?"*

"To invite her to a barbecue? Yes. To ask for her help in her official capacity as a member of the Myrmidons and use my resources? Hell no." She gritted her teeth and mentally kicked herself. Another dollar for the swear jar.

A doughy man sitting nearby glanced up from the legal pad on which he'd been pretending to take notes. Tam gave him a look that said, *Mind your business,* and he immediately looked away, his pad slipping from his hands and falling to the floor. He snatched it up, but not before she saw the doodles of sailboats and large-breasted stick figures.

Classy, she mouthed.

The man grinned, his face turning a delicate shade of

pink.

"I'm sorry about that. I just didn't want to bother you with it."

"Sure." She rolled her eyes. "So what's this about? Social call?"

"Sorry, no. I need your help."

"Don't you make me cuss again," she warned.

"What?"

"You turned down my offer to be a part of my team, but you still want to use my resources? Is that how you treat all the women in your life?" She turned and walked out into the hallway before she said something unprofessional.

"We're friends. Friends help each other out."

"All right, but you know I expect favors to be repaid. Go on, and make it quick. I'm about to go into a meeting with the director of the CIA."

"Do you know anything about a man named Ibrahim Shawa?"

Tam knew the name, but not a great deal else. "Sure. Spiritual guru? Trying to make peace in war plagued parts of Africa?"

"That's what he claims, but my friend Jimmy has evidence that he not only has connections to Boko Haram, but that he's also a bigwig with the Trident. Maybe the leader."

That was a surprise. Tam chewed on this bit of information. Jimmy was another man who had declined her invitation to join the Myrmidons. Oh well, no need to hold a grudge. "Maddock, you know I can't get involved investigating the Trident. The Dominion isn't nearly as dead in America as we hoped. I just dealt with a big old mess on the Mexican border."

"Dealt?" Maddock said. *"Past tense. So that means you're free to help me."*

Tam had to laugh at that. "Maybe, but it depends on what you need. And have Jimmy send me his Intel. If it's good stuff, I'll consider that as your payment for the favor I'm about to do you."

"Deal," Maddock sounded relieved. *"As for the favor, Bones and I need to sneak inside somewhere very secure, and we need to take one more person with us."*

As Maddock explained where he needed to go and what he hoped to find, a rueful grin spread across Tam's face. The things that man got himself into.

"Lord Jesus, I swear you are going to be the death of me. You know, I think the only reason you keep Bones around is so you don't look arrogant by comparison."

"Fair enough. So, is that a yes or a no?"

Tam closed her eyes and rubbed her forehead. The man was impossible.

"It's a yes," she finally said, "and I've got the perfect person to help you out."

CHAPTER 29

Maddock marveled at the grandeur of St. Peter's Basilica. All around him were sights so magnificent he felt he could scarcely take them in: intricately carved wood and marble, magnificent paintings and mosaics, exquisite stained-glass, and gleaming precious metals. As he, Bones, and Dima made their way up the stairs, he reflected on the centuries of history contained in this place. One could probably spend a lifetime exploring the Vatican and still not unlock all its mysteries.

"It's pretty cool," Bones said, looking around, "but don't you think they could sell some of this stuff and, I don't know, feed hungry people?"

"You can't sell history," Maddock said.

"I suppose." Bones made a sudden move and in a flash he held a thin, swarthy man by the wrists. The man struggled and cursed him in a variety of languages. "Don't waste your time," Bones said. "Just hand me back the wallet." The man pleaded ignorance in broken English, but Bones squeezed his wrist until he changed his tune.

"I will give it back. It is in my left pocket."

Maddock retrieved the wallet, opened it, and frowned. "There's only a couple of dollars American in here. Where's everything else?"

The pickpocket gaped at Maddock. "I didn't... I mean, I don't..."

Bones let out a harsh laugh. "It's a decoy wallet, genius. Now, how about I rip your arms out of their sockets so you can't steal anymore?" He began to twist the man's arms.

"No, please! I will leave right now," the man begged, his brown eyes wide with terror. Maddock reckoned the man had never been faced with so frightening a sight as the huge, angry native.

"See that you do." Bones released him and gave him a hard shove that sent him falling down hard on his backside. He spared one frightened glance at Bones before springing to his feet and hurrying down the stairs.

"Do you think that'll teach him a lesson?" Dima asked

"Probably not, but it felt good."

At the top of the dome they paused to take in the magnificent view. The city lay spread out below them, a living monument to one of the greatest civilizations the world had ever known, and the religion it single-handedly spread across much of the world. It was truly a remarkable site.

"It's something else, isn't it?" A tall, lean man with brown hair and sharp eyes sidled up to them.

Maddock nodded. "It's my first visit here, so everything is pretty impressive."

"If you like the view from up top, you should see what's down below," the man said.

That was a signal. Maddock smiled. "I'm Maddock, this is Bones and Dima."

"Gavin Stone." Stone didn't offer to shake hands. Instead, he got right down to business. "Remember, you are tourists taking the Scavi tour, the same tour your friend Robert booked a spot on, and I'm your guide. Follow my lead. We have a tight window so let's not dawdle."

Stone led them back down the stairs and through the main level of the Basilica. From here, beneath a sign that read "Sepulcrum Sancti Petri Apostoli," a tourist could get a limited view of the area designated as the tomb of Saint Peter, but Maddock and his friends were going to get a much closer look.

"We will first make our way down to the Vatican grotto," Stone said in a perfect tour guide voice, "which lies one level above the remains of St. Peter."

They descended an ornate staircase and passed through marble-lined hallways. As they walked, Maddock thought he could understand Bones' discomfort with the obscene displays of wealth. Then again, such magnificence seemed fitting for what was essentially the capital city of one of the world's major religions. When they descended into the lowest level, their surroundings changed. Here the walls were brick and stone and showed signs of great age.

Stone continued to play his role, speaking in a voice intended to carry to anyone within earshot. "The lowest level, called the Vatican Scavi, is sixteen-hundred years old. Also known as the Vatican Necropolis, the Tomb of the Dead, or St. Peter's Tomb, this area was discovered in the 1940s when excavations were carried out in preparation for the burial of Pope Pius IX. Though this place had been long reputed to be the resting place of St. Peter, no one expected to find anything down here."

Stone paused, but picked up the narrative almost immediately as two men in the multi-colored, striped uniform of the Swiss Guard strode past. To his credit, Bones did not so much as crack a smile. He knew as well as Maddock did that despite the absurd-looking uniform, these men were trained soldiers. Neither Maddock nor the others made eye contact with the guards, not wanting to be remembered should things go awry.

"As they dug, the archaeologists found a burial ground that dated back to the fourth century. They found the temporal of Emperor Constantine, and even ancient graffiti that translated to the phrase 'Peter is here.' Initially, the remains they found were not promising. Of the three human skeletons they located, the only one that was of appropriate age and build to be the apostle turned out to be the skeleton of a woman. They also found animal bones mixed in with those of humans.

"Eventually, a new set of remains was found in a hollow niche in the wall upon which the graffiti was written. These bones were determined to be of a robust man sixty to seventy years of age. The skeleton included bones from all parts of the body except for the feet, which would be consistent with the way a crucified body was treated, since it was common practice, after the victim expired, to cut the feet off when taking the body down from the cross. Furthermore, the bones were covered in Imperial Roman purple dye, which typically reserved for the emperor and other high-ranking men. Finally they discovered a section of the wall near the place where the bones were found on which 'Peter is within' was inscribed in Greek."

Stone paused, took a moment to listen, and then nodded. "Okay, enough of that. If we hear anyone coming I'll start doing the tour guide stuff again." He glanced at his watch. "We've got about forty minutes until we're expected to be out of here, but I'd hate to cut it that close."

"Agreed," Maddock said. He turned to Dima. "Where do we start?"

"At the place where the bones of St. Peter were found," she said. "At least, that's what the legends say, for whatever that's worth."

Maddock and Bones had seen enough in their lives that they no longer automatically doubted legends. They stepped aside as Dima bent to examine the niche where the bones of the apostle had been found. She ran her fingers all over the wall, examining every inch. After a few minutes she stood and took a step back.

"I don't see anything."

"Maybe it's in the floor," Bones said. He knelt to examine the spot beneath the niche.

"It's solid rock," Stone said.

Bones brushed the ground at the base of the wall, frowned, and leaned in close until his nose was inches from the spot where the wall met the floor. He let out a puff of breath and then another. Next, he traced an invisible square with his fingernail, and then blew again.

"There's something here. It's hard to see but there's definitely something." He began working at the spot. Seconds passed, and then a minute. Stone kept checking his watch and looking around. Finally, Bones shook his head. "Screw this." He drove the heel of his palm into the spot he'd been working. With a crack, a square section of rock came free. Bones looked up with a smile. "Sometimes you just need the proper tool to do the job right." He removed the square and shone his Maglite into the opening. "Whoa. Check this out."

Everyone moved closer and knelt down for a better look. Embedded in the wall of the dark recess was something that looked like a child's puzzle. It was a rectangle containing three rows of tiles. Letters were carved into 15 of the tiles and two more were blank, leaving one empty space so that the squares could be rearranged.

"Like we really have time to do a puzzle," Bones said.

"Lucky for you, I sort of have a knack for puzzles. It's one of the reasons Tam hired me. Let me take a look." Stone switched spots with Bones. He examined the puzzle for a minute and then a sly smile crept across his face. "It's Latin, he said, "and since this is the tomb of Peter, let's try this." He reached inside and began shuffling the tiles, spelling out 'super hanc petram.' "Upon this rock," he said as he slid the last tile into place.

There was no time to wonder if Stone's solution was the correct one. The room began to shake. Maddock felt the floor move beneath his feet and he grabbed Dima and leaped back. Bones and Stone moved to the side and the four of them watched as a manhole sized circle, its edge invisible until this moment, slowly turned and descended, revealing an opening in the floor.

"I guess that was it," Stone said.

"Nice job on the puzzle," Maddock replied. "Now, let's see what's down there."

CHAPTER 30

Maddock slipped down into the hole, which was only about two meters deep. He hit the ground and looked around. Walled by the same ancient rock that comprised the crypt above them, the passageway in which he now stood descended at a steep angle. Not waiting for the others, he moved on, working his way down until he reached a stone staircase. He paused at the top while the others caught up.

"You know, this underground passageway stuff is getting old," Bones said.

"If the past few years are any indication, it's our destiny to explore them all."

"I guess. So what's down there?"

The staircase led down into what appeared to be an antechamber with a tiled floor and a high ceiling. On the far side of the room stood a door, but it was not at all what Maddock had expected to find beneath an ancient crypt.

"Holy crap. That thing is high tech," Bones said.

The door was modern, made of sturdy metal. On the wall to its left hung a security device, some sort of card reader by the look of it. And above the door a security camera looked down on the antechamber.

"I suppose if the Vatican really does keep their super secret books down here, they rely on more than puzzles and trapdoors to protect them." Maddock turned to look at the others. "This changes things. Even if we can get past that door, we have to assume security will know we are here and will send men in after us."

"And even if we get away, our faces will be captured on camera," Dima said. "We will be international criminals."

"I can get us past the door," Stone said.

"And I can take care that camera if you've got some

lipstick on you," Bones said to Dima.

"How about lip balm?" Dima reached into her pocket and pulled out a tube of ChapStick. "I figured I wouldn't need to try and look beautiful on this trip."

"Like you even need to try." Bones gave her a wink and took the tube of lip balm. "Perfect." Bones moved to the far side of the staircase, hugged the wall, and hurried down. When he reached the antechamber he again pressed himself against the wall and circled the room, remaining out of sight of the camera as he made his way to the door. When he arrived at the door, he uncapped the lip balm, reached up, and coated the camera lens with the waxy substance.

"I'm sure that raised an alarm somewhere," Maddock said. "We'd better hurry."

Stone was down the stairs and across the antechamber in a flash, his long legs eating up the ground in great strides. He took out an object the size of a credit card with a short cord attached to it. He slid it into the security card reader and plugged the other end of the cord into a cell phone-sized object. He tapped a few buttons, the screen on his device flashed in a series of numbers scrolled across. Maddock held his breath until the light on the card reader flashed green and the door swung open.

"Tam can be a bear to work for," Stone said, "but occasionally she gives us some great toys to play with."

They stepped inside a small room, their way barred by a plexiglass wall with a small door set in the center.

"Climate controlled," Dima said. "To help protect the documents." She pushed the door open and stepped inside, the others following.

This room was tiny, no more than five meters square. A small wooden table and two chairs sat at the center and against the far wall stood a glass case containing perhaps forty books and scrolls, all of which looked very old and very fragile.

Dima hurried over to the case and let out a gasp. "I can't believe this. *The Gospel of Mary Magdalene, The*

Gospel of Judas..." She opened the case and reached for one of the scrolls but quickly pulled her hand back. "What am I thinking?" She reached into her pocket and pulled out a pair of cotton gloves which she slipped on before retrieving the scroll. She unrolled it enough to see the first line of text. "*The Book of Lucifer,*" she whispered. "I didn't believe this one existed. Positively amazing."

"Not to rush you or anything," Stone said, but I have a feeling the Swiss Guard headed our way the moment we opened that door. Unless, of course, they noticed what Bones did to the security camera, in which case we have even less time."

"I'm sorry, it's just that these books... Never mind." Dima hastily scanned the shelves, reached in, and took out a tiny leather bound volume. "This is bound in human skin," she said, her face twisting into a grimace. She opened the cover and smiled. "This is it. Let's go."

They quickly exited the room, but Stone raised his hand immediately, bring them all to a halt. "It's too late. The guard is coming." Indeed, voices and footsteps echoed through the room. "You three hide. I'll let myself get caught and you can sneak away once I've gone. Tam can get me out."

"Thanks for that, but it might not be necessary," Bones said. He didn't explain, but turned and headed back inside the room. "Let's play a game I like to call follow the conspiracy theorist." He hurried to the small table and dropped to the ground. "According to one of my favorite web forums, the Templars had trapdoors and tunnels all around the Vatican, though nobody knows where they might lead. All of them were marked by the Templar cross." He pointed to the large stone tile on the floor beneath the table. It was marked by the famed red cross.

"It wouldn't be the first time this cross has shown us the way," Maddock said. He joined Bones and the two of them tugged at the tile. It came free immediately, revealing a square shaft and a series of rusted iron rungs.

"Everybody down," Bones said. "If we're quick, I can have this thing back in place before the pajama patrol gets here."

Dima went down first, followed by Stone, Maddock, and then Bones. They didn't know how deep the shaft might be or whether the iron rungs would hold, but it was the best option available to them. They descended in the darkness until Dima announced that she had hit the bottom.

When Maddock's feet hit solid ground, he stepped quickly to the side, but not before Bones shouted, "Look out!" Maddock hit the ground hard as his friend's bulk landed atop him.

"Did you forget how to climb?" he grunted.

"The rung gave way. You must have weakened it. I keep telling you to lose weight Maddock."

"You have got to stop falling on me."

"Where are we?" Dima asked.

Bones looked around. "Ancient sewer system," he said.

"And how do we get out?"

Bones grinned. "No clue."

They began exploring the maze of tunnels that twisted and turned in the darkness far below the Vatican. Several times they hit dead ends and were forced to backtrack. These ancient tunnels were crumbling in places and water dripped from the ceiling. Maddock hoped everything would not come tumbling down on top of them.

"Are we lost?" Dima finally asked.

"Not at all," Bones said. "We're just eliminating all the dead-end passageways first. Once we've taken all the wrong turns, the only way left will be the way out."

"That's not very comforting," she said, but she did not raise any more questions.

After two hours of exploring, or, more accurately, wandering, the passageway began to slope upward. Here, the walls were sturdier and showed no signs of leakage. Heartened, Maddock picked up the pace. They climbed and climbed until he was certain they must be approaching ground level.

"Do I hear voices?" Bones asked.

They stopped to listen. Sure enough the dull sound of conversation emanated from up ahead. They hurried on, turned a corner, and skidded to a halt in front of a blank wall.

"Holy crap. You've got to be kidding." Bones lashed out with a vicious front kick, slamming his booted heel into the wall. With a loud crash, the aging mortar crumbled and several of the stones flew outward, opening a gap in the wall large enough for a man to fit through. Bright light and fresh air streamed in.

"I guess we found the way out." Bones flashed a sheepish grin and then peered out the hole he had unintentionally made. "Uh oh."

"What is it?" All of Maddock's senses were on high alert. Had the Swiss Guard caught up with them, or perhaps the Trident?

"Just follow me. And run." With that, Bones plunged through the hole and took off.

Dima and Stone followed, and Maddock brought up the rear. When he burst out into the open he was surprised to find himself looking up at the stands of an ancient arena. The years had been unkind, it still retained hints of its previous majesty. Even now, he had to marvel at the skill of the hands which crafted this ancient wonder. All around, tourists gaped at them. He didn't waste time trying to explain. He just ran.

Leave it to Bones to bust a hole in the Colosseum.

CHAPTER 31

Tyson navigated the throng of tourists outside St. Peter's Basilica. He hated crowds, especially when he was in a hurry. The intel he had received indicated that Dima Zafrini had left Turkey on a flight to Rome. Also, he finally had names for the two men with whom she was traveling: Dane Maddock and Uriah Bonebrake. Both were former Navy SEALs who had turned to treasure hunting. Oddly, the Trident's best men had been unable to learn much about their backgrounds. Great portions of their service records were locked down tightly, and bits of their civilian lives seem to have vanished. It was highly suspicious and suggested that they had powerful connections. He didn't need a report, however, to realize Bonebrake was related to the old man whose family had protected the secret of the Noah Stone for so many years. That made this personal for Bonebrake, which meant the man would not be easily diverted. That was fine by Tyson. He looked forward to evening the score with the two men when he finally caught up to them.

"You think they're here?" Ahmed asked, his hand resting too close to the spot where his pistol was concealed.

"A traffic camera spotted them heading in this direction." Tyson never cease to be amazed at the sorts of connections the Trident had. They even had eyes among the Polizia in Rome. "Bonebrake stands out in a crowd. Once they picked him out, the other two were easy to recognize."

"I can't wait to catch up to them," Ahmed said. "I owe Maddock for what he did to Felipe."

Tyson felt his hackles rise at the mention of their friend whom Maddock had taken down in the ice cave. Felipe was still hospitalized with a concussion. It further galled him that, once again, Zafrini had gotten away. If he and Ahmed didn't catch them soon, things could get ugly.

"Any idea where they would have gone?" Ahmed asked, craning his head to see over the mass of humanity that milled about the famed basilica.

"I think the tomb of St. Peter makes the most sense considering its history." Tyson had heard rumors of secret places beneath the ancient tomb. Perhaps Zafrini had found something more definite. "The rest of the place is like a museum, so it's doubtful they'd bother with it."

"We'll have to hurry to catch them."

Tyson shook his head. "The tomb area is a dead end so we should be able to trap them there."

"Fine. Let's get on with it. I'm tired of Zafrini's narrow escapes. If we could just get these bloody tourists out of the way." Ahmed shot an angry look at an elderly man with a walker who barred their way.

Growing impatient, Tyson forced his way forward until he reached the spot where the Scavi tour began. An annoyed-looking man in a Swiss Guard uniform moved to block his way. Tyson's first reaction was to knock the fellow down, but nothing good would come of that.

"Excuse me, but we were supposed to meet some friends for the Scavi tour, and I'm afraid we are running late. Have you seen them? A tall American Indian, a blond man, and a Jordanian woman? Fairly attractive?"

The guard's frown deepened until his eyebrows almost touched. "I think you should come with me, sir."

Tyson was suddenly aware of the other guards milling about. He had been so focused on looking for Maddock's party that he had failed to notice something was very wrong. All around him were the subtle signs of a major disturbance: men in suits interviewing witnesses; other men, hands pressed to their ears, speaking rapidly in Italian; members of the Swiss Guard in their colorful uniforms stalking back and forth, looking like caged dogs ready to be released for the hunt.

"What is it?" Ahmed asked.

"Nothing. This gentleman was just about to help us find our friends." Tyson smiled.

And then punched the guard in the temple with all his might. The man crumpled silently to the ground.

He turned and gave Ahmed a shove toward the exit. "Run." As they barreled toward the door, upending anyone to slow to get out of their way, Tyson had only one thought: How was he going to explain this to Shawa?

CHAPTER 32

The sun shone brightly in the afternoon sky. The wind rustled a pleasant tune in the trees that lined the garden. Among their branches, colorful birds added their tunes to the harmony. It was a perfect day.

From the corner of his eye Ibrahim Shawa spotted Yusuf waiting at the garden gate. He could tell at first glance that the news, whatever it was, was not good. He closed his eyes, closed the book he was reading, and placed it carefully on the table. Next, he took three deep breaths to calm his nerves. He had been on edge of late and it would not do to lose his temper with Yusuf. After all, the man was only the bearer of bad news. He opened his eyes and forced his lips into a patient smile.

"Come," he said.

Yusuf hurried in, stopped in front of Ibrahim, and bowed deeply, the sinuous movement of his long, slender frame affording him a serpentine quality. His small, dark eyes and light brown skin, so like that of the inaccurately-named black mamba, added to his snakelike appearance. Of course, there was nothing venomous about Yusuf.

Ibrahim return the bow with a slight bob of his head. He sat back, steepled his fingers, and waited.

"I have news, Mu'alim." The word was Arabic for 'teacher', a title Ibrahim had chosen for himself long ago. Yusuf paused, his eyes flitting from side-to-side as if he could somehow escape this moment.

Ibrahim felt his anger began to rise, but he maintained his calm façade. "Please tell me, my son."

Yusuf stiffened, and raised his chin. He didn't quite meet Ibrahim's eyes as he spoke. "Tyson has failed. More than once." He cleared his throat. "I fear I do not hold out much hope for his success."

Ibrahim's fingers twitched, the desire to ball his fists

and strike someone strong within him. Calm, he told himself. He waited patiently until the man summoned the courage to continue.

In a shaky voice, Yusuf outlined the events of the previous several days. Tyson and Ahmed had caught up with Dima Zafrini in a small coastal town in the United States, but had failed to take her, or to acquire the page from the *Book of Noah*. They had succeeded in finding clues to the locations of two of the three stones. However, one lead had proved to be false. They had infiltrated the bank in which it was supposedly kept, but the stone was not there. They caught up with Zafrini again as she attempted to recover the second stone from a shipwreck in the Atlantic Ocean, off the coast of some place called South Carolina. Tyson and Ahmed had taken the items that Zafrini and her companions had recovered, but none of them proved to be a Noah Stone.

Ibrahim began to tremble with suppressed rage as Yusuf outlined Tyson and Ahmed's latest blunders. They had followed Zafrini and two other men, former United States Navy men named Maddock and Bonebrake, to Turkey, and then to the Vatican. Both times, Zafrini and the others had eluded them. "Felipe was injured. He is recovering in a hospital in Turkey."

Ibrahim kept his silence until he could speak calmly.

"The Vatican?" he said. "Zafrini was wasting her time there. I have placed researchers in the secret archives many times. *The Book of Noah* is not there."

Yusuf's lips moved, but he made no sound. He winced and lowered his gaze.

"What is it?"

"She did not go to the secret archives," Yusuf said to the ground.

That was a surprise. "No? Where did she go?"

Yusuf muttered a reply to soft to reach Ibrahim's ears.

"Speak up!" he snapped.

"She took the Scavi tour. Down into the Vatican Necropolis."

"The Tomb of the Dead. What did she think she would find down there? There's nothing but dry bones and graffiti."

"I don't know. All we can say for certain is that she and her companions went down into the catacombs and never came back out again." Yusuf flinched as he spoke the last words.

Ibrahim looked up at the clear blue sky, a canvas for his thoughts. If Zafrini had indeed vanished beneath St. Peter's, that meant there were places down there yet to be discovered. He would have to find a way to get men inside there as soon as possible.

"Zafrini must be found. If she has, in fact, recovered any of the stones, or the *Book of Noah*, we will take them from her. I need not remind you how important to me those stones are."

Yusuf shook his head.

Ibrahim stood, reached out, and clasped Yusuf's trembling hand. "I do not blame you. The fault lies with Tyson. Tell him I will permit him to correct his mistakes, but my patience is nearing an end. We will change the world, and we will begin by bringing peace to our land through the power we will unleash." He did not miss Yusuf's small frown. "What is it? Speak freely, man."

"Forgive me, Mu'alim, but I always find it odd when you speak of peace, given the work that we do and the way that we do it."

Ibrahim smiled and gave the man's hand a squeeze.

"There are many paths to peace, my son. Some look to the dove, but I will bring peace by the sword."

CHAPTER 33

"**All right. Do** you want to hear what I've got?" Dima said through the doorway to the balcony where Maddock and Bones sat drinking coffee. Stone had secured them a room in a hotel on the outskirts of Rome, registering it under his name so they could fly under the radar. He had further assured them that they need only contact him he would use the Myrmidon's resources to get Maddock and the others out of the country whenever they were ready to leave. In turn, they were expected to share whatever they learned with Tam, and to turn over the *Book of Noah* to her when they were finished with it. Dima had balked at the last condition, but had finally agreed. Maddock had decided he rather liked Stone. The man was smart, capable, and sensible. He also didn't flinch at breaking the rules when necessary, which meant he had a friend in Bones.

"Let's hear it," Maddock said.

"As much as I would like some fresh air, let's do this inside. I know I'm being paranoid but you never know who's listening." She had stayed up all night poring over the *Book of Noah*, translating it bit by bit, along with the image of the fragment they had found in the frozen monk's hand. Though her eyes were bloodshot and her hair disheveled, she seemed invigorated.

Maddock and Bones picked up their coffee cups and followed her inside where they found seats on the small sofa. Dima stood in front of them like a schoolteacher lecturing her pupils.

"The book is not in perfect condition. Far from it, in fact, but I did the best I could. There's always some guesswork when it comes to translation, but I'm confident that what I've got is very close. I won't read every word. Just the high points. This first bit is consistent with the bits of the *Book of Noah* that were preserved in the *Book of Enoch*." She cleared her throat and began to read.

"I saw written on them that generation upon generation shall transgress, until a generation of righteousness arises, and transgression is destroyed and sin passes away from the earth, and all manner of good comes upon it. You who have done good shall wait for those days till an end is made of those who work evil; and an end of the might of the transgressors, for their names shall be blotted out of the book of life and out of the holy books, and their seed shall be destroyed forever, and their spirits shall be slain, and they shall cry and make lamentation in a place that is a chaotic wilderness, and in the fire shall they burn. And when Methuselah had heard the words of his father Enoch—for he had shown to him everything in secret—he returned then and showed them to his son Lamech. And Lamech called the name of that son Noah, for he shall comfort the earth after all the destruction."

Bones held up a hand. "Fire? I thought we were talking about a flood."

"I assume it's talking about Hell," Maddock said.

"Possibly," Dima agreed, "but I can't say for sure. The next part is very close to the Genesis story with which we're all familiar." She continued reading.

"And it came to pass, when men began to multiply on the face of the earth, and daughters were born to them, that the sons of Yahweh saw the daughters of men that they were fair, and they took for themselves wives of all which they chose. And when the sons of Yahweh came in to the daughters of men, and they bore children to them, the same became mighty men which were of old, men of renown. There were Watchers in the earth in those days, but they were not of man."

"Sorry to interrupt," Bones said. "I know the sons of Yahweh were the non-humans, you know, the Nephilim and the like." He shot a knowing glance at Maddock. The two of them had some experience in that regard. "But what's this about Watchers? Is this *The Book of Noah* or the script of that crappy Russell Crowe movie?"

"The Watchers aren't in the Bible, but they're mentioned in extra-Biblical sources, like the Book of Enoch. Now, any more questions or are you going to shut up and let me read?" Dima put a hand on her hip and tapped her toe impatiently.

Bones chuckled, sat back, and took a sip of coffee. "Go ahead. I'm not stopping you."

Dima made a face and returned to her translation.

"And Yahweh saw that the wickedness of man was great in the earth, and that every imagination of the thoughts of his heart led to transgression. And it repented Yahweh that he had made man on the earth, and it grieved him at his heart. And Yahweh said, I will destroy man whom I have created from the face of the earth; both man, and beast, and the creeping thing, and the fowls of the air. Yet a remnant I shall save, as I have foretold.

"Noah found grace in the eyes of Yahweh, for Noah was a just man and righteous among his generations, and Noah walked with Yahweh. And Noah begat three sons, Shem, Ham, and Japheth. And Yahweh said to Noah, The end of all flesh is come before me; for the earth is filled with wickedness and violence through them; and, behold, I will destroy them with the earth. Make you an ark. And, behold, even as I do bring a flood of waters on the earth, to destroy all flesh, with you will I establish my covenant, and you shall come into the ark, you, and your sons, and your wife, and your sons' wives with you. And living things, two of every sort, shall you bring into the ark, to keep them alive with you; they shall be male and female."

Maddock noted some differences in this account, namely the lack of specific instructions for the construction of the ark. No mention of gopher wood, pitch, the number of levels, or the specific dimensions.

"And Yahweh sent to Noah three stones, and they fell like fire from the heavens. And Yahweh said to Noah, bring not the three stones together, for in that moment

you shall surely die. And Noah took up the first stone and commanded the Watchers to build the ark. And for forty days the watchers labored. And Noah took up the second stone and his blood was on the stone, and he called out to the creatures that walk the earth, and they came two by two and seven by seven into the ark. And Noah took up the third stone, and his blood was on the stone, and the fountains of the deep and the floodgates of the sky were opened."

Dima paused, her brown eyes intense. "Now we know what the three stones do."

"So the stone we recovered from the sinkhole can bring down the rain?" Bones asked.

"Or bring up water from below the earth." Maddock's hand moved to his pocket. He had taken to keeping the stone with him at all times, while Bones kept the one that had belonged to his ancestor. "I don't think I'll try it out just yet. I'd hate to turn this place into Venice."

"I don't know," Bones said. "I wouldn't mind taking Dima on a romantic boat ride."

"In your soggy dreams," she said, rolling her eyes.

"Keep reading," Maddock said. "Bones can hit on you later."

"And the waters rose to cover the land, and the men came to the ark, and they cried, Let us inside for we shall surely die. And Noah took up the first stone, and his blood was on the stone, and the men were driven away by the Watchers. And Noah took pity upon the Watchers for they were not of man, and he brought them into the ark and he called them adama for they were of the earth."

Here, Dima paused. "Some extra-Biblical sources claim Noah brought the body of Adam onto the ark. I suspect this is the source of that legend."

"And among his sons, Ham contended with Noah, for he saw his father loved the adama and that the stone was precious to him. Thus Yahweh blotted out every living thing that was upon the face of the land, from man

to animals to creeping things and to birds of the sky, and they were blotted out from the earth; and only Noah was left, together with those that were with him in the ark. And the water prevailed upon the earth. But Yahweh remembered Noah and all the beasts that were with him in the ark and Yahweh caused a wind to pass over the earth, and the water subsided. And the fountains of the deep and the floodgates of the sky were closed. And on the seventh day of the seventh month Yahweh spoke to Noah and said, Go forth from the ark and take your wife and your sons and your sons' wives with you. Bring out with you every living thing of all flesh that is with you, birds and animals and every creeping thing that creeps on the earth, that they may breed abundantly on the earth, and be fruitful and multiply on the earth. And give to each of your three sons a stone, that they may take them far across the earth, for if the stones come together you shall surely die.

"But Noah heeded not the words of Yahweh for the stones were precious to him. And Ham, the father of Canaan, said to his brothers, It is not good that our father has taken the stones. Let us contend with him and take the stones that are rightfully ours. But his brothers said, We shall not rebel against our father.

"And Noah began farming and planted a vineyard, and when he drank of the wine he became drunk. And Ham saw his father's drunkenness, and vowed to take the stones for himself. But Noah kept the first stone beneath his head, for among them all it was most precious to him, and thus Ham seized only two stones. And when Noah saw what his youngest son had done, he sent forth the adama, but Ham had fled to the land of Canaan. And Noah said, Cursed be Ham, a servant of servants to his brothers he shall be. So all the days of Noah were seventy-seven years upon the mountains of Meri."

A thoughtful silence settled over them as Dima finished her translation. Finally, Maddock spoke.

"So, Noah had three stones that fell from the sky.

They're powerful individually, but together they can…"

"Make a mess," Bones provided.

"That's one way of putting it."

"And the Trident wants all three," Dima said. "That guy who tried to snatch me said so."

"Which proves they're up to no good." Maddock sat up straight. "Think about it. I could see how either of the stones we currently have could be used for the common good. If you had the second stone, you'd never have to worry about drought decimating your crops. With the first stone you could keep predators away from your livestock. If Ibrahim Shawa only wanted those two stones, it could be for benevolent purposes, even if we don't like his underlings' methods."

"But the fact that he wants to bring them together proves he wants somebody to die." Bones nodded slowly.

"If he gets that third stone, he'll stop at nothing to get the other two," Maddock said. "We need to find the last stone before he does."

"What do we do with the stones we have?" Bones asked. "I mean, if bringing the three together causes some sort of catastrophe, aren't we tempting fate if we bring our two stones along?"

"But we need them," Dima said. "Think about it. The tests we've run indicate there's nothing special about the stones. They don't give off any sort of radiation signature or anything that would help us find them. You only found the second stone because of the way the first one reacted to its presence."

Maddock scratched his chin and nodded. "I also can't think of anywhere secure to put them at the moment. I guess the hotel safe is out of the question." He smiled and winked at Dima, whose sudden, panicked look indicated she'd taken his suggestion seriously. "I'll think on it. The most pressing question right now is, where do we find the last stone? What is this Meri?"

Dima bit her lip. "I have a theory about that, but you're not going to believe it."

CHAPTER 34

"**Africa? Are you** serious?" Bones asked. "That sounds totally wrong."

"Hear me out. It's not as crazy as you might think." Dima sat down in the armchair facing Maddock and Bones and placed her translation on the table in between them. "First of all, we've got the translation. It says the ark came to rest in the mountains of Meri. Meri and Meru are often used interchangeably to describe a particular mountain in Africa."

"But is that enough to go on? Words can change form," Bones argued.

"That's hardly everything. Hear me out. First of all, there's a scholarly tradition that Noah was African, perhaps even nobility. We know he was the grandfather of Kush, from whom the nation of Kush got its name."

Maddock nodded. Kush was an ancient African kingdom located in present-day Sudan.

"What's more," Dima continued, "many nobles in that time kept menageries with male and female specimens for breeding purposes, so Noah might have simply led his own menagerie into the ark. And the rulers during that period controlled the Nile, the Tigris and Euphrates, and Lake Chad, and they used the various waterways as their roads. Noah would have been quite familiar with boats."

Bones rubbed his chin. "It's thin."

"Not as thin as my patience will be if you keep interrupting me." Dima shifted in her seat, crossed and uncrossed her legs, and folded her hands. "What if I told you there's only one place in the world that claimed to be Noah's homeland? It's called 'Borno' or 'The Land of Noah' and it's located in the center of Africa, near Lake Chad, in fact."

Bones nodded but didn't interrupt this time.

"The African connection rang a bell with me, and I did a little research. Listen to this Nigerian flood story." She took out her cell phone, tapped the screen, and began to read.

"The first man, Etim 'Ne, and his wife Ejaw came to earth from the sky. At first, there was no water on earth, so Etim 'Ne asked the god Obassi Osaw for water, and he was given a calabash with seven stones. When Etim 'Ne put a stone in a small hole in the ground, water welled out and became a broad lake. Later, seven sons and seven daughters were born to the couple. After the sons and daughters married and had children of their own, Etim 'Ne gave each household a river or lake of its own. He took away the rivers of three sons who were poor hunters and didn't share their meat, but he restored them when the sons begged him to. When the grandchildren had grown and established new homes, Etim 'Ne sent for all the children and told them each to take seven stones from the streams of their parents, and to plant them at intervals to create new streams. All did so except one son who collected a basketful and emptied all his stones in one place. Waters came, covered his farm, and threatened to cover the whole earth. Everyone ran to Etim 'Ne, fleeing the flood. Etim 'Ne prayed to Obassi, who stopped the flood but let a lake remain covering the farm of the bad son. Etim 'Ne told the others the names of the rivers and streams which remained and told them to remember him as the bringer of water to the world."

Maddock had to admit he was intrigued by this new piece of information. "Obviously the minor details are different, but that's the only flood story I ever heard, before we found the *Book of Noah*, that is, that connects stones with flood mythology. I suppose the actual events of the *Book of Noah* could be the source of that legend."

"And the difference in the number of stones can be attributed to storytelling techniques," Dima agreed. "Seven is considered a powerful or lucky number in many cultures."

Maddock tried to picture a map of Africa in his mind. Chad lay in central Africa, while Tanzania, where Mount Meru was located, lay in the east. "But how do you get from Lake Chad to Mount Meru? That's a long way. I suppose if it were a worldwide flood." He shrugged.

"That's unlikely, given the archaeological record." Bones held up his hands. "Sorry, I figured I'm allowed to talk now."

Dima ignored him. "Remember that Noah lived at a time when the Saharan region, and much of Africa for that matter, was experiencing a wet period, so the boundaries of the major waterways were different than they are today. According to studies done of satellite imagery, Lake Chad, or Mega-Chad as they refer to the old incarnation of the lake, was once a massive body of water. It covered an area at least five times the size of Lake Superior with depths of two hundred to six hundred feet. It's believed to have extended hundreds of miles beyond its current boundaries, even encompassing Lake Victoria and beyond. It's a little over two hundred miles from the center of the Chad Basin to Mount Meru, so it's not impossible that the water could have reached the mountain itself. Add a major flood to that, and there's no reason the ark couldn't have settled somewhere on the slopes of Mount Meru."

"I'm not trying to give you a hard time here," Bones said, "but we're stringing together evidence from different parts of Africa, which is a pretty big place. How confident are you that the *Book of Noah* is accurate? We've already seen some differences between it and the Bible story."

Dima nodded. "Obviously, we won't know until we investigate, but you can't deny it's the best lead we have. The Trident must also believe in its worth or else they wouldn't be coming after it...and me."

Maddock sat back and let it all sink in. It was a lot of new information to process.

"You know, there's something we still haven't

considered, Maddock," Bones said.

"What's that?"

"Stones with mysterious powers. We've seen that before, and it wasn't the power of God at work."

Maddock nodded. On several occasions, they had encountered such stones, and had reason to believe their origins were not supernatural, though not of the earth.

"Would you two care to fill me in?" Dima asked.

Maddock quickly summarized a few of their exploits and the discoveries they had made. "Of course, that's not to say there aren't items out there with miraculous powers. We've found a couple of those, too."

Dima sat slack-jawed, staring at the two of them as if she expected them to admit it was all a joke. Finally, she let out a weary sigh and shook her head. "You're really not winding me up, are you? You've really seen this stuff, or at least you believe you have."

"Come on, now." Bones reached into his pocket and pulled out his stone. "You watched Maddock use this to take control of the mind of an animal. You're really going to tell me you don't believe in the supernatural? Heck, you're a Noah researcher, which tells me you've always been a believer on some level."

Dima looked down at her hands, which she held folded in her lap. "A dreamer more than a believer. I guess I hoped to find proof of God but expected to find a much more pedestrian source of the myth. Which is looking like it wasn't that much of a myth after all." She looked up, her eyes cloudy. "What I didn't expect was to learn that little green men were behind it all."

"That's not at all what we're saying," Maddock reassured her. "Even if these stones didn't come from God in the way the story claims, they got their power from somewhere, and what they do is nothing short of miraculous."

"I suppose. But why didn't you two tell me about all of this before?"

Maddock grinned. "Would you have believed us?"

CHAPTER 35

The city of Arusha, the capital of the district of the same name in Tanzania, lay near the Kenyan border. Located on the eastern edge of the Great Rift Valley, the city of nearly half-a-million people was both a diplomatic hub and a center of tourism, with such noted sites as Olduvai Gorge, Serengeti National Park, and Mount Kilimanjaro all located nearby. As he guided their rented four-by-four through the outskirts of the city, Maddock admired the lush, green landscape, with Mount Meru looming just to the north, so close he felt he could reach out and touch it. At fifteen thousand feet, Mount Meru was Africa's fifth highest mountain. Though not nearly as well-known as Kilimanjaro, which stood forty miles to the northeast, Meru drew many serious climbers. Its slopes were also home to Arusha National Park, known for its varied wildlife and spectacular landscapes.

"So that's where we're headed," Bones said, gazing out the window at the tall peak. "Should be a heck of a climb."

"Supposedly it can be climbed in two to four days, depending on your experience and physical condition," Dima said, scanning a web page devoted to the mountain.

"Maddock and I can handle it no problem. Have you done much climbing?"

"Enough that I won't be a burden, and I stay in shape."

"I've noticed that." To his credit, Bones didn't punctuate the comment with a leer, wink, or even a smile.

"If the mountain is climbed regularly," Maddock said, "it's a wonder no one has found any clues to the ark."

"You have to figure that, in this climate, there's

nothing left of the boat itself," Dima said. "All that's left are the legends, and hopefully the stone."

"Are there any local legends about the ark?" Bones asked."

"Believe it or not, tourist agencies refer to Mount Meru as 'Noah's Ark.' Supposedly, it's because of the tremendous variety of species that live on and around the mountain, but maybe there's more to it than that."

"So, how do we proceed?" Bones asked. "Do we start by climbing the mountain?"

"We're going to visit the park first," Maddock said. "The ark didn't necessarily land right on top of the mountain. We'll split up, do some hiking, and see if either of the stones pick anything up." They had reluctantly brought both of the Noah Stones along, figuring they had a large area to cover and having two stones would double their chances of locating the third. "We might also be able to pick up some clues from the locals. If that doesn't work, we'll try the peak."

"All right." A touch of disappointment rang in Bones' voice. He hated to miss an opportunity to climb.

"Cheer up. I think you'll like the lodge where we're staying tonight. It's got great food, hot tubs…" Out of the corner of his eye, Maddock caught the sly wink Dima sent in Bones' direction.

Bones returned the wink. "Sign me up." I assume the rooms are coed?"

"We've got two rooms. Maddock gets one, I get the other. Where you sleep depends on your behavior."

"In that case, you're definitely bunking with me," Maddock said to Bones. He wondered at Dima's flirtatious behavior. One moment she seemed to like Bones, the next she was putting him in his place. Not that he didn't deserve it most of the time.

"What's the political situation in Tanzania?" Bones asked.

"It's stable overall, but there have been some terrorist attacks, mostly against religious sites. There are rumors of connections to Boko Haram, but it's not definite."

Bones sighed. "Good old Islamic fundamentalists."

"The Christians' hands aren't clean either. They've made their share of reprisals and done their share of rioting. It's a mess."

"Sorry if I gave offense," Bones said quickly. "I never thought to ask if you're Muslim."

"I'm not really anything. Growing up in the Middle East, you get to see the darker side of religious devotion firsthand. I haven't missed it since I moved to the States."

They skirted the national park, riding on in silence until the Hatari Lodge came into view. The so-called "luxury bush hotel" consisted of three buildings, one of which had once been the home of actor Hardy Kruger. Located near the boundary of Arusha National Park, the idyllic setting offered sweeping views of open plains, acacia forests, as well as Kilimanjaro and Mount Meru.

Inside, a short, balding man in khaki greeted them at the front desk.

"Welcome to the Hatari Lodge." He punctuated his friendly greeting, delivered in lilting, accented English, with a broad smile.

"Wayne Shipman checking in," Maddock said, giving the false name under which the reservation has been made.

The desk clerk's demeanor changed immediately. Lines creased his brow and he pursed his lips.

"Yes, Mr. Shipman and party," he said flatly. "Two rooms?"

"Yes, that's correct." Maddock was puzzled by the man's sudden change in attitude. "Is there a problem?"

The man hesitated and then shook his head. "No, sir. It's just that we were forced to relocate some guests to another lodge in order to accommodate you."

"I assure you, that was never our intention. We didn't actually make the reservations ourselves." Maddock suppressed a grin. Leave it to Tam to let no one stand in her way, including paying guests. "I would apologize to them myself if I could."

"I did not mean to suggest you were at fault. But when a government official arrives to claim the rooms personally, it is a bit disconcerting." He looked at Maddock, Bones, and Dima through narrowed eyes, probably thinking to himself that these three did not look at all like government agents.

"We are on a government-sponsored research trip," Dima said. "And again, we never dreamed that anyone would be inconvenienced by our presence. We are truly sorry."

Now, the desk clerk relaxed, and his smile returned. "It is all right, of course. We are happy to have you here. What sort of research are you doing?"

"Archaeological surveys," Bones said. "No actual digging, just comparing landforms to places described in ancient documents."

The clerk's smile slipped, though whether it was disapproval of their intended work, or the fact that he preferred talking to Dima over Bones, Maddock could not say. "I hope this will not be a precursor to conducting future digs here in the park," he said.

"Not at all," Maddock assured him. "This is strictly information gathering for the purpose of verifying data."

The clerk did not try to hide his skeptical frown. "That is good to know." He turned, leaned down, and began rummaging through items piled behind the counter. A few moments later he produced a black, leather briefcase. "The men who… reserved your room, left this for you. He pushed the case across the counter to Maddock.

"Thank you," Maddock said, passing the case to Bones.

"It is very heavy," the clerk said.

"Reading material. Very boring, unless you like topographical charts and climate data."

"No thank you." The clerk finally managed a smile as he handed Maddock two room keys. "I will show you to your rooms. Dinner will be served in the main hall in," he checked his watch, "three hours. All the guests dine together, family-style."

"I don't care how you serve the food as long as there's plenty of," Bones said.

The clerk looked him up and down. "Perhaps I shall tell them to roast an extra chicken. We don't often serve men of your stature."

"Did you hear that, Maddock? My own chicken. I like this place."

Maddock nodded but kept his thoughts to himself as they follow the clerk to their rooms. The lodge seemed nice enough. He only hoped they could stay ahead of the Trident long enough to find what they were looking for.

CHAPTER 36

The tiny hotel room felt like a prison cell. Everything in Europe was too small for a man of Tyson's size. His feet hung off the bed, the pitiful stream of water in the shower wet only a hand's breadth of flesh at a time, and passing through a doorway meant risking a concussion. Curse this place!

He looked out the window and down at the throngs of tourists wandering the streets of Rome, taking in the sights. What must it be like to live so free, without a care? Suddenly he couldn't remember what it felt like to live without a death sentence hanging over your head. There was no question—Tyson was a dead man walking unless he could find Zafrini, and thus far she had eluded him at every turn. The thought of the woman and her companions, Bonebrake and Maddock, set his teeth on edge. Somehow he had to find them, and when he did, he would take his sweet time making them pay for putting him in this position.

His phone rang. When he saw the identity of the caller, he considered hitting the ignore button. A call from Yusuf was seldom good news. Did this mean the clock had run out on Tyson and Ahmed? Was Shawa's right-hand man calling them to account? Perhaps he shouldn't answer. Then again, it wasn't like he could avoid Shawa forever. There was no leaving the Trident, much less escaping its reach. He glanced at Ahmed, who nodded once. Reluctantly, he accepted the call.

"This is Tyson." He hoped his voice didn't tremble. He hated sounding weak.

"Tyson, it's Yusuf." The voice was scarcely audible.

"Why are you whispering?"

"Just listen. There isn't much time. I think I might know where Zafrini is."

Tyson's heart skipped a beat. "Go on," he said, not

daring to get his hopes up, yet dying to get out of this dingy hotel and back on Zafrini's trail.

"I received a report that the large Indian she is traveling with was spotted leaving an airport."

"Bonebrake." Tyson uttered the name like a curse. "Are you certain it was him?"

"He wasn't wearing an identification tag, but he's unique. And he was traveling with a man and a woman. Besides, he's looking for the ark. What are the odds another giant American Indian would show up in Arusha?"

Tyson forced a laugh that came out as a grunt. "Arusha? Then they are following a cold trail. We have searched that mountain thoroughly."

"The trail doesn't matter right now," Yusuf said. *"What matters is that you and Ahmed must catch up with Zafrini and her party and recover any documents or items they might have in their possession. Shawa will permit you this last chance to make things right, but he will not tolerate more failure."*

Tyson did not have to ask about the items to which Yusuf referred.

"It would also be a good idea for you to take Zafrini in," Yusuf continued. *"I think Shawa will want her questioned. There's no telling what she might know."*

Tyson breathed a sigh of relief. The chase wasn't ended yet.

"Yusuf, I can't thank you enough for this. You just might have saved my neck."

"Don't thank me yet, my friend. Just get this mess sorted and get yourself back into Shawa's good books before he calls you in to answer for your blunders."

That last bit stung, and even seemed a touch unfair, but Tyson was not foolish enough to express surprise. Shawa despised incompetence and he accepted no excuses for failure. "I understand."

"Good," Yusuf said. *"If you need more men, you will have to hire them from among the locals. I can't help you in that regard without risking Shawa finding out. And*

keep your eyes open. We have reason to believe that Boko Haram has planned something for Arusha, and it could happen soon."

"I owe you."

Yusuf chuckled. *"Yes you do. And don't think I won't collect when the time comes. Good luck."*

Tyson ended the call and pocketed his phone. He wasn't sure what Yusuf met by that last comment, but that was the least of his worries right now.

Ahmed looked up from his magazine, his gray pallor belying his feigned nonchalance. "What did Yusuf say?"

"He says it isn't over just yet. Grab your things. We need to catch a plane."

CHAPTER 37

"Now this is what I call a meal." Bones smiled as he piled his plate high with roast chicken, steamed vegetables, and bread.

"Leave some for everyone else," Dima said.

Down the long table packed with tourists, people stared at Bones with looks that ranged from amusement to deep concern. Maddock couldn't blame them. If Bones didn't slow down, the people at the far end stood a very real chance of going hungry tonight.

"Oh, sorry about that," Bones said. "I always got fed last growing up, so I'm not used to leaving food for everyone else." He smiled and slid the plates on down the table.

"Nothing wrong with a healthy appetite," said a broad-shouldered man with a walrus mustache. "I've been known to clear a few plates myself." He chortled and patted his ample belly. "I'm sure I don't have to tell you that." He filled his own plate and passed the food along. "So," he said to Maddock, "I understand you are archaeologists."

Maddock tensed. The fellow looked harmless enough, but who was to say? "We are."

"Excellent. I am something of a biblical archaeologist myself, though with me it is a hobby, not a profession. Douglas Schrader. This is my wife, Alice." He inclined his head to the woman seated on his left. Alice, a slender woman with silver-streaked brown hair, smiled. "And my daughter, Melanie." Melanie was an attractive girl of about sixteen, with long, brown hair and big, hazel eyes. She blushed and made a little wave.

Maddock introduced himself, Bones, and Dima, using false names for each, and they all shook hands with Schrader.

"If that's your hobby, what do you do for a living?"

Bones asked

"I'm a missionary. My family and I are opening a school for orphans outside of town. We thought we would get in a little sightseeing before we open our doors. Who knows? I might even find Noah's Ark."

Only the years of military discipline instilled in him kept Maddock from reacting to the statement. He took a bite of chicken and chewed slowly, considering what Schrader had just said. Was it merely a coincidence? Surely if the man had ill intentions he wouldn't be so reckless as to reveal himself to Maddock and Bones.

"Noah's Ark?" Dima asked. "I thought that was somewhere in the Middle East. Turkey, perhaps."

"That is what common wisdom holds," Schrader said. He leaned across the table and lowered his voice. "I've made a fair study of the Noah stories, and I believe the ark might have actually landed in this region."

"Really?" Dima cocked her head. "That sounds far-fetched."

"Oh ho. A skeptic!" Schrader laughed. "You are hardly the first. Believe it or not, there's an old tradition that this region is, in fact the home of Noah. Why, Mount Meru is referred to by many as 'Noah's Ark.' But what people don't know is that Mount Meru is not the same as…" He paused when his wife, a slender woman with long, silver streaked brown hair, laid a hand on his arm.

"Please, Douglas. These nice people are trying to enjoy their meal, and so are Melanie and I. None of your lectures at the dinner table."

"It's all right, really," Dima said. "Actually, it sounds interesting."

Schrader's wife smiled. "That's very kind and more than a bit indulgent of you, dear, but he knows better."

Schrader made a small shrug and turned his attention to his meal. They ate in relative silence, with only an occasional bit of small talk breaking the monotony. Schrader and Alice described their plans for the school, which included housing and religious instruction.

"Most of the community has been supportive," Alice explained, "but a small contingent opposes educating young women. Fortunately, Arusha is a modern city and such attitudes are rare."

"I think it's a wonderful cause," Dima said. "And I also hope Mr. Schrader gets a chance to search for the ark."

"I shall, first chance I get," Schrader said around a mouthful of roast plantain. "As I was about to say earlier, I found an account that claims…"

"Nice try, dear," Alice interrupted, her tone as soft as her eyes were sharp. "Now, please stop talking with food in your mouth."

Schrader rolled his eyes and his daughter giggled.

When they finished eating, Alice ushered her family away quickly, much to Maddock's disappointment. He was interested in hearing what Schrader knew, or thought he knew, about the ark. Perhaps it was nothing useful, but it wouldn't hurt to find out. Maybe he'd have the chance later.

Bones and Dima went out for a walk, so Maddock returned to his room where he inspected the contents of the case that had been left for them at the front desk. It contained two handguns: a Walther for him and a Glock for Bones, along with ammunition and a spare magazine for each. When he was satisfied both were in good working order, he returned them to the case and slid it under his bed. He took a few minutes to examine a map of the park and sketch out a plan for the following day. They'd hit the slopes and work their way up, hoping one of the Noah Stones would react to its missing counterpart.

When he couldn't come up with anything else to busy himself, he tried calling Angel, but couldn't get a decent cell phone connection. Disappointed and weary, he fired off a quick text message in hopes it would get through, stretched out on the bed, and drifted off to sleep. His slumber came to an abrupt end shortly thereafter when Bones banged through the door and flipped on a bedside lamp.

"I thought you were bunking with Dima," Maddock said, opening his eyes but not bothering to sit up. The bed was comfortable and he was stiff from the series of tunnels they'd crawled through and the many airplane rides they'd taken in the past week. He wasn't sure which was harder on his body.

"I thought so too," Bones grumbled. "Apparently, the hot tub thing was a test and I failed. She said if I really liked her I wouldn't be in such a hurry." He sat down heavily on the bed on the opposite side of the room.

"*Do* you like her?" Maddock asked. "I mean, for more than a hookup? You've been acting kind of strange around her."

Bones frowned "You know what? I think I do. How do you figure I ought to handle this?"

Now Maddock sat up. "Seriously? You want my advice about women?

"Yeah. I mean, you suck at picking up chicks, but you're pretty good at holding onto them once you find one you like. Except for Jade, but you kicked her to the curb, so I guess that still counts."

Maddock let that pass. "What is this? A teenage girls' slumber party? I guess we could play Truth or Dare."

"Come on, bro. When is the last time I actually liked somebody? You know, *really* liked her?"

Maddock groaned. Here they were in search of a potentially deadly ancient stone, the Trident was breathing down their necks, and Bones, of all people, wanted to talk about relationships.

"I don't know," Maddock admitted. "I just try to be myself."

Bones sat staring at him, as if he expected more. Finally, he shook his head and flopped back onto the bed. "Maddock?" He said to the ceiling.

"Yes?"

"You suck at giving advice."

CHAPTER 38

The sun was a golden ball balanced on the edge of the horizon when Maddock called it a day. He'd spent more hours than he cared to count wandering the slopes of the mountain, searching for caves, passageways, or even depressions where a huge boat might have once come to rest. He'd seen lots of amazing sights: broad vistas of lush greenery and a dozen zoos' worth of native wildlife, but as for the mission, he'd struck out at every turn. The Templar Stone, as he'd come to think of the artifact they'd recovered from the wreck, remained in his pocket. Not once since he and Bones had split up to begin their search had it radiated even the tiniest measure of heat that might indicate the presence of the third and final Noah Stone.

Out of habit, he checked his cell phone to see if he had a message from Bones, but still no signal. He hoped his friend and Dima had enjoyed better luck than he. His head pounding with frustration, he began the long walk back to the lodge. When he got there, he would track down Schrader, preferably when his wife wasn't around, and listen to his stories. The feeling that the man knew something useful had not entirely left him. Schrader had made the comment that Mount Meru "wasn't the same as…" something. Given today's failure, Maddock was already wondering if they were on the wrong track. In any case, what would it cost him, save some time, to sound the man out? And, if Bones continued his pursuit of Dima, Maddock would have plenty of spare time to fill this evening.

As the Hatari Lodge, a chunk of sandy brown in the midst of all the green, came into view, he paused and looked back at the mountain. If they didn't come up with any new clues, he supposed they'd arrange some climbing gear and try the peak next. He'd hoped it wouldn't come to that. He didn't mind a good climb, but three days uphill, all the while facing the possibility that they'd meet with more failure, held little appeal for him.

When he arrived back the lodge, Schrader was nowhere to be found. It wasn't a large place, so it didn't take much looking to confirm that the missionary was not on the premises.

His disquiet growing, Maddock returned to his room. Stripping down, he folded his sweaty clothes and laid them on the bed. He'd have blamed the military for his fastidious behavior, but it was his parents who had instilled that particular discipline in him long ago. Smiling at fond memories, he headed for the shower. The pressure was low, but it was better than nothing. He stood beneath the shower head, letting it wash away the dirt, sweat, and memories of a fruitless day's work. By the time he shut off the water, he felt halfway ready to tackle Mount Meru. He was just toweling off when he heard a door bang open.

"Maddock!" Bones' voice cut through the calm. "Are you in here?"

Towel wrapped around his waist, Maddock stepped out into the room to find Bones and Dima waiting there.

"What's going on?"

"Get dressed and grab your Walther. Somebody just snatched Schrader and his family in broad daylight, not a hundred yards from the lodge. If we hurry we can catch up with them."

Maddock dropped the towel, not worrying about Dima, and began tugging on the same dirty clothes he'd stripped off a few minutes before.

"Any idea who did it or why?" he asked.

"Not really. The Schraders did say that not everyone around here approved of them educating girls. That's a Muslim extremist idea."

Maddock looked up. "Boko Haram?"

Bones shrugged. "Does it really matter?"

"Not a bit."

Maddock laced his boots, stood, and headed for the

door, but Dima barred the way.

"I don't see why you two have to be the ones to go after them. Shouldn't you let the authorities handle it?" Fear shone in her eyes.

"The authorities might not get here in time. We're here now and they don't have much of a head start. We can do something about this," Bones said.

"And Bones is an amazing tracker. He'll be able to find their trail," Maddock added.

Dima bit her lip. "But what if something happens to you?" Her eyes were locked on Bones, who seemed at a loss for words.

"Here, take this." Maddock handed her his cell phone. "If we aren't back by morning, there's a number in here for Tam Broderick. Get to a place with a signal and call her. She'll take care of you and she'll send people to find us. Of course, we'll owe her the favor from Hell if that happens."

He put his hands on her shoulders and gently turned her so he could slip by. Behind him, Bones and Dima exchanged whispered words, and then Bones was at his side.

"Let's do this. I've been in a bad mood for a while now and I'm ready to take it out on someone."

"So, that's the camp. I think it's safe to say they're staying put for the night." Maddock pointed at the flickering light of the campfire in the distance. He and Bones had spent two hours tracking the kidnappers over rough terrain and back to their encampment.

"Idiots. Trying to hide in plain sight," Bones said. "Why wouldn't they hop in their trucks and get the Hell out of Dodge?"

"Maybe they're counting on strength in numbers, or they just didn't figure on anyone knowing where to look for them."

"Either way, it works to our advantage. Most of them have probably bedded down for the night. They think they're safe, and they'll be sleepy, which will slow their reaction time." Bones ran his hand over the Glock at his waist. "Have you seen any sign of the Schraders?"

"No, but it's got to be the big tent in the center. They've got a guy standing guard in front of it."

Bones nodded. "I've counted a dozen men in total moving through camp and in and out of the tents. They're idiots if they don't have at least a couple of guys minding the perimeter a bit farther out."

"Agreed." Maddock cast a baleful glance at the full moon hanging low in the clear night sky. A little more darkness would be welcome, but there was nothing to be done about it. They would just have to be extra stealthy. "We'll need to work our way in quietly, taking the perimeter guys out in complete silence if at all possible. If we start shooting, it'll put them on full alert and we'll be hard-pressed to break through their defenses."

"Plus, they'll take off with the Schrader's, or do something worse." Bones didn't need to elaborate. "So, it's knife work, or do you have any other bright ideas?"

"I've got a plan. Do you have your stone with you?"

CHAPTER 39

The night was too quiet. Hassan hated it. Give him a city, a town, even a village. Anywhere he could be around people and away from this nature that everyone found so peaceful and exhilarating. Insects buzzed about his head, their high-pitched whines the only sounds on this desolate place. He smacked at one of the offending gnats and managed to cuff himself across the ear. It set up a lovely ringing sound, but at least that drowned out the gnats.

He heard a low rumble to the east. Dark clouds were rolling in quickly. They'd soon blot out the moon, and leave Hassan in darkness.

It was foolish to make camp here, this close to Arusha. The authorities could catch up with them any time. But Faid, their leader, claimed he had connections in town who would make sure the pursuit went in the wrong direction for the first forty-eight hours. By then, they'd be long gone, though not nearly soon enough for Hassan's liking.

He sighed and glanced at the closed flap of the tent he guarded. The infidels were inside. The man had ceased his cursing and the woman her wailing hours ago, but the girl still whimpered the occasional plea. The Christians disgusted Hassan, but there was something about the young girl's frightened tone that stoked the fires inside him. Perhaps, once the others were sound asleep…

Something moved out of the corner of his eye, snapping him from the depths of his depraved musings. He looked around but saw nothing.

"Ezekiel?" he whispered. Ezekiel was guarding the perimeter but it was possible he had circled in close to the tents. He wasn't the most steadfast about his duties and Hassan wouldn't put it past him to wander so far afield. "Ezekiel, is that you?"

No reply.

He looked, listened, but nothing. It had probably been his imagination. That was the thing about silence and darkness—his mind started filling in the blank spaces.

"Stop being a child," he scolded himself. He let the barrel of his AK-47 fall to the ground, as if lowering his weapon were a statement to the night that he would not be cowed. "Two more hours and then you can sleep." At least he had not drawn middle watch, so he would have six uninterrupted hours of rest. He was ready. The stress of the day had sapped him of his energy.

He closed his eyes and, for a moment, let the fatigue wash over him. It would be so easy to fall asleep standing here.

The underbrush nearby rustled and his eyes snapped open. What *was* that? He turned and took a few steps in the direction from which the sound had some, straining to see.

Another flash of movement, this time off to his left, lightning fast. He raised his rifle but saw nothing at which he could take aim. Nor did he hear anything. What in the name of Allah?

As he stood there, heart drumming, the stories came back. Campfire tales, meant to frighten young children, echoed in his mind. The spirits of the dead gathered in valleys like this one, waiting for a moonless night. Waiting to rise.

Movement to his right. There and gone.

"Who's there?" He hated the plaintive tone that saturated his words with fear. He cleared his throat, steeled himself, and tried again, this time stronger. "Show yourself."

Nothing.

"You can't wake the others and tell them spirits have invaded our camp," he whispered. "Move your feet."

Step by laborious step, he moved out beyond the ring of tents. His finger brushed the trigger of his rifle.

How he longed to fire, to pierce the darkness, shred the silence. But not until he had a target.

Beyond the tents, he began a slow circle around the perimeter, all the while keeping the center tent in the corner of his vision. The prisoners were bound tightly and weren't going anywhere, but they were his responsibility until his watch ended.

As he walked, he cursed his superstition and his fear. He was a soldier of Allah, a warrior for the cause. What had he to fear when God was on his side?

By the time he completed his circuit around the camp, seeing nothing, his nerves had settled and he returned to his guard position with a renewed sense of confidence. He was not afraid of shadows in the night.

He drew back the tent flap and peered inside. Three pairs of eyes stared back at him, and the fear he saw there added fuel to the nascent fire of his renewed courage. He was not a pathetic creature such as these. He was a soldier. He bared his teeth, enjoying the way the girl flinched and the man thrashed against his bonds. Weak. All of them.

He turned back to face the night and his smile melted. There, in the dim light that filtered through the clouds, stood a distinctive silhouette.

A lioness.

She sat there on her haunches, head slightly tilted, and gazed at him like a house cat waiting for a bowl of cream. A sudden warmth ran down the inside of his thigh and he took a step back. "Go!" he hissed. Yet the lioness remained still. "Get out of here," he gasped, struggling to hold his rifle steady. "Go away."

The longer he stood there, soaking in his own urine and his shame, the angrier he grew. This creature had made no move. Clearly, she posed no threat to him, but she deserved to die all the same.

He looked down the shaking barrel of his rifle, struggling to take aim.

He didn't see the second lion until its jaws closed around his throat.

The only thing Douglas Schrader could do now was pray. From the moment the terrorists had surrounded them he'd been helpless to do anything else to stop them. He'd watched in impotent rage as the devils had taunted his family, tormented them. They'd poked and prodded the women with their knives, threatened in heavily accented English to cut off various body parts and make Schrader eat them. And when they weren't making threats, they were casting lascivious grins at his daughter. Every time they did so, they turned to him and raised their eyebrows, as if to ask, "What are you going to do about it?"

Why was this happening to them? They were doing God's work, yet God had forsaken them. A dark pool of despair welled up inside him as he assessed the situation for what seemed like the thousandth time. He was bound, unarmed, and hopelessly lost. He could only hope for a miracle.

The tent flap opened and one of the guards peered in. Schrader twisted, fighting at his bonds, but failed to break free. Beside him, Melanie let out a fearful whimper. The guard smiled, turned, and closed the tent.

Moments dragged past, and over the roaring in his ears, Schrader heard a voice. He heard it again. Then a surprised cry. And then nothing.

He waited.

He wasn't sure how much time had passed before the tent opened again. This time, a different man peered inside.

"Where is Hassan?"

Schrader had no idea which one Hassan was, much less what had happened to him. He just sat there, glaring at his captor, held fast by his bonds and his utter helplessness.

"Never mind. We are almost ready for you." The man held up a machete, the dim light glinting on its curved blade. His eyes locked with Schrader's and then he drew a finger across his own throat. "Such is the fate of infidels," he growled.

Schrader's insides turned to water and his head began to spin. He wondered if the devils would record it for posterity, release it to the world, perhaps. At least he'd die a martyr—that would be something. *Kill me but spare my family*, he prayed. *It's my fault they're here. Let them go.*

Melanie had not missed the man's threat. She began to sob loudly. Schrader tried to meet her eye, to give her a reassuring look, but he hadn't the strength. It was all he could do to remain upright. He kept his focus on the open tent flap and the back of the machete-wielding man.

And then a tawny blur flashed across his field of vision and the man was gone.

Surprised cries rose outside and figures began running to and fro. He saw more flashes of lightning-fast movement and then heard a burst of gunfire. Somewhere close by, but out of his field of vision, he heard a cry of fear suddenly squelched in a gurgled gasp, and then, to his utter amazement, he watched as a lioness backed past the tent flap, dragging a limp man. Her jaws were clamped tightly just beneath the base of her victim's skull.

He felt a moment of exultation at the grisly sight. Perhaps this was the miracle he had been praying for. And then a new thought struck him. If lions were attacking the camp, how long before they found their way into the tent?

As if in response to his thought, he heard a tearing sound. He turned to see a knife blade slicing through the back wall of the tent. What in the name of all that was holy? That was certainly no lion, and any of their captors would come in through the front door.

Alice had awakened, and she and Melanie scooted over to huddle against Schrader. As they watched, two hands parted the tent wall and a familiar head poked inside. It was the blond man from the lodge! What was his name?

"Shipman?" he rasped.

"Actually, it's Maddock," the blond man said, "but that's not important right now." He stepped inside the tent, deftly sliced their bonds, and then motioned for them to follow him. Holding hands with Alice and Melanie, Schrader stepped out into the cool night air. He couldn't believe his good fortune, but he knew it wasn't over yet. They still had to get away from the kidnappers…and the lions.

"Do you know about the lions?" Schrader whispered. "They're attacking the camp."

"Don't worry about it. We've got it under control. Just stay with me."

Behind them, more gunfire split the night. Schrader stole a glance over his shoulder but could see little. He prayed no one was following them. The way before them began to rise, and he turned and focused his attention on what lay in front of him. Snatches of moonlight filtered through low-hanging storm clouds, shining down on the slope that lay before them.

And on the dark figure that rose up in their path, aiming a rifle in their direction.

Schrader had scarcely processed what he saw when Maddock raised a pistol and, without breaking a stride, fired off two shots. The first bullet took the figure in the chest, the second in the throat. By God, the man could shoot! Schrader had some skill with handguns but he wasn't on Maddock's level. Who was this strange fellow who'd saved them?

The shots seemed to have drawn the attention of the men in the camp, because sharp cries punctuated by gunshots rang out. A bullet buzzed past Schrader's ear, and another pinged the ground at Alice's feet.

"Veer left and keep running!" Maddock turned, hit the ground, and squeezed off a shot in the kidnapper's direction.

Schrader did as he was told, half-dragging his wife and daughter toward the crest of the hill. They were so close. He heard Maddock fire off another round. The man wasn't wasting his ammunition. That sort of efficiency spoke of a high level of professionalism.

The top of the hill loomed just a few yards ahead. "Just a few more steps, girls," he huffed.

And then hot fire pierced his side. For a moment, he thought an insect had stung him, but then the fire grew into an inferno. He cried out, pressed his hand to his side, and pitched forward, hitting the ground face-first.

"Daddy!" Melanie dropped down by his side. With Alice's help, she rolled him onto his back. He stared up at the two people he loved most in the world, and he had only two words for them. "I'm sorry."

"It's not your fault." Tears ran down Alice's cheeks, but she managed a ghost of a smile. "You'll be all right."

Schrader shook his head. "Shouldn't have brought you here."

"Don't talk, Daddy." Melanie caressed his cheek. "Save your strength."

Schrader knew time was short and suddenly there were so many things he wanted to say, so many things he hadn't done. And then a single thought hit him hard. Something he hadn't done.

Maddock appeared out of the darkness. "Let me take a look." He knelt over Schrader and began inspecting his wound, but Schrader barely felt it. There was only one thing on his mind.

"Listen to me."

"Just relax," Maddock said.

"Listen to me!" Schrader poured all his remaining strength into the words. "What I told you about looking for the ark...I have a secret and I don't want it to die with me."

CHAPTER 40

Maddock's heart raced as the sign reading *Lake Natron* flashed past. "Almost there." They'd managed to get Schrader and his family to safety, and with the help of a local pride of lions, decimated the kidnappers. Those that survived had scattered. Maddock hoped the lions, none of whom had suffered so much as a scratch in the encounter, would not become man-eaters. Considering they'd acted under the influence of a Noah Stone, he hoped they would return to their natural states afterward.

Now, armed with information from Schrader, they had driven the two hours to the Ngorongo Conservation Area. Considered one of the natural wonders of the world, this vast protected area stretched from Lake Natron in the northeast to Lake Enyasi in the south and Lake Manyara to the east. The area incorporated the Olduvai Gorge and the Ngorongoro Crater, the largest unbroken caldera in the world. The eight million-year-old crater had once been an active volcano. After going dormant, its collapsed cone formed a crater more than six hundred meters deep and covering an area of more than three hundred square kilometers. It was huge, and it was the place Schrader believed the ark lay.

"So tell me again what Schrader said." Dima held a legal pad in her lap and was mulling over various notes she had taken.

"He said quite a bit." Schrader had been convinced he was going to die, and had confessed to Maddock that he had in his possession an ancient stone tablet he had stolen from a dig years before. Furthermore, if his translation was correct, it confirmed the location of the ark in the Arusha region. Fortunately for him, the bullet had passed through the ample layer of fat at his midsection. It was a painful wound, to be sure, but hardly fatal.

"First, he said that Mount Meru and Mount Meri were not the same place. Then he said, 'Look to the Mountain of God. The truth lies there.'"

"All right." Dima made a mark on her notepad. "Ol Doinyo Lengai is the only mountain anywhere in the Arusha Region that is called by that name. So far, so good."

Called "Mountain of God" in the Maasai language, Ol Doinyo Lengai was an active volcano in the Gregory Rift, located south of Lake Natron within the Arusha Region of Tanzania. Part of the volcanic system of the East African Rift, it uniquely produced natrocarbonatite lava, a darker, cooler form of lava than what was commonly found in most volcanos. Cooler was, of course, a relative term, as the lava still reached temperatures of more than five hundred degrees.

"He also said, 'Find the city of stone. The place of sacrifice.'"

"Which could refer to Engakura." Dima bit the tip of her pen and gazed at her paper. "It's a stone city with a complex irrigation system, but there's no tradition of stone construction in this part of Africa, which makes it unusual. So, it would be the logical place to look."

"It narrows things down a bit," Maddock agreed. "If we have to search the entire area, we might never find it."

"I don't see anyone around," Bones said, craning his neck to look out over the crater as they drew close to the rim.

"The northern area is the most remote," Dima said. "Tourists usually stick to the places that are most easily accessed."

Bones nodded. "Works for me. Fewer people to get in the way."

Maddock had to agree. The last thing they needed was bystanders interfering, or perhaps being harmed, should things go sideways. "Let's hope the rangers stick to the other parts of the crater." Strictly speaking, one was not permitted to descend into the crater without a ranger guide, but they had ignored that rule for obvious reasons.

"If one shows up, we'll deal with it," Bones said. "We've come too far to let park rules stand in our way."

Maddock slowed their four-wheel-drive as they began the steep descent. Down below, a vast expanse dotted with wildlife swept out to the horizon. It was a spectacular sight, one he'd have paid more attention to were he not focused on trying to avoid plummeting to his death.

"Do you think Schrader knew what he was talking about?" Bones asked. "He was frightened and losing blood."

Maddock shrugged a shoulder in a gesture of noncommittal. "I suppose we'll find out soon enough."

"According to this website," Dima said, looking at her phone, "the crater is home to almost every species of African plains mammal. Even the endangered black rhino resides here. Giraffes might have lived here at one time too, but probably migrated away due to the lack of trees which provide their food. There are no impalas or topi, but that's likely due to competition with wildebeests. There's even a huge bird population and the continent's densest group of predators. It definitely sounds like a place where someone might have restocked the continent's animal population sometime long ago."

"You're missing a major upside to what you just read." Bones held up his Noah Stone. "We don't have anything to fear from a population of predators. I am the boss of them. But if the Trident catches up to us, those guys will be fair game."

Maddock nodded. Perhaps, just this once, the Trident wouldn't catch up with them.

It took Schrader a long time to remember where he was. Stress, fatigue, and pain medication had clouded his mind. The bed, the nightstand, and the view of the city through the window were all unfamiliar. What had happened? Where were Alice and Melanie? Why did he hurt?

It was the antiseptic smell that struck a chord. He was in a hospital. Someone had brought him here, but who?

Like watching a movie running backward, a series of murky images swam past his mind's eye.

Blood and bandages.

A huge man with a ponytail carrying him like a baby into the emergency room. That couldn't be real.

A breakneck ride in a stolen jeep. But whose jeep?

Lying on the ground, gazing up at a man with eyes the color of the sea. What was his name?

And then it all came back in a rush. He and the girls had been kidnaped and held captive by Muslim extremists. They had been rescued by two men whom he had met at the lodge. Maddock and Bonebrake were their names—their real names, that is. Schrader had been shot. Fearful that his secret, no, the secret he had stolen, would die with him, he had told Maddock everything.

He felt his cheeks warm at the memory of his confession. What would Maddock do with the information? Would Schrader get the chance to find the ark first, or would Maddock spill the secret, maybe even try to locate the ark himself?

The door to his room opened, and a tall, black man with a shaved head stepped inside. He wore a white coat, but nothing else about him suggested he was a doctor. The man moved with the lithe grace of a predator, and he stalked to Schrader's bedside with grim purpose in his eyes. He didn't consult any charts or monitors, but instead folded his powerful arms and stared down at Schrader.

After a few heart-pounding seconds of wondering who this man was and what he wanted, Schrader finally summoned the courage to speak.

"Can I help you?"

The man smiled. "Yes you can." He had a slight accent, Jamaican, perhaps.

Schrader waited, but the man said no more. "What do you want?"

"I want to know about the men who brought you here."

Schrader frowned. "Why? Are they in trouble?"

"No, but you and your family will be if you do not tell me what I want to know."

A jolt of fright shocked Schrader to wakefulness. He tried to sit up but lacked the strength. "Where are my girls?"

"They are in another room in the hospital, being watched over by one of my associates. The quality of the information you give me will determine their fates, and yours." The man pulled up a chair, sat down, folded his hands, and looked at Schrader with polite interest. "You may begin whenever you are ready. I suggest you make it soon."

Once again, a feeling of helplessness overwhelmed Schrader, and he was reminded how weak he truly was. What use was the armor of God against powerful people who seemed bent on harming him and his family?

"Are you one of them?"

"The people who abducted you? No. My organization and its aims are not so pedestrian as all that. Please, time is short, and the sooner you help me, the sooner I can return your family to you and leave you in peace." He laid a hand on Schrader's arm. "You are not a threat to me, Mister Schrader, so I truly have no interest in doing harm to you and yours." His long fingers closed around Schrader's wrist and he began to squeeze. "But I promise you, you *will* work with me, voluntarily or otherwise."

Schrader had managed to summon a measure of resolve, but he was wise enough to see he had few, if any, options here. The story spilled out of him like an upended bag of marbles. He told the man all he knew about Maddock, Bonebrake, and the attractive young woman with whom they traveled. It wasn't much. When he finished, he searched the man's eyes, trying to read his thoughts.

"Thank you. That is helpful."

Schrader relaxed and closed his eyes.

"Where did they go after they left you here?"

Schrader's eyes snapped open. "I can't say."

"You can't say, or you won't say?"

While Schrader sat, tongue-tied, the man reached inside his coat, took out two syringes, and held them up. "Pancuronium bromide and potassium chloride—two of the chemicals used in lethal injection. The first causes complete paralysis, impairing even your ability to breathe. The second stops your heart. If I inject you with these you will be dead in a matter of minutes."

Schrader found his voice and what remained of his pride. "Kill me, then. If I know something that's of use to you, it will die with me."

The man sighed and clicked his tongue. "I thought you might say that. You are, indeed, a man of strong will."

Schrader hated that a small part of him enjoyed the praise.

"My patience and courtesy are almost at an end. Dane Maddock is looking for Noah's Ark. I have it on good authority that, while you were being treated last night, you were mumbling something about the ark." He stood and took out his cell phone. "My associate has in his possession similar syringes. Perhaps a video chat is in order? You can watch him administer these chemicals to your daughter."

"No, please." Schrader took a deep breath. "All right. I'll tell you." He swallowed hard, fighting against the bile rising in his throat. Was he condemning Maddock to death? He couldn't say for sure, but he was definitely issuing a death sentence upon his own daughter if he didn't tell this man what he wanted to know.

"They've gone to Engaruka."

CHAPTER 41

The remnants of Engaruka spread out across the hilly terrain. First recorded by explorers in the late nineteenth century, the system of ruins was regarded as one of the region's most important archaeological sites. Though explorers had compared the features to castle ruins, and had remarked on its stone circles and impressive structures, its significance was due to its irrigation and cultivation structures. Even knowing this, the site was hardly what Maddock had expected. Rather than impressive feats of masonry, what remained of the ancient city amounted to little more than terraces and the foundations of buildings. In some places, only a few piles of stone remained.

"Doesn't look like much, does it?" Bones mopped his brow and squinted against the midday glare.

"Who cares what it looks like as long as we find what we're searching for?" The heat and their fruitless search were clearly getting to Dima. She rounded on Maddock, hands on hips. "Tell us again what Schrader said about this place."

"Like I said, he was getting less and less coherent. The first thing he said was, 'They came up from the ground.' He didn't say who 'they' were, but given the context, I can only assume he meant Noah and his family, and maybe the animals."

"But he also mentioned the Mountain of God," Bones said, turning his eyes toward Ol Doinyo Lengai looming on the horizon. "It makes it sound like Noah didn't come down the side of the mountain, but instead he came out through an underground passageway."

"Volcanic tubes," Maddock agreed. "We know from experience that's a possibility."

"Yeah, but that's an active volcano up there." Bones nodded toward the peak. "Even if we find the passageway, do you really want to go inside?"

"Tell you what, when we find it, Dima and I will go in and you can stand guard out here. How does that sound?"

"Screw you, Maddock. What else did he say?"

"He said, 'Remember the sacrifice.' I seem to recall Noah made sacrifices to God after the flood waters subsided."

"*Then Noah built an altar to the Lord and, taking some of all the clean animals and clean birds, he sacrificed burnt offerings on it,*" Dima recited.

"So we're looking for an altar?" Bones asked.

"Makes sense to me," Maddock said. "I've kept my eyes open but haven't seen anything." He turned to Dima. "Any suggestions?"

"Engaruka isn't nearly old enough to have been here during the time of Noah, but if it, or an older settlement, grew up in the wake of Noah's arrival, it would make sense that the altar might have been central to their culture." She glanced at a map she had found online and then took a look around. "I think the middle of town, so to speak, would be that way." She pointed to the northeast. "Just over that hill."

Twenty minutes later they found themselves in the midst of a cluster of low walls and stone circles. Maddock turned slowly around, taking it all in. Nothing leaped out at him. What if they were wrong and this was another false trail?

"Are either of your stones reacting at all?" Dima asked with no trace of hopefulness in her voice.

"As cold as my sex life," Bones said.

Dima smirked. "Maybe things will turn around for you once we find the ark." She gave him a wink.

"You hear that, Maddock? Leave no stone unturned! Andale!"

Maddock froze. "What did you say?"

"You already forgot your high school Spanish? Speedy Gonzales. Arriba! Andale! Get your big white butt in gear."

Dima giggled and gave Bones a playful shove.

"No. Before that," Maddock said.

"Leave no stone unturned?"

"Exactly." Maddock turned toward what he estimated to be the very center of town. There stood the remnants of a large building. Only the foundation remained, but its former size and grandeur was clearly evident. He imagined it had once dominated this stretch of the landscape. "Look at the outline of the walls. What does it remind you of?"

Dima saw it immediately. "Six points! The Star of David!"

"What do you say we take a look underneath that big pile of rubble in the middle?"

Bones didn't have to be told twice. He vaulted the wall, climbed up onto the pile of rocks, and began moving stones with surprising vigor considering the amount of time they'd already spent walking in the heat of the day. Maddock and Dima joined in and they fell into a rhythm, working the stones loose and tossing them aside. Little by little, they reduced the heap of stone to a small mound, but they turned up nothing of note.

Maddock was just beginning to wonder if he'd steered them onto the wrong track when Bones whooped. "Jackpot! Take a look at this."

The sun shone down onto a smooth, black stone, so unlike the native rock of the region. They attacked the pile with a renewed sense of purpose. An hour later, they'd cleared a space around a massive, rectangular slab of black stone the size of an ox. Maddock began brushing the surface of the stone, clearing away the dust and dirt to reveal a crude, six-pointed star carved in its surface.

"I think this is it." Reverence reduced Dima's voice to a whisper. "What now?"

Maddock remembered the next thing Schrader had said. "Blood is the key." He slid his belt knife free of its sheath, pricked his thumb with the tip of the blade, and let a few drops of blood dribble onto the stone right at the center of the six-pointed star.

They waited.

Nothing.

"I think you need more blood," Bones said. "Or maybe it has to be an animal sacrifice."

"Maybe, but…"

The ground shifted beneath Maddock's feet and he sprang back. The altar slid to the side, revealing a gaping hole.

Bones clapped Maddock on the back. "Nice job, Maddock. I keep forgetting you aren't as dumb as you are ugly."

"The feeling's mutual." He took a deep breath, sheathed his knife, and took out his Maglite. "What do you say we find Noah's Ark?"

CHAPTER 42

Maddock shone his light down the broad, gently sloping stone ramp that descended into the depths of the earth. Once again he felt the familiar thrill of excitement that came on the precipice of discovery. Despite whatever perils might lie ahead, and the very real dangers that followed behind them, he was now focused on the prize. Were they about to discover the source of perhaps the greatest legend in history? He moved forward, scanning every inch of the space ahead, watching for potential pitfalls, either natural or wrought by human hands. Their footsteps echoed in the hollow stone passage, every breath they took sounded like a thunderclap in the quiet of this domain that hadn't felt the tread of feet in perhaps thousands of years.

"Maddock?" Bones said.

"Yes?"

"I'm sick of lava tubes. Too much sameness." Bones reached out and rapped the wall, making a hollow thump that echoed in the wide passage.

"I think you've said that before."

"I know. I just wanted to make sure you hadn't forgotten. Next time we head off on one of your... adventures, let's keep it above ground if we can."

Maddock stopped cold. "*My* adventures? It was your family's lost stone that got this started, you know."

"Will you two cut it out?" Dima said. "There's something up ahead."

Maddock turned to look. Ten paces in front of them, the passageway divided.

"Decision time," Bones said. "Let's check it out."

When they reached the spot where the passage split they stopped short. Here, the floor was strewn with bones and trinkets.

"What the..." Bones began.

"I think it's a place of sacrifice," Dima said. "Think about it. All the years people lived here, they must have figured out how to make the altar open up."

"If they were using it for sacrifice, it would have opened every time they spilled blood on it," Maddock said. "Unless it requires human blood." He didn't pursue that line of thinking any further.

Dima nodded, chin cupped in her hand, eyes taking in the scene. "I'll wager this is as far as they dared go, so they left offerings here to appease, I don't know, the god of the mountain?"

"That would make sense," Maddock agreed. "In some ways, religion is a byproduct of humankind trying to control the uncontrollable. You make a sacrifice and pray for rain for your crops, or for safety from an erupting volcano." He glanced up as if he could still see the steaming peak of Ol Doinyo Lengai.

"Or escape from your mortality," Bones added.

"Let's not get too deep into theology," Dima said. "We need to decide our next move. Did Schrader offer any hints?"

"I think he finally lost it. He just kept muttering, 'They came two-by-two.' Nothing else." Maddock picked his way across the bone-strewn floor and examined the entrances to the passageways one at a time, shining his light as far down each tunnel as he could He saw nothing amiss with any of them. "What am I missing?" he whispered. He shone his light on the space above the tunnel where he stood. His eyes caught a faint irregularity in the stone.

"Bones, take a look at this."

"Let me guess, you need a boost."

"No, just take a look tell me what you see."

Bones moved to Maddock's side, rose up on his tiptoes, and squinted. "There's something scratched here. Looks like two animals. Doves, I think."

"Two by two," Dima said. "And the dove is a powerful symbol, connected with water and the spirit. Plus, Noah sent a dove out to see if the flood waters had subsided. This must be it." She took a step forward but Bones held her back.

"Hold on, chick. There's always a catch. First, we see if there's an image above the other passageway."

Dima frowned, her eyes flinty, but she didn't argue.

Bones moved to the second passageway and inspected the rock directly above it. "Two pigs. Mmm, bacon."

"I still say we go with the doves," Dima said. "In the Old Testament, the pig is an unclean animal."

"You're right," Maddock said. "And that's why we should avoid the doves."

Dima and Bones turned twin looks of bemusement his way.

"Come again?" Bones said.

"Schrader said they came two-by-two, but not all animals came onto the ark in two's, did they?"

Dima smacked herself in the forehead. "I'm an idiot."

Bones frowned. "If you are, then I'm even worse because I still don't get it."

"Noah needed animals for sacrifice," she began, "but he could only use so-called 'clean' animals. Remember that bit from the *Book of Noah*? 'Two by two and seven by seven.' Obviously, if he brought only two clean animals and sacrificed one…"

"A miniature extinction event," Bones said.

"Exactly. So while Noah brought two of every animal considered unworthy of sacrifice, he brought seven of every clean animal so he could make sacrifices without eliminating his breeding stock."

"So," Maddock said, "the doves didn't come two-by-two, but the pigs did." He moved to the tunnel where Bones stood, the one marked by the unclean animals, and took a deep breath. "Here goes nothing." Taking one last, long look inside, he took a step.

The ceiling didn't fall, the floor didn't collapse, and nothing shot out of the walls to impale him. *I've watched too many Indiana Jones movies.* He took another step, and then another. When he'd taken a dozen, he felt safe enough to tell Bones and Dima the way was safe. They entered as slowly as he had, Dima clutching Bones' arm.

"You might have saved my life, you know," she said to Bones. "If you hadn't stopped me from walking into that tunnel, who knows what might have happened?"

"Yeah, saving hot chicks is sort of my thing. You can thank me later."

Shaking his head, Maddock moved on into the darkness.

CHAPTER 43

"Tyson! I've found something." Ahmed stood in the center of a crumbled building at the center of Engaruka, waving like an idiot. The cloth he'd wrapped around his head had come loose and now dangled off his shoulder like a woman's scarf, yet he seemed oblivious to how he appeared to the men.

Between the heat and the dire nature of their circumstances, Tyson was quickly losing patience with his colleague. If this were a false alarm, Tyson might have to punch him. He strode through the fallen stones and crumbled walls that passed for an ancient city, making his way to where Ahmed waited. A dozen men circled around him, mercenaries hired to help them finish the job. He'd have preferred Trident regulars, but Shawa would never permit it. It was up to Tyson to earn his way back into the man's good books, and he felt he was on the precipice of doing just that.

"What is it?"

"A ramp leading underground." Ahmed beamed. "Right here. There was a giant black stone covering it, but it's been moved aside."

That was interesting. Tyson clambered over the loose stones until he reached Ahmed's side.

It was just as Ahmed had described—a strange, dark stone had been moved, displacing the rubble around it. Down below was a stone ramp leading down to a passageway of some sort. "Well done," Tyson said.

"I found three sets of boot prints. One set was large enough to be the Indian's, and another small enough to be Zafrini's."

"I'd say that seals it. Let's get them." Knowing it was important to instill confidence in the mercenaries, who could be a fearful and superstitious lot, Tyson went first. Finger on the trigger guard of his pistol, he stalked down into the tunnel, shone his light around until he was certain the way was safe, and then called up to his men. "It's clear. Come on down."

One by one, the mercenaries made the drop, with Ahmed last. When they were all together, Tyson gave brief instructions.

"No talking. No flashlights or headlamps unless I give the order. We don't want to warn them of our approach."

The men nodded, recognizing reason and good sense when they heard it.

"Rifles at the ready and safeties on until I give the word. One stray bullet can do a world of damage should we find ourselves in tight quarters."

As he turned and moved forward into the darkness, he allowed himself a smile. He had Maddock and crew cornered, and his men outnumbered theirs nearly five to one. This time he would not fail.

He moved as quickly as he could without making unnecessary noise. He wasn't worried about booby traps. If there were any, Maddock and the others would have exposed them on their way in. Hopefully this would allow him and his men to make up for lost time.

When they came to a place where the passageway split into two, an unsettling place where old bones covered the floor, he barely hesitated. He chose two mercenaries and sent each down a tunnel with instructions to scout ahead fifty meters and report back. The two men nodded, seemingly happy to get away from the great heap of bones, and rushed ahead.

Ten seconds later, a loud crash and a cry of pain rang out from the passageway on the left. Tyson turned on his flashlight and moved to the mouth of the tunnel. Twenty paces in, a solid block of stone had fallen, crushing the mercenary.

"Rock fall in the tunnel," he called over his shoulder. No need to alarm the mercenaries, who didn't seem to have considered there might be dangers beyond that which their quarry presented. "Hopefully the other tunnel is solid."

While they waited for the other scout to report back, Tyson made a quick inspection of the chamber in which they stood. He immediately noticed primitive carvings above each: doves above the booby-trapped tunnel and pigs over the other. He wasn't sure what significance, if any, the images held, but he filed them away for future reference.

Moments later, the scout returned, declaring the way ahead clear. Emboldened, Tyson once again took the lead. He would catch Maddock.

"I don't see any symbols here." Bones stood gazing at the blank wall where the tunnel they followed had come to an abrupt end. "Could we have missed a turn somewhere?"

"Not if our theory about clean and unclean animals is correct," Maddock said. They'd encountered numerous places where the tunnel split or intersected other passageways. Every time, only a single passageway was marked by the unclean animals. He was convinced it was more than good fortune that had brought them this far. They had to be in the right place. "Check everything," he said. "Walls, floor, ceiling. There's got to be something to show us the way."

He dropped to one knee, inspecting the floor, while Dima searched the walls and Bones scanned the ceiling. Maddock saw nothing but rough, gray stone.

"This place is weird-looking," Bones said. "Instead of the usual stalactites and stalagmites, there's all these lumpy, twisty rocks all around. I've never seen anything like it."

"It's a product of the carbonatite magma," Dima said. "It was mentioned in an article about Ol Doinyo Lengai. Because of the magma's low temperature and unusual composition, it doesn't flow like normal lava. It's thick and slow-moving, and thus can harden in unusual shapes. There's no other place like it in the world."

This gave Maddock an idea. He ran the beam of his light down the cavern wall, inspecting the odd shapes that had formed in spots along the walls. One immediately caught his attention. "Maybe I'm just missing Key West, but that looks an awful lot like a lobster to me."

He knelt beside the figure that had caught his attention. Up close, there was no doubt. Someone had worked on this formation, perhaps selecting one that vaguely resembled the sea creature, and carved out claws and a tail to enhance the resemblance.

"Shellfish are unclean," Dima said. "But I don't see any trap door."

Maddock had a feeling he knew what to do. "Blood is the key." He reached for his knife, but Bones stopped him.

"Let me do it this time." Bones drew his own blade, made a small cut on his forearm, and held his arm out.

The moment the first drop of blood hit the stone, it sizzled. They all took a step back and watched as the sculpture turned a deep shade of scarlet. The cavern began to shake, and Maddock feared they had just made a big mistake. Then, with a sharp crack, a huge section of rock broke free and slowly tipped backward and crashed down with a hollow thud.

Silence reigned as they stood enraptured by the secret they had just uncovered. It was hardly the first hidden door Bones and Maddock had discovered, but there was something about what they knew lay behind this one that made it different.

"I think," Maddock said, "we found it."

CHAPTER 44

Maddock could tell the moment he stepped through the doorway that he stood inside a massive space. He swept his light in a circle, revealing a mammoth cavern a good two hundred paces in diameter. All around, alcoves had been walled off with planks, creating makeshift stalls. In some places, the formations created by the magma formed ramps that led up to more alcoves. In total, three levels of irregularly spaced stalls and pens were set in the cavern walls. Water dripped from the ceiling and gathered in a huge pool that took up nearly half the floor space.

"It's incredible." Dima uttered the words in a soft, reverential tone typically reserved for sacred spaces.

"This must be where Noah tended the animals until the flood waters subsided," Maddock said.

Bones walked over to the closest stall and tested one of the boards. "Sturdier than I expected. I wouldn't put any weight on it, though. Where do you think they got the wood?"

"I don't know, maybe from that big wooden ship they floated in on?" Maddock said.

"Fair enough. Excuse my slow brain. This is freaking awesome, so I'm a bit distracted."

They rounded the pool, inspecting the stalls, but all were empty. No artifacts, no animal remains, only bare stone.

"Where do you think we are?" Bones asked. "Inside the mountain?"

"Somewhere far beneath it, I'll wager," Dima said, taking out a camera and snapping pictures.

"Deep enough for water to filter down, probably from the lake." Maddock took one more look all around. "Since there's nothing but stalls here, Noah and his family must have lived somewhere else. Let's try the upper levels."

Since not all the levels were connected with one another, it took a while to cover them, but after some searching, they found a passageway on the third level that led out of the cavern. The way was barred by a wooden gate that shattered when Bones tried to open it.

"Sorry. I thought I was being careful." The big Indian eyed the ceiling of the passageway. "Watch your heads. Lots of low-hanging lava formations here. I wonder if Noah was pint-sized, like Maddock."

"You know Maddock's not short," Dima said, smiling.

"It's my thing. Don't ruin it for me."

"You seem to have a lot of 'things'," she said, ducking down to follow Bones into the tunnel. "Like collecting women?"

"Where did you get that idea?" Bones glanced over his shoulder at her and managed to crack his head on a low outcropping. "Crap! See what you did?"

"Sorry. I just wanted to see how you'd react."

Bones winced and rubbed his head. "Let's just say I'm capable of change if someone gives me a good reason."

Maddock cleared his throat. "If you two would take a break from your episode of *The Bachelor*, you'd see what's through that doorway."

They'd come to the end of the passageway. Beyond it lay another cavern.

Bones turned slowly, careful not to hit his head again. "Whoa!"

This cavern was easily as large as the one from which they'd just come. Here, too, water dripping from the ceiling formed a pool in the center. Up above, the slow flows of magma formed twisted, bulbous shapes like deformed fingers interlaced. Six large, evenly-spaced alcoves stood around the perimeter. Inside those closest to them, Maddock saw signs of habitation: roughly-hewn furniture, stone bowls, and stone and iron implements.

"This is where they lived," Dima said. "It's hard to

believe we actually found it."

They took a few minutes to examine the living quarters up close, Dima recording it all with her camera. The furnishings and implements were crude, but their age and the history behind them made them remarkable. Maddock felt dizzy looking at evidence that Noah had, in fact, lived, and that the ark story was, at its essence, factual.

Bones picked up a stone knife and ran a finger along its edge. "I gotta say, this never gets old. I'm always blown away by what we find."

Smiling, Dima reached out and gave Bones' hand a squeeze. "What do you know? You do have a soul."

Something about the shape of the cavern gave Maddock pause. He moved toward the center, stopped at the edge of the pool, and looked around. And then it struck him.

"All the alcoves are triangular," he said. "They're all about the same size and spaced evenly."

"So?" Bones asked.

"Picture a floor plan of this space. What would it look like?"

Dima gasped. "A six-pointed star! Do you think this place was the original inspiration for the Star of David?"

"Could be. If Noah and his family found shelter here after the flood, this cavern with its safety and fresh water must have seemed like a gift from God. That would explain why Noah carved the shape on the altar stone."

"Speaking of the altar stone," Bones said, "that thing is huge. How do you think they got it from here to there?"

"I don't know," Maddock admitted. "Maybe the answer lies through there." He aimed the beam of his light toward another passageway to their left. "I think we should give it a look."

Up ahead loomed a high, arched opening. Tyson held up a hand, signaling for the others to stop. He could tell by the shape that this was an actual doorway, not another of the many tunnels through which they'd passed. It had taken a bit of trial and error and two more lost mercenaries for him to intuit the meaning of the symbols above the passageways, but he'd finally gotten them here.

Ahmed sidled up to him and craned his head, trying to peer into the darkness. "Do you think this is it?"

Tyson flashed an angry look at Ahmed. "If it is," he said in a voice that carried only to his comrade's ear, "let's not announce our presence to anyone who might be inside. Understand?"

Duly chastened, Ahmed nodded and took a step back.

Tyson turned to face his men. He held a finger to his lips to indicate they should remain silent, and then he turned, moved to the doorway, and listened. He heard nothing, save dripping water. He doused his headlamp, moved forward a few paces, and listened again. Still nothing. Tyson considered this. It was possible that Maddock's party had wandered down the wrong passageway and fallen prey to one of the same traps that his own men had, but he doubted it. Zafrini was brilliant and Maddock and Bonebrake had proven themselves to be resourceful. Tyson had to assume his quarry waited somewhere up ahead. He would have to take a chance.

He turned on his light and stepped out into a cavern. He could tell immediately that this had been a barn of sorts—the place was filled with pens and stalls, with a pool suitable for watering livestock at its center. His heart raced at the thought that thousands of years ago, Noah had tended animals here, and had probably guided them down the very tunnels up which Tyson and his men had come before releasing them into the world.

He looked around, taking in the sights, and felt tension knotting his muscles. This was a dangerous place. All around were spots from which an enemy could stage an ambush. Maddock and Bonebrake could hide in any of the alcoves and fire at him and his men from cover. But what choice did Tyson have but to advance?

They would move quickly and quietly, and strike with ferocity.

The Trident would prevail.

CHAPTER 45

Maddock led the way up a steep incline and out into another cavern, this one smaller than the previous two. What he saw there stopped him in his tracks. Though their entire search had been aimed at this moment, he hadn't fully expected to find it.

"The ark. It's here!"

Before them lay the shattered remains of a wooden boat. Despite its present condition, he could still make out the bow and stern, which remained largely intact. It was huge. Noah and his family could have scavenged boards from it for their entire lives and there would have been plenty to spare. He took a few dizzied steps forward, letting the sense of wonder wash over him. They had done it.

Dima hurried forward to run her hands along the boards of the legendary ship. "I can't believe it." She stepped back, took out her camera, and began snapping pictures. "It's real! I always believed there was truth to the story but I figured even if the ark had existed, it would have crumbled to dust by now." She paused, lowered her camera, and stood beaming at the magnificent sight. "It's magnificent."

"There's something that doesn't make sense," Bones said. "How did the ark get underground?"

"I have a theory." Maddock shone his light up at the ceiling, where the tangles of magma formed a latticework of stone. "I think this was a deep depression or a place where a section of the mountain collapsed and formed this chamber. If the water subsided quickly enough, the ark could have been sucked into it. Unable to climb out, Noah and his family made their home in the caverns. Over time the slow-moving magma formed the ceiling we see now. Like you said, it's still an active volcano, after all."

"Let's hope it doesn't blow until we get out of here." Bones shot a nervous glance at the stone above them. "I don't fancy a race against molten rock, not even the slow kind. We should hurry up and…" Bones froze.

"What is it?"

Bones pointed to the wall to their right. "Dudes. Big stone dudes."

Maddock followed Bones' line of sight. Standing like sentinels against the wall were three stone men. Truth told, they were barely men at all. They resembled vaguely human-shaped stacks of thin, flat stone. Maddock didn't know why he was surprised—the stone men had been a key part of the *Book of Noah*, but to see them in the…not flesh, exactly, was still a shock.

"The Watchers," Dima said.

"They look like Rock 'em Sock 'em Robots," Bones said. "Big, blocky bodies, broad shoulders, square heads and fists."

"Hopefully they don't wake up and start punching us." Maddock moved in to get a better look. Seen up close, each was a mottled pattern of various shades of gray. The stones that formed the creatures were fitted together with such precision that he wouldn't have been able to see the seams were it not for the contrast in the rocks that formed them. He ran a hand along the forearm of the closest Watcher and felt warmth spread through his body. Whether the sensation was real or imagined, he could not say.

"You know, these guys are sort of the heroes of the Noah story," Bones said. "They built the ark and protected Noah and his family. I'll bet they're the ones who placed the altar stone over the entrance to the passageway."

"I can't think of a word to describe them. All the superlatives I know just fall short." Dima once again raised her camera and began snapping photographs of the stone sentinels.

Maddock would have been content to stand there and admire the Watchers, but Bones nudged him.

"Do you feel warm?"

"I do. I think it's…wait a minute." He reached into his pocket and drew out his Noah Stone. "The third stone! It's somewhere close by!"

"It's got to be on the other side of the ark. Let's go!" Bones hurried over to the broken middle section of the ship, which now was little more than a giant heap of broken boards, and climbed over. When he reached the top, he whistled in surprise. "Bro, you have got to see this."

"I see another passageway up ahead. Do you want me to investigate?" Ahmed seemed to have finally mastered the art of speaking softly. Perhaps being brought up short in front of the men had finally made an impression on him.

"No. I'll go first." After the booby traps, Tyson had sensed the mercenaries' confidence flagging, and he'd made certain to take the lead as often as possible. Long ago he'd learned what he called the Teddy Roosevelt Principle—men would willingly follow a confident leader who was not afraid to put himself in the line of fire.

The passageway was steep, and he moved slowly along it. He had a strong feeling they would catch up with Maddock soon. They'd already found the place where the animals were kept, and the place where Noah and his family had apparently lived. What was left, except the last stone?

And the prize he coveted most.

When the mouth of the passageway came into sight, he halted. The others stopped behind him.

All was quiet.

Tyson concentrated, bringing his senses to bear. He heard the beating of his heart, the rush of blood in his ears, the slow intake of breath from the men who stood close by.

And then he heard the sound of voices up ahead, so soft he could not make out the words, but there could be no doubt—they had finally overtaken Maddock. Smiling, he turned to his men and nodded. The moment was at hand, but there was no cause for haste. This had to be done properly. It was time to plan their attack.

CHAPTER 46

On the other side of the remnants of the shattered ark, a dozen steps led up to an alcove. Maddock went first, the stone in his hand growing hotter with every step. He couldn't yet see what waited for them at the top of the stairs, but he could tell that the alcove had been carved with images of the sea: cresting waves, leaping dolphins, and coiled tentacles. His breath caught in his chest. This had to be it. When he reached the top, he froze, his eyes locked on a wondrous sight.

"What do you see? Is it..." Dima choked on her words when she reached his side. Behind her, Bones cursed and stopped short.

The body of a man lay on a simple block of stone. His wizened skin was a light shade of brown and stretched tightly across his frame. Long white hair spilled over his shoulders. His snowy beard was knotted in a braid that ran down the center of his chest. He wore only crumbling loincloth and a shark's tooth necklace on a silver chain.

"Noah." Dima dropped to her knees before the legendary figure. "I can't believe he's real."

But Maddock wasn't looking at the body of the Biblical patriarch. "I, for one, can't believe what he's holding."

His words seemed to rouse Bones and Dima from their stupor, and they finally took notice of the object Noah held in a literal death grip.

"A trident!" Dima said.

Lying diagonally across Noah's chest was a golden trident. A little more than a meter in length and the thickness of a man's thumb, the ancient weapon gleamed in the triple beams of their flashlights. Maddock's eyes followed the line of the three-pronged fork upward to the tip of the center prong, where a familiar-looking black stone was embedded.

"The third Noah Stone," he said.

"What does this mean?" Dima asked. "The *Book of Noah* said God sent the stones from the sky. This doesn't seem to match the story."

Maddock glanced at Bones, who nodded. They were clearly thinking the same thing.

"It could have come from the sky," he said.

"What do you mean?"

Before Maddock could answer, the sound of running feet caught his attention. He whirled about and saw nearly a dozen bobbing lights moving into the cavern.

"Turn out your lights. The Trident is here."

Dima dropped to the ground as bullets buzzed through the air like angry hornets, ricocheting off the half-dome of the alcove where Noah had been laid to rest. All around her, the brittle lava shattered, spraying her with sharp fragments. She couldn't believe what was happening. It was all she could do not to scream and run in panic. Somewhere close by, she heard Maddock and Bones return fire. She forced her eyes to open and looked to see what transpired.

It was a dizzying scene played out in darkness. The attackers had turned out their headlamps, and now only bits and pieces of the cavern were illuminated for a split-second at a time by the strobe-like bursts of muzzle flash. She could track the movement of the Trident's men by their torrents of gunfire, and Maddock and Bones appeared to be waiting to target those flashes. She spotted Bones, kneeling atop the ark's broken stern. He fired off a single shot and then rolled to the side as bullets tore through the spot he'd occupied an instant before.

More gunshots, and then a distant cry of pain. She could tell by the spot from which the sound had come that one of the Trident's men had gone down. Good! Of course, based on her observations, she estimated another ten or so remained. What were they going to do?

Maddock and Bones couldn't possibly hold out against so many, could they?

A flashlight flicked on in the bow of the ark, and the Trident replied with a torrent of lead. What was Maddock doing? He was going to get himself killed.

As soon as the thought passed through Dima's mind, Maddock rose up from a spot three meters away and fired into the knot of Trident men. One screamed in agony. But the others returned fire.

A bullet clipped the ground inches from Dima's outstretched hand and she cried out in alarm. "Oh my God!"

"Dima! Find cover!" Bones shouted.

His words jolted her into action. She belly crawled around behind the bier on which Noah's body lay, and curled up in a ball, trembling.

"Running low on ammo," she heard Bones say. Maddock didn't reply

She'd always thought of herself as capable and independent, but now she was entirely out of her depth. She cursed herself for her cowardice and her inability to do anything to save them. A sudden rage flooded her, and with it came a renewed sense of determination.

Think, Dima. There's got to be something you can do.

But what? There would be no miracle this time. Bones couldn't use his stone to call in another pride of lions. And then it struck her. There was another stone within her grasp. She only required the courage to stand and take it.

Trembling from head to foot, she climbed to her feet and felt for the trident. Her hands found something stringy and her stomach twisted in revulsion as her fingers tangled in Noah's hair. Focusing, she felt along his leathery corpse until she felt cool metal. The trident!

She tugged at it, but it wouldn't come free. Even from the grave Noah would not relinquish his prize so easily. She pulled again, and it slid and inch, but no farther.

"No, no, no." She slid her hands down the length of the metal shaft until she found one of Noah's hands. "So…very…gross," she muttered as, one at a time, she pried his fingers back until they snapped. She repeated the operation with his other hand and drew the trident free.

Down below, bullets still flew. The men who attacked them hadn't made it past the ark yet. Maddock and Bones were putting up one heck of a fight.

"This had better work."

She closed her eyes and pressed her palm down on the point of the stone.

Tyson sprang to the side and rolled as the sharp crack of breaking rock reverberated through the air all around him. He looked up, straining to see in the darkness. Another crack, and then another. What was that? Were the walls coming down on them?

The floor beneath him shook as loud, booming thuds echoed around the room. Those weren't gunshots; they were deep, thunderous sounds that shook him to his core.

One of his men screamed, the sound dying in a wet squelch.

More bursts of gunfire, but the shots were no longer aimed at the ark.

"What are you doing?" he shouted.

A headlamp flicked on, and in the glow, he recognized Ahmed. Idiot! He'd be dead in an instant.

But no shot came. Were Maddock and Bonebrake out of ammunition? Perhaps it was time to rally the men for an all-out charge.

And then the beam of Ahmed's lamp, bouncing wildly about the cavern, fell on an ungodly sight.

Three stone giants moved slowly, inexorably toward a cluster of Tyson's men. They were hideously human in their general form, but their bodies were featureless stacks of shifting stones. The mercenaries gave way, blazing away with their automatic rifles as they drew back from the monstrosities, but the bullets pinged harmlessly off the giants.

As Tyson's men continued to fire in vain at the oncoming creatures, a single shot rang out from atop the ark and one of the men fell. So the enemy wasn't out of the fight just yet.

Tyson fired off a single burst in the direction of the shooter, though he knew it would be too late to hit his target. The emergence of the giants had dulled his senses and slowed his reaction time. He had to do something to pull his men together.

In the middle of the chamber, Ahmed suddenly found a measure of reckless courage. He let loose a cry of rage, punctuated with a burst of gunfire, and charged the giants. It was a heroic sight, to be sure.

Until one of the giants stepped forward and brought his hands together, crushing Ahmed's skull like a grape.

That did it. The men scattered. A few turned on their headlamps and ran for it, barreling down the passageway that led out, the giants in steady pursuit.

When the last stone man disappeared into the tunnel, all fell silent.

Tyson sat motionless, focusing his thoughts. He knew only a couple of his men had fled down the tunnel. By his calculations, he had five remaining. More than enough to finish the job.

"The giants are gone!" he shouted. "Charge the ark!"

CHAPTER 47

The cavern was quiet. Too quiet. Maddock knew all the Trident's men had not fled when the Watchers came to life. The rest were still here, hunkered down, waiting to resume the assault.

That was not good. Up to this point their attack had been disorganized, and that had worked to his and Bones' advantage. The men had been too fearful for their own lives, too cognizant of their own mortality, to commit to full-out onslaught. They had moved around, putting a heap of bullets in the air, hoping to take him and Bones out without fully engaging. Now, with their ammunition dwindling, a full-scale attack would put an end to things.

"I'm out," Bones whispered from somewhere close by. "Got any ideas?"

"The giants are gone!" a voice rang out. "Charge the ark!"

"That's it," Bones said. "Dima, can you bring them back?"

"I couldn't control them," came her frightened voice. "I'm sorry. The stone was so powerful. It was just too much for me."

The stone! Perhaps it wasn't over yet.

"Bones, take my Walther. I've got four bullets left." Maddock held the weapon out in the direction of Bones' voice and felt his friend's hand close on it.

"What have you got up your sleeve?" Bones asked.

"A Hail Mary."

Maddock ducked as the Trident's men opened fire again. He dug into his pocket and took out his Noah Stone, the Templar Stone, and pressed it hard into his palm.

From his spot in the bow of the ark, he reached out with his thoughts, searching for water.

It was all around them. It flowed through tiny cracks in the stone up above, seeping down into the pools they had seen before. It moved downward to an underground river far below them. It was there if Maddock could only make use of it.

He tuned out the sounds of battle, trusting Bones to keep them alive just a little bit longer, and concentrated with all his might.

Pressure, like invisible hands, closed in on him. His head spun as the breath was slowly squeezed from his body. He felt the water, he called to it, but would it heed him as it had done for Noah so many thousands of years ago?

More gunshots, more footsteps coming closer. Time had almost run out.

It began with a trickle.

A few fat drops fell on his face. All around came the drip drop of falling water, quickly rising to a thunderous crescendo like a thousand storms.

Confused shouts rose from the attackers, followed by a sharp command to keep going.

Maddock opened his eyes.

A lightning-sharp crackle split the air as the ceiling shattered and a torrent like waterfall gushed down from above.

The bullets stopped flying. Lights flickered on as the surviving men tried to comprehend what was happening. Nearby, Bones had dropped the Walter and was struggling to crawl back toward the stone steps atop which Dima waited. Beneath him the mountain of wood that was the remains of the ark shifted as, piece by piece, the surging waters began to carry it away.

Down in the chamber below, Maddock sensed the pool rising, slowly filling the massive space, spinning in a wicked maelstrom. The Trident's men were now in full retreat. Maddock watched the bobbing lights as some ran and some were swept toward the whirling maw down below. Beneath his feet, the ark began to break apart and he felt himself falling.

"Maddock, you've got to stop it!" Bones called above din.

"I know!" he shouted. But could he?

Once again he pressed the stone into his hand, letting the blood flow across its smooth surface. Once again, he reached out with everything he had, everything he was, and found the water. This time, he pushed back against the surging force of nature.

It was like trying to hold back the tide. Pushed forward by its natural momentum and drawn along by the hands of gravity, the water above them continued to pour down upon them. Maddock's mind was battered by the resistance to his efforts as surely as the falling water pounded his body. The ark continued to crumble and he fell hard, and began to slide. It was hopeless. He couldn't overcome the force of nature.

But the stone could. He needed to find another way.

He couldn't close the broken ceiling above them, but perhaps he could redirect the flow. He cast his mind out, following the water through the twists and turns as it flowed through the broken magma, through the bedrock, and back to its source in the lake far above them.

Find another way.

The lava tubes! The mountain was filled with them. With the full force of his will he drove the water toward the hollow spaces beneath Ol Doinyo Lengai. He pressed it into the tiniest fissures, through the soft earth, through the tiniest crevasses.

As he pushed, the pressure seemed to rebound on him tenfold. He stopped sliding across the floor, held fast by an unseen force. Water sluiced over and around him filling his mouth and nostrils. Heavy planks from the shattered ark pounded his body. He struggled for breath, fought to push the water from his lungs, but he could not.

If these are my last moments on earth, I'm going to make them count.

He poured his last drops of strength and will, paltry as they were, into the effort.

And he felt it.

At its headway, the water broke through. It poured into the lava tubes and flowed back into the heart of the volcano, boiling, hissing, and steaming as it met the inferno deep in the heart of the earth. Fire and water, forever at war.

The downpour abated, slowing to a steady drizzle. Maddock rolled over, pushed himself up onto all fours, and vomited a small pond onto the smooth stone. He sucked in a deep, wet breath, relishing the sweet oxygen that filled his lungs. Slowly, the pressure subsided, the fatigue drained away, and he staggered to his feet.

The ark was gone. All that remained was a tangle of wood partially blocking the passageway through which they had come. He turned around, eyes searching for Bones, and spotted him standing at the base of the steps, looking up.

Maddock took one step and then froze.

Tyson stood in the alcove where Noah's body lay. He had one arm around Dima's waist and a gun pressed to her temple.

"It's over," Tyson said. "Give me the stones."

CHAPTER 48

"Give me the stones," Tyson repeated. He had tossed his headlamp aside, and it lay at his feet, shining up and casting him in sinister shadow. His eyes gleamed with a zeal bordering on madness. "They rightfully belong to the Trident. Hand them over now."

"We're not giving you anything," Maddock said.

Tyson's laugh chilled his marrow.

"You will give them to me, voluntarily or otherwise. I have enough bullets to finish the three of you." He twisted the gun, grinding the barrel into Dima's head for emphasis. "Starting with her."

"You think you're that good?" Maddock began to slowly move forward, mind racing, hoping to find a way out of this.

"I don't have to be good to put a bullet in Zafrini's brain. And unless you've grown wings, neither of you can make it up the steps in time to stop me." He sneered, baring his straight white teeth. "The way I see it, you have two options: give me the stones and I let the three of you walk away; or watch Zafrini die, after which I will kill you and take the stones. Make up your mind quickly. My offer expires in about ten seconds."

An icy certainty, colder than the water that still rained down from the ceiling, enveloped Maddock. There would be no diverting Tyson from his course. He would kill Dima without a moment's hesitation.

"What's to stop you from killing us once you have the stones?" he asked.

"Nothing. But I assure you, I only want the stones. Once I have them, you will be as insects to me. Sometimes an insect gets crushed beneath the boot, but often they scurry away into the holes from which they came. I am offering you that chance."

"Don't do it," Dima said. "This is all my fault. I

should have destroyed that page the moment I got it."

"No," Bones said. "They still would have come looking for this." He took out his family's Noah Stone and held it up.

"I mean it!" Dima shouted. "If the Trident gets the stones, who knows what they'll do? They might destroy the world with them, for all we know."

This time, Tyson's laugh held a touch of mirth. "Destroy the world? The stones are not weapons of mass destruction. I thought you were an expert, but you know nothing." He looked down at Bones. "Last chance. Bring the stones, lay them on the top step, and back away."

"You'll let her go?" Bones asked.

"Of course. She's useless to me."

Bones turned to Maddock. "Give it to me."

"Bones, I…"

"Give it to me, Maddock." He lowered his voice. "I can't let her die."

There was such pain in his friend's voice that Maddock couldn't possibly say no. Besides, Tyson was correct—they had no choice. He searched Bones' eyes for any indication that he had a plan, but all Maddock saw there was desperation.

Maddock handed the Templar Stone to Bones and turned his eyes toward Tyson. Disgust filled every fiber of his being. He hated losing, and even more, he hated giving up. There had to be something he could do.

Bones made his way up the steps, hands held out at his sides, moving slowly to show he wasn't about to try anything stupid.

"That's far enough," Tyson said when Bones neared the top. "Put them down and back away."

Maddock could tell it was costing his friend everything to comply. If Maddock hated surrender, Bones despised it. Maddock moved to the base of the steps to stand behind Bones.

"Send Dima down to us and we'll leave," he said.

"In a moment." Tyson shoved Dima to the ground, took three steps forward, and scooped up the stones. He returned to the top of the stairs and stood gazing down at the body of Noah. Dima sat nearby, frozen in fear.

"The trident," Tyson said, raising the golden weapon aloft. "With this we shall once again claim the power of Poseidon himself!"

"Poseidon! Are you saying Noah was the Greek god of the sea?" Maddock asked, their perilous situation momentarily forgotten in light of Tyson's bizarre statement.

Tyson's lips curled in a sneer. "Simple man. Poseidon is much older, much greater than any of the so-called patriarchs of the Bible. The trident, the vessel for his power, was lost ages ago, long before the fall of Atlantis. It fell into the hands of Noah, and he abused that same power."

"What are you talking about?" Dima rose to her feet and inched toward the steps, keeping as far from Tyson as possible. "He used the stones to do God's bidding."

"That is the story you've been told, but it is a lie. Noah thought himself better than those around him, believed his line purer. He committed genocide, used the power of the stones to purge his lands and begin again. The power of earth, water, and life." He held up the other two stones.

"That's crap," Bones said.

"Believe anything you like. The trident is the ultimate power. Look at it." He held the weapon high. "The power of three, the Trinity itself, sprang from the loins of the trident. Even the holy menorah is the offspring of this, the earth's greatest force. And now you shall witness its power for yourself."

"No!" Dima shouted. "Bringing the stones together means death. The *Book of Noah* said so."

"Another lie, spread by Noah himself to prevent anyone else from daring to harness the power. His son, the ancestor of my leader, tried to take it for himself but failed. Now the power is mine."

"You can't." Dima snatched at the trident, but Tyson batted her hand aside and gave her a shove, sending her tumbling to the ground.

"Dima!" Bones mounted the stairs but Tyson quickly drew his pistol and trained it on Bones.

"Stop."

Bones froze, hands in the air.

"It would be a shame if I killed you all before you saw the true power of the trident." He took one of the Noah Stones and slid it into one of the trident's empty tines. It clicked into place with a metallic hum.

"Please, I'm begging you," Dima said. "You don't know what it might do. You'll kill us all."

"I know exactly what it will do. It will bring us one step closer to harnessing the power of the ancient world." With a smile, he clicked the final stone into place.

CHAPTER 49

Maddock shielded his eyes as brilliant light erupted from the trident. He staggered backward, regained his balance, and dared an upward glance.

Tyson stood in a nimbus of gold, head thrown back in ecstasy, the trident upraised in his clenched fist.

"I can feel it!" he cried. "It is so…" Whatever it was, the words escaped him. He turned slowly on the spot, enraptured by the power of the shining artifact of another world.

Dima scrambled down the steps and hurled herself into Bones' arms. "Isn't there anything we can do?" she gasped.

"Let's just get the hell out of here." Bones turned and headed for the door.

"Stop!" Tyson's voice was a thunderclap that shook the chamber. "You will stay and witness my glory."

He loomed over them like the Greek god he so ardently worshiped. The golden light began to creep along his arm. Where it touched him, flecks of gold like tiny stars shone in his dark skin. "Yes! Come to me, Poseidon. Bestow upon me your power."

"If I had even one bullet left, I'd shoot him," Bones growled.

As the light continued to consume Tyson, sparks began to fly from the points of the trident. They shot up to the ceiling and clung there. Soon the sparkling light danced all over the cavern, sizzling where it touched the still-falling drops of water.

"This place is changing," Tyson boomed. "It will be my throne room. From here shall the Trident rule."

"His throne room?" Dima said. "That thing is doing something to his brain."

"I think he was already unhinged," Bones said softly. "Dima, why don't you see if you can slip out of here?

Maddock and I distract him. Don't worry, we'll catch up with you as soon as we can."

"I won't leave you." She shook her head, long dark hair spilling over her face. "This isn't over yet."

Tyson cried out again in a sound a touch too inhuman to be a laugh. Maddock and the others covered their ears as the shrill sound pierced their eardrums. Behind them, a chunk of ceiling broke off and crashed to the ground.

The light now covered Tyson's body. His clothing had burned away, and he stood there cloaked in flashing gold. The light began to pulse, slowly at first, and then faster, and with each flash, an image began to form.

Maddock squinted to make it out, but it quickly resolved into the outline of tall, muscular man with mahogany skin, long, white hair, a twisted beard the color of seaweed, and flashing golden eyes. Faster and faster the image flickered like an old projector skipping frames. Tyson, then the image, and then Tyson again. Back and forth it went.

The glowing form seemed to grow firmer, more tangible by the second. Inside it, Tyson began to struggle. He twisted and jerked, teeth gritted, spittle dripping from his lips.

"What…is…happening?"

"It's trying to take control of him!" Dima shouted.

As if the figure carried real weight, Tyson's shoulders hunched, his waist bent, and then his knees buckled and he dropped to his knees. All around the cavern, the golden lights burned with searing intensity, and the dripping water turned to steam, filling the air with hot mist.

Snarling, Tyson regained his feet, and for a moment, he seemed to be winning the battle against the force that fought to overcome him. His eyes turned toward Maddock and the others, standing frozen at the foot of the steps.

"That's it. A sacrifice!" he cried. "Poseidon demands a blood tribute." He leveled the trident at Dima.

"No!" Bones threw himself in front of Dima as triple bolts of fine, golden lightning crackled from the points of the trident and shot toward him.

Maddock was already in motion as the surge of electricity blew his best friend off his feet. In one fluid motion, he drew his knife and hurled it at Tyson as he ran.

Tyson never saw it coming. He screamed as the blade took him in the eye. He thrashed about, lightning still bursting forth from the trident. All around them, the walls began to crack and water once again poured through.

Maddock was up the steps in a flash. As Tyson turned, half-mad with pain, to face him, Maddock leaped and struck the man full in the chest with a double side-kick that sent Tyson crashing into the wall. The trident slipped from his grasp and clattered across the floor, coming to rest against the back wall, which cracked and split as the still pulsing weapon struck it. A section of wall fell away to reveal a previously hidden passageway.

The golden sparks still spun around Tyson, who struggled to rise. Maddock lashed out with another kick, connecting with his temple, then followed with a vicious knee to Tyson's forehead. Tyson slumped to the ground, unconscious. The golden nimbus flickered and died, but golden sparks still danced in his skin.

"Maddock! Help me!" Down on the floor, Dima was performing CPR on Bones.

Maddock's knees nearly buckled at the sight of his friend, his brother in all the ways that mattered, lying still on the floor. He hurtled down the stairs, dropped to the ground beside Bones, and pressed an ear to his friend's chest.

He heard nothing.

Maddock quickly took over the resuscitation efforts. First two rescue breaths, and then a series of chest compressions.

"Come on, Bones," he urged.

All around them, the chamber was coming apart.

Water gushed in from holes burned in the stone by the golden sparks. It was a deluge that Maddock knew wouldn't be stopped this time. If Bones didn't come back to them soon…

And then Bones coughed, and his chest began to rise and fall on its own. He hacked, coughed again and sat halfway up, resting on his elbows.

"Come on, buddy, let's get you on your feet." Maddock tried to slip an arm around his friend, but Bones shoved him away.

"No time for hugging. Let's get out of here." Bones lurched to his feet, wobbled, and took a look around.

"Nice waterfalls. Are we screwed, or what?"

"Maybe not," Maddock said. "I think there's a way out behind Noah. Come on."

They hurried up the stairs, shielding their heads from the falling rock. At the top, they rounded the bier and headed for the passageway the trident had blasted open.

The trident!

Maddock searched for it, but it was gone, washed away by the pouring water or crushed beneath falling rock. Either way, it was probably better off buried here.

"Maddock!" Bones grabbed Maddock by the belt and yanked him back into the shelter of the passageway as a huge section of ceiling collapsed, burying Noah, perhaps for all eternity.

"Thanks."

"No sweat. Just answer one question for me." Bones stared intently at Maddock.

"What's that?"

"Did you do the rescue breathing, or was it Dima?"

Maddock threw back his head and laughed.

"I'm serious, Maddock," Bones protested. "I need to know."

"We'll talk about it later. For now, let's see where this passageway leads."

CHAPTER 50

It was well past midnight when they emerged from the warren of underground passageways that twisted and turned beneath the slopes of Ol Doinyo Lengai. It had been a long, difficult climb, with only their cell phones for light, but they'd kept at it, taking every passageway with even the slightest uphill slant, hoping to find a way to the surface. All the while, the sounds of destruction had chased them along as the chambers that had lain hidden for thousands of years were washed clean by the deluge and buried beneath a mountain of stone. It was a shame, Maddock thought, but fitting in a way that a flood should be the agent of its demise. Again and again the ground shook beneath their feet, but the tunnels through which they traveled held fast.

They lay on the rocky mountain slope, battered and bloodied, but alive. The chill night air sliced through their sodden clothing. Dima pressed her body against Bones for warmth, but Maddock kept his distance. After the CPR incident, he knew Bones would have no interest in sharing body heat. He didn't care; he was happy to be alive.

The moon hung high in the velvet sky, casting the land beneath in silver light. It amazed him that the world could lie at peace, blissfully ignorant of the destruction wrought far beneath the mountain. After witnessing the terrible power that had been unleashed, it somehow seemed wrong to bask in the serenity of the African night.

Maddock gave their group a half-hour to rest before he insisted they begin working their way down the mountain. Climbing after dark wasn't exactly safe, but hypothermia was a real threat considering the temperature and their thin, wet clothing and weakened conditions. At least they were down on the lower slopes and the moon provided more than enough light for them to find their way. It should be a safe descent.

"I don't suppose there's any chance of recovering the trident?" Dima clung tightly to Bones' arm as if she feared he might get away if she were to let go.

Maddock had a feeling his friend would have no easy time shaking that girl.

"I doubt it. My gut tells me the whole place caved in. You heard the sounds."

"And felt them, too," Bones added.

"It's not that I want it, or anything," Dima said. "But if it can be recovered, I would hate to see it to fall into the wrong hands."

"Amen to that, sister." Bones gave her a squeeze.

"Don't call me 'sister.' It's creepy."

"True. Besides, Maddock is the one who's into sisters."

Maddock stopped in his tracks. "Wait a minute. She's not *my* sister. As a matter of fact, someone in this group did date my sister, and it wasn't Dima and it sure as hell wasn't me."

"Is that a fact?" Dima quirked an eyebrow at Bones. "Funny, I don't recall you mentioning that."

"I've dated a lot of chicks. It's hard to keep track." Bones paused. "That didn't make it any better, did it?"

"Not even a little bit."

Buoyed by the joy that only comes from narrowly averting death, they kept up the light banter as they continued down the slope and into the valley.

"Where's our car?" Dima asked when they'd finally come down off the slopes.

"A few miles that way," Maddock said. "Still a bit of a hike, but we can handle it."

"You know what I just realized?" Bones rose up on his toes and looked around. "This valley is full of predators and we lost the stone that lets us make friends."

Maddock shook his head. "It's all right. After what we've been through, I'll take my chances."

EPILOGUE

It was a balmy day in Key West. A stiff breeze blew in from the Gulf, filling the air with a pleasant hint of the sea. Maddock and Angel sat on the deck of Maddock's condo, soaking in the sun and suds. Maddock tried to lie back and relax, but Angel's skimpy bikini, a star-spangled, red, white, and blue number, kept him pleasantly distracted. From inside, the sounds of boisterous conversation drifted out, along with strains of The Police playing on the stereo. Bones and Dima were regaling Willis, Matt, and Corey with the story of their search for the ark. As usual, Bones was doing most of the talking and all of the embellishing.

"Dude, I'm serious. Big, freaking, stone giants!"

"C'mon," Willis said. "Dima, is he messing with us?"

"If Bones says he saw them, I'll take him at his word," Dima said mildly.

Bones sputtered a protest over the raucous laughter.

Maddock smiled and closed his eyes. Things were just as they should be.

"Maddock, we need to talk." Angel rolled over onto her side, tipped her sunglasses up, and fixed him with her doe-eyed gaze that he always found difficult to resist.

"What about?" he said with a touch of trepidation.

"First of all, we need better music. You know, something from this century."

Maddock chuckled. "Talk to Corey. He's spinning the discs."

"That's what I'm talking about. Nobody says 'spinning discs.'"

"What can I say? I'm an old soul." He took a swig of Dos Equis and gave her a wink.

"We also need to talk about redecorating this place. It's all boats and ocean crap."

"I like boats and ocean crap."

Angel smiled, reached out, and caressed his arm. "But it's not going to be your bachelor pad much longer. It needs a bit of a woman's touch. And we'll also have to get the baby room ready."

Maddock's beer slipped from his limp fingers and clattered to the deck, spilling its frothy contents. He sat bolt upright. "Baby? What?"

Angel fell back onto her deck chair, laughing. It took her several seconds to catch her breath. "It's too easy with you," she said, wiping tears of mirth from the corners of her eyes. "I swear, I wish I had that on video."

Maddock took several deep, slow breaths before he trusted himself to speak. "You are a wicked woman."

"And that is why you love me." She sat up, leaned over, and kissed him deeply. "But on a serious note, we do need to talk about setting a date."

"Sorry to interrupt." Avery stepped out onto the deck. "I heard you made it back safely from another of your shenanigans."

"Great to see you, sis." Maddock stood and made to give her a hug, but she pushed him away.

"I don't need your sweat on me," she said, grimacing at the sight of his dripping body.

"I'll take a hug. I don't mind a little sweat." Tam Broderick poked her head out the door, smiling. She was clad in short shorts and a form-fitting tank top. "I even dressed for the occasion."

"You don't look right in anything but a power suit," Maddock joked as he leaned in to hug her.

"Thanks, I guess. I was hoping we could talk."

"Sure." He turned to Angel and Avery. "Will you two excuse us?"

Angel nodded, then mouthed, "This isn't over."

Maddock had to laugh. That was one talk he wasn't going to be able to weasel his way out of. He slipped on a shirt and he and Tam found an empty room where they could speak privately.

"Thanks again for the help you gave us," he said. "Stone was a lifesaver."

"I've found him useful. Speaking of Stone, he wants to put the *Book of Noah* back where you all found it. He thinks he can do it without raising any alarms this time. He seems to have taken it as a personal challenge."

"Are you going to let him do it?"

"Hell, no. The Vatican already knows it's gone, so the damage is done. I'm going to put it somewhere safe. Who knows when we might want or need it again."

"So Dima did give it to you?" Maddock had feared she might renege on the deal.

Tam nodded. "She couldn't wait to get rid of it. Now, tell me everything."

Maddock took his time recounting events since the assault on Bones' grandfather. He left nothing out. Though Tam always had a hidden agenda, she had demonstrated herself to be his ally, and a useful one at that. When he finished, she nodded thoughtfully, mulling things over.

"Do you think the stones were Atlantean?" she asked.

"I don't know. Tyson used the phrase, 'Long before the destruction of Atlantis.' I don't know how literally we should take that, though."

"So the Trident's goal is to reclaim the powers of the ancient world, and I assume they are talking *really* ancient. Even a few years ago I would have thought the whole thing was crazy. I'll say this much—my life has been very different since I met you."

"Join the club. I'm the one who keeps running afoul of these nuts. If the Trident has a naughty list, I assume I'm now on it."

"Lord Jesus, I thought the Dominion was a headache." She pressed her fingers to her temples and turned to gaze out the window at the street below. "I'll bring this story to the powers-that-be. Since our big discovery I've got a bit more credibility when it comes to this mystical stuff, but I still don't think many people believe me, and dealing with it is above my pay grade."

"Don't present it to them as mystical. Tell them it's

extremely advanced technology."

"You think I don't already do that?" She turned, tilted her head, and gave him a sly smile. "If you're on the Trident's list, the safest place for you is working for me. You know you've got a standing job offer."

"Right. Then it'll be my job to put myself in danger every day instead of just every once in a while. I'll stick to my treasure hunting."

"If you say so." Tam turned around to face him. "How's that going, by the way?"

"Are you trying to tell me you don't already know?"

Tam held up her hands. "All right, I admit I keep tabs on you, but I haven't seen any of your financials since you left the squad."

"You're a piece of work, you know that? Do I have any privacy where you're concerned?"

"I promise there are no cameras in your toilet."

Maddock wished he could stop himself from laughing. He resented the way Tam intruded on people's lives and sometimes wielded private information like a club. At least she didn't seem to be doing that now.

"For your information, after Bones and I left for Turkey, the crew went back to the Templar wreck site and made a nice haul. It should bring a hefty price and keep us afloat for some time."

"Good for you." Her smile seemed genuine, but you never knew with Tam. "Speaking of treasure hunting, I've got something I'd like for you to look into that's right up your alley. I'll pay you, plus anything you salvage will be yours, but it can't be known you're working for me."

"Tam, I just said I don't want to work for you."

"You'll be an independent contractor. Come on. A paycheck, treasure, and the chance to erase the red from your page in my ledger."

"Somehow I think I'll always be in your debt." He sighed. "All right. Tell me about this job."

End

ABOUT THE AUTHOR

David Wood is the author of the bestselling Dane Maddock Adventures and Dane Maddock Origins series and many other titles. Writing as David Debord, he writes the Absent Gods fantasy series. When not writing he hosts the Wood on Words podcast and co-hosts the Authorcast podcast. David and his family live in Santa Fe,New Mexico. Visit him online at davidwoodweb.com.